EXILES

JERRY AUTIERI

1

Consul Cato strode across the small parade grounds in front of camp headquarters. The sun pushed over the eastern horizon and already heat prickled his skin. He dressed in a simple tunic and sandals. Given the work ahead, he would not want to soil any of his good clothes, and the men enjoyed seeing him dressed this way. In fact, the adjutant following behind looked more formal. The distant shouts of centurions and optiones rousing their men for the day ahead might have comforted him, but today it was background noise.

Varro and Falco had escaped. Centurion Longinus had, of course, warned him of it, and even tried to prevent it. But those slippery worms once more proved they hid more potential than their dull and battle-scarred faces indicated. Flamininus had been correct to bring them into Servus Capax. He was correct in wanting them under his control versus those damned Hellenes. He was so close to breaking all three, and now this.

They had pushed him too far now. At least he had Curio in hand. The other two were irredeemable.

He arrived at the tent where Centurion Longinus held his prisoner. Two guards stood at rigid attention outside, young principes in the bloom of adulthood. They were fine soldiers, men from the fields who could take orders and act with intelligence. He suffered no less under his command. They offered crisp salutes as he approached. Cato returned the salute and waited for them to open the tent. He sighed at what would happen next. The sweet scent of cooking fires from headquarters drew into his nostrils. He had skipped his breakfast for this.

Cato swept under the tent flap with his adjutant following. The scent of blood and fear assailed him, odors familiar enough to fade as he filled the entrance. Centurion Longinus stood from his wooden stool and saluted. The night had been hard on him, and his relentless beard had thickened again. Cato simply nodded to him and scanned down the light of a clay oil lamp to the figure trussed on the ground.

He was a country lad by his build, with strong shoulders, and a face like a bull. These types made fine soldiers, and Cato regretted seeing him broken and bloodied on the ground.

"He was the signifier in Varro's command group, sir." Centurion Longinus prodded the man with his toe. "We knocked him off his horse while the others got away. He broke his shoulder and knee in the fall."

Cato's brow flicked up. "I'll have the full report on that escape, Centurion. You and all your men could've expended more effort than catching one man with all his bones shattered."

Longinus lowered his eyes. "Of course, sir. But this one, Lars, knows their plans, sir. I'll be certain to run them down after you've satisfied your questions."

Cato appreciated Longinus's positive attitude. He was as loyal a man as ever served him and competent. He should've been elected to Servus Capax rather than Flamininus's lot. But Cato had misunderstood the implications and now regretted it.

"You will make it a priority," he said, then gestured for Longinus's stool. The centurion dutifully placed it beside the captive and he settled on it. Then he dismissed his adjutant to prepare a later breakfast for him. Seeing the condition of the captive, he would finish early enough to still enjoy a meal.

The one called Lars tried to appear as defiant as a gagged and bound man with a shattered body could. It was not much, but Cato appreciated the effort. He detested weak men and would punish them much harder.

"Signifier is a position of honor," Cato said, leaning on his knee. Centurion Longinus stood at attention beside him. "Only the best soldiers may bear the century standard. Now look at you. You have traded all that honor, all the glory that you could have brought to your family, for what? I intend to find out."

He gestured to Longinus to remove the leather gag. When he did, Lars let out a panting breath, and a string of drool spread to the floor. But he did not look at Cato and stared into nothing.

Again, Cato drew a long sigh. "Lars, you are dead. You know this, of course. They caught you deserting, so there isn't any recourse for me. Too many know of what you've done for me to order anything but execution. I'll let you think about that a moment."

Cato sat back, noting that Lar's expression allowed a hint of distress. He looked up at Centurion Longinus and nodded. The centurion drew his pugio and kneeled beside the prisoner.

"Now, I'm sure you are thinking I will send you through the fustuarium. That is a possibility and the most likely judgment. But here we are in the privacy of this tent. They carried you inside during the night, your bones broken and flesh bleeding. A swift and peaceful death is preferable to a long beating with clubs. You are young still. I assume you have not witnessed the fustuarium yourself."

He waited, watching for signs of Lars's capitulation to his ultimate fate. But he continued to stare as if deaf.

"All the men of your century will be issued clubs." He spoke while staring into his memories of this brutally efficient disciplinary action. "Normally, you would have to run through them naked as they beat you. I've seen no one survive to the other side, since usually a good friend will break your skull early to limit suffering. But my understanding is you don't like me or many others. So in your case, I'm not sure. Anyway, you cannot run with a broken knee. So they'll all take turns clubbing you. I'm sure you'll feel every blow. And if you survive, they will club you again. By that time, you'll make a better bowl of blood soup than a soldier."

Lars's eyes at last shifted to Cato. "You want me to tell you where they went?"

Cato gave a light smile. "Details, Lars, I want details. They went north, and so they are simply fleeing. Tell me where they planned to hide and where they wanted to end up. Tell me why you helped them. Are you one of their organization that I don't know about? That would seem impossible, but I have to admit it might be true."

"What will you do for me if I tell you?" Lars's voice was breathless and rough with fear. He tried to act as if he held any bargaining power. But Cato was here more for curiosity than anything else. He knew Varro and Falco would eventually head to the Ilegertes as their only potential allies.

"I will give you that swift death right now. Otherwise, you will be flogged and subjected to the fustuarium, ensuring the greatest suffering I can devise for you within the limits of the law. But there is also suffering you can experience outside of the law while it is just the three of us in this tent. Let's save all that. You know you've nothing to bargain with. Redeem yourself to me at least, and say what you know."

"I don't care what you think of me. You pretend to be one of us, but you're just a snake."

Centurion Longinus punched Lars's broken knee. The big man strained against his bindings as he tried not to cry out. But his eyes crushed shut and he grit his teeth as he endured what must be a terrible afterglow of agony.

Cato nodded to Longinus. "Thank you. Lars, you must not forget to address me properly as the highest authority in Iberia. No more foolishness. Tell me everything."

Lars growled and shook his bullish head. The words flowed like clumps of honey at first, but then streamed as whatever reservations he had sloughed aside.

He described much of what Cato had already guessed. The Iberian, Aulus, had corrupted the command group and convinced them to rescue Varro and Falco in exchange for future rewards. They created a hasty breakout plan, clubbed the guards senseless, and aimed only to flee.

The only revelation was that this native claimed membership in Servus Capax, which couldn't be true as far as Cato knew. But he tucked that away as Lars detailed how Servus Capax would award them with wealth and lands, and therefore a step up in society that absolutely would never happen. He had to puff out his cheeks or else burst into laughter at the extent of this man's credulity. Truly, he was a country boy who did not know how society worked, and who misunderstood his place in it.

When Lars finished, he blew out a long breath. He remained lying on his side while Longinus squatted beside him, jittering his pugio in hand as if eager to put it to use.

"So, you would hide out until I gave up, then skirt around me to reach the Ilegertes. And you expected they would happily throw away their alliance with Rome to aid your lot and put you on a ship to wherever you wanted to go? I had to hold my breath a few times during your confession, I'll admit. But honestly, how could you believe any of what you said? Are Centurions Varro and Falco that good?"

Lars's face darkened, and for the first time, he looked up at Cato. "Or maybe you're that bad that I'd choose desertion over you."

Cato laughed. It was a witty if useless quip, so he had to appreciate that much. But Cato never appreciated disrespect.

"Thank you for your cooperation, Signifier Lars. You confirmed my expectations, but I needed to hear it from the source. And I believe you. You were a victim in all of this, I'm afraid. You let greed cloud your thoughts, and so undo you. What a shame, really."

"Just end me," Lars said, closing his eyes. "There's nothing left for me now."

"That is so." Cato shook his head and nodded to Centurion Longinus.

"Reapply the gag. Cut out both of his eyes and stuff them into his mouth. Then finish him however you wish. Throw his body outside the camp. We do not bury traitors among heroes."

Lars stared up at him and shouted as Longinus cut it short and thrust the leather gag back into his mouth. His eyes were wide with fear and shock. Cato simply sighed.

"I warned you to respect me as consul. You never once looked at me or addressed me according to my status. You slandered me and showed only the greatest disgust toward me. Even if you detest me, you must respect my rank. I could have ordered much worse. This is still better than the fustuarium."

Cato sat up as Longinus, short but incredibly strong, rolled Lars onto his back. He was not one to look away from his bloodiest orders. He just stood back to allow more working room.

Even tied and with broken bones, Lars offered a tough struggle. It was such a shame to put down a spirited man. But it had come to this, and he had to taste the pain of his own insolence before he died.

Longinus pinned Lars's face down with one hand and set the

point of his dagger under the left eye. Lars stiffened, cross-eyed, looking at the blade in his face.

The blade slid into the fatty flesh and dark blood bubbled up from the wound. Longinus worked like a doctor, incising around the orbital bone while Lars thrashed and screamed against his gag. But Longinus sawed out the eye to leave a disgusting, bloody hole in the face. Cato marveled at how big the eye was once out of its socket. He had of course seen this before, but each time it reminded him how much hid under the flesh.

Lars was delirious with suffering for the second extraction, which proceeded faster for it. The second eyeball popped out with a bloody puff and now both eyeballs were set beside Lars's head. He hardly seemed human with the gag and the thick blood flowing over his face.

"This is what traitors get," Longinus said as he scooped up two eyeballs and the dangling bits of meat clinging to them. He then removed the gag and crushed them into Lars's mouth and now Cato did look away. The squelching and squeezing sounds revolted him, and he studied the far tent wall while Longinus worked on his choking and squealing victim.

When finished, he sat back with both hands covered in dark blood. He studied his victim as if choosing a favorite technique. Cato folded his arms and waited for his orders to be completed. Lars's identity was lost under the bloody fluid that gleamed on his ruined face in the lamplight.

At last, Longinus shrugged and shoved his pugio into Lars's throat, then carved lengthwise to open his arteries. Cato again stood back from the blood spurt, having expected it from the first cut. A drop did patter against his hem, and he curled his lip at it.

But Longinus had mercy, even if it did not seem so. Lars went limp and his eyeless head rolled to the side, ending his suffering in a stroke.

"Clean up and have the body removed as instructed," Cato said. "Then meet at my tent for your orders."

"Sorry, sir." Longinus's voice was rough. "I got soft at the end. He should've suffered like all the other deserters."

"I think he went to the grave in pain, Centurion. Don't waste your thoughts on this one."

Outside the tent, Cato felt relieved to be done with this. He would have to track down Varro and Falco as loose ends. As they had only one viable option, he would not waste time in pursuit. They would either perish in the wilds of Iberia or else find their way to the Ilegertes. It would be a simple matter to bag them there.

He crossed back to his tent alone, plainly dressed and with no guard or attendant to follow. It was a requirement of rank, but he honestly detested such power displays. Who here does not know his rank? He was a capable fighter and did not need anyone to guard him at least while in his own camp. Any of the thousands surrounding him would rush to his side if he called. But even on such a short walk, guards sprinted from his headquarters to meet and escort him back. It was their duty, and he did not fault them. In fact, had they failed he would've placed them on charges.

Inside, he enjoyed a simple breakfast while reviewing strength and inventory reports, scouting intelligence, and a slew of other information needed to take his men north and crush the last of the natives. No matter what transpired with Varro and Falco, this was his primary objective.

But his mind kept returning to the two of them. Now with Curio under his control and the others either lost in the wild or soon to be recaptured as deserters, Flamininus no longer had majority control over Servus Capax. It had been a bitterly foolish mistake to let him recruit three of his own men at once. But then he and Galba had focused only on Varro and left the other two as some sort of junior members or the like. It was his own fault for not questioning this, and before he knew it, Flamininus was nearly running the entire operation. Well, he and his fellow Hellenes.

Cato stared at the wax tablet in hand, but his eyes saw only his triumph over Flamininus. Certainly, he would seek reprisal for this upset. But Cato had what he wanted, which for now was an even hand in this operation. Flamininus might feel burned, but he could see behind Cato to the true power. Let him stew and scheme, Cato thought with a tight smile, but that wiry little Helene would not throw himself against the likes of Flaccus.

He snapped the tablet down on his austere desk with a clack. His bowl of puls, real soldier's food, cooled as he stared at it.

Yet if Varro and Falco somehow returned to Rome—no, he shook his head. Even those two were not so fortunate. The Ilegertes might be inclined to treat them well, but would not betray their alliance for nothing in return. Yet...

Cato thrummed his fingers on the desk. He would apply pressure on Curio to gain insight into what those two might do. After all, they were taken into Servus Capax expressly for their uncanny ability to escape the most hopeless situations and still come away with a victory. Were they somehow—and this was fanciful thinking, but an important mental exercise—to connect with Flamininus they would be certain to reveal Cato's unorthodox methods.

He wondered if that mattered. It might stain his reputation in some circles, but elevate it in others for sure, he thought. Reputation was a man's principal wealth. He did not want to risk tarnishing it before the wrong people. But more importantly, Flamininus would still have his men. Cato was uncertain he could make desertion charges stick if Flamininus, Galba, and—may all the gods forbid it—Scipio himself decide to oppose it. The Scipio family already owed gratitude to those two for handling the Paullus situation in Macedonia.

With a growl, he returned to reading his reports. This was a pointless exercise since Longinus will bring the two of them back to be tried before Flamininus knows any better. This afternoon, he would call in Curio and get his opinions on what approaches they might take. Curio made a show of appearing eager to serve, but it was overdone. Cato knew he was not completely convinced of his decision to part with his two friends. So he would be as gentle as he could, but as firm as he needed.

By now, he had wondered at Longinus's absence. The First Spear would not be mopping up blood from that tent, but would have detailed men to it. So why was he not here? The tribunes should assemble soon. There was much to discuss after last night and for the campaign ahead.

Yet the moment his patience tipped into irritation, the tent flap opened and his guards announced Centurion Longinus.

He swept into the tent without Cato's acknowledgment. Normally, Cato would bristle at this breach of protocol, but when he saw the centurion's expression, he sat back.

"Sir, sorry for the delay. I have bad news, sir."

"I am prepared for news of all kinds, Centurion. What is the situation?"

Longinus's face had grown so dark it was hard to tell where the thick, dark stubble of his beard ended.

"There has been a theft from the treasury. All the guards are in the hospital now. And Centurion Curio along with his command group have vanished."

Cato's fists balled white and he felt his temples throb while he growled, "Flamininus, you rat."

2

The camp was in chaos, at least as far as Cato was concerned. He had just visited the treasury to inspect the scene along with the paymaster tribune and centurions. Now he headed to the hospital where doctors tended to the sickened guards. The chaos as he saw it was the onlookers trying to figure out what had happened. First Spear Longinus and several tribunes and their retinues fluttered behind him as he stamped down the roads.

"What are these men doing?" He waved angrily at the few who watched this column of might streak past. "Tribunes, you are dismissed. All but you, Tribune Carius. The rest of you, get all the men marching and drilling. I don't want an idle moment today. I want the men exhausted before noon. No time for idle chatter. Run them up the mountains and down again until they beg for mercy, and give them none."

He paused his march, nearly causing the entourage to crash into themselves. He glared at them until they acknowledged his orders and turned away. This left him with only his adjutant,

Longinus, as well as Tribune Carius and his centurion, both in charge of the payroll and treasury.

With a dark glare, he turned back toward the hospital.

"What sort of treasury do you run, Tribune Carius? I thought you a far more meticulous man than you are proving to be."

"Sir, you've inspected us personally. I assure you, we are thorough in checking the men we select. We have redundant security procedures, sir, so that no one man can break security through idleness or error."

"Fine words," Cato quipped. "But your rigorously selected men are all in the hospital and an entire pay chest has gone missing without the slightest hint of how it vanished. Not even a wagon rut. So explain it to me."

Cato drew up to the hospital, and Carius's answer did not follow. It mattered not, since clearly, no one knew anything about this breach. He hoped the men themselves could explain it.

Already he heard his command being executed in the distance as centurions bellowed out marching orders. A finch perched on the top of the hospital tent, which was a wide and billowing structure of heavy cloth turned yellow and stained from the campaign. The bird flew off as if Cato's snarling face frightened it. Emerging from the tent, the senior doctor saluted.

"Sir, I understand you want to question the men."

Cato marshaled his anger. No matter what he felt, he was now in front of the men and he must appear collected. So he slid a smile as heavy as lead onto his face.

"That is correct, doctor. But can you tell me how they were sickened?"

The doctor touched the back of his head and glanced over his shoulder as if checking that his hospital had not fled him.

"It would seem they imbibed some sort of poison, sir, that sickened them."

"Imbibed poison?" Cato turned darkly to Tribune Carius who

now seemed to shrink behind his centurion. At least the centurion had the temerity to stand at attention. "So this word you choose, imbibe. Are you covering for these men, doctor? Did they drink while on duty?"

"I cannot say, sir." The doctor's good-natured smile trembled. "I mean to say, I cannot say how they came to ingest the poison, sir. Given what I've learned from those coming around, it appears most of them fell ill after their evening meal. But some might have ingested the poison at a later time. It's not clear if those were on active duty or not, sir."

"I can make it clear," Cato said, staring into Carius's horrified face. "Treasury guards all have a responsibility to remain clear-headed just like any other soldier. If a poor velite is forbidden from excessive drinking while in the field, then so it is for so-called elite, carefully selected treasury guards."

"My men don't drink on or off duty, sir." The centurion spoke up, his voice firm and clear. "I'll take every one of their floggings if you find they did, sir. They drink what's rationed to them, no more or less."

Cato stared at this man. Now that was a true centurion, brave enough to risk a flogging for his insolence. Given the state of his camp, however, Cato would overlook this outburst. He did not need more rumor and disquiet from flogging a centurion standing up for his men.

"There are a dozen guards in there, Centurion. You would not survive your promise."

The centurion did not show any fear, such was his conviction.

"And what of the slaves assigned to your men?" Cato realized the slaves who delivered the rations might be part of this theft.

"Same as the others, sir. Sick as dogs and talking like madmen. At least I assume so, since no one knows their language. Just wouldn't bother sending them to the hospital. They'll either pull through or die, sir."

The tension seemed to release with this centurion's confidence. Even Longinus gave an admiring grunt, which was rare enough for him.

"Very well, Doctor, how long do you expect before we know if they will all recover?"

"I cannot say." Again, the doctor touched the back of his head. "Without something to sample, we do not know how to treat them. I've fed them such mixtures I know to ease sickness. We have forced the more wakeful ones to vomit, but it seems of little use. Whatever they consumed is in their bodies now, and must work itself out. If I had to guess, mushrooms must have been part of the recipe. But otherwise, it is totally foreign to us."

Cato invited himself inside the hospital and found the twelve treasury guards in their own section of the tent, cordoned off from the others with mobile screens. Other injured or sick men lay on their cots and tried to salute as he passed. But he was so intent on the poisoned guards, he failed to return them.

The moaning and senseless babble of the victims filled the area. Once beyond the screens, Cato saw their conditions. Most were curled up as if frozen in a spasm. They drooled on themselves and stared into nothing. Some laughed, others cried, and others spoke in unconnected sentences.

"By the gods, Doctor, they have been ruined. Look at how that one's hands have turned to claws. What they have done to my men?"

"Sir, I wish I could say. Here, speak with Arrianus. He is mostly recovered, and we separated him from the others so his spirits would not be lowered at their condition."

Arrianus looked as if he had seen death with skin sweaty and pasty and eyes sunken and staring. He did not immediately recognize Cato, but did his centurion and tribune. So he made to rise from his cot, but Cato waved him down.

"Save your strength for my questions," he said. "Let's set aside rank for a moment and speak as fellow soldiers. Somebody deceived you into consuming a vile poison. How did you come to this?"

Arrianus's eyes shifted from side to side as if hearing warnings. He folded his arms tightly over his chest, but he spoke in a clear voice.

"We all got dizzy after supper, sir. I was cleaning up when I felt dizzy and heard sounds. I saw lights flashing. Then I remember little besides mad things I'd rather not repeat, sir. I think I saw the way to Hades, sir, and it is too horrifying to think upon. There were monsters there. Monsters that tried to eat me."

He mimicked the pawing of a lion as his eyes unfocused to look inward at whatever horror he remembered. While Cato was impatient to hear more of the circumstances of the poisoning, he was also curious about what a man so close to death might encounter.

"But the beasts couldn't catch me, sir. I ran faster than I ever did before. And I escaped back here." He now rubbed his shoulders. "But something from that place followed me. It sticks to my skin, sir. I fear it will never come off, and I will carry the foulness that stained me forever."

"Be at peace," Cato said. "The drug has not fully worn off, that is all. Do you remember anything about the meal you ate? Who prepared it? Did anyone unfamiliar touch it before eating?"

The confused Arrianus shook his head and scratched at his shoulders. He seemed about to deny anything unusual, then his eyes widened. But Cato saw realization turn to guilt and an immediate instinct to hide what he was about to say.

Cato used the voice he reserved for the battlefield. "Soldier, tell me what you were about to hide from me. I need to know what happened. If you are honest with me, I will be merciful in any required punishments. But if you try to deceive me, I will go to the limit of the law to ensure you regret it."

Even in his confusion, Arrianus straightened his shoulders and dropped his crossed arms. "Yes, sir. It was our wine, sir. It seemed nothing different until we drank it, and we realized someone had mistakenly sent us wine reserved for the officers, sir, rather than our usual ration."

"And there it is," Cato said. "You enjoyed an upgrade to your rations and were thusly taken down by an unseen foe. That is the price of greed, Arrianus. You should have put down your cups and reported that mix-up. Instead, you guzzled like hungry children."

"Sir, we drank only what we were allowed, and maybe a sip more for the delicious taste. We did not know it was a mix-up. We thought we were being rewarded."

"For what, I wonder," Cato said. "But you have been honest and told me what I need to know. It is clear how this robbery happened."

"Robbery?" Arrianus's face turned even paler. "Sir? Is that why we were poisoned?"

"The lot of you on duty that night were all so poisoned, and some badly. So I wonder how much you reckon is a sip more for flavor. A pay box of denarii was stolen, hardly a massive theft, but still a substantial amount. There will be a price to pay for it. Still, you have all suffered enough. Just focus on recovery and I will discuss what follows with your tribune, if anything at all."

"Thank you, sir." But it sounded more like a question than gratitude.

Cato left the hospital with Tribune Carius trailing behind and spluttering excuses. The two centurions both knew to keep silent as Cato's anger rose with each new insipid excuse.

"That is enough, Tribune. You will begin investigations into what happened. Your first order is to determine where Centurion Curio and his command group went. I know he is behind all of this. When you locate him, bring him in chains back to camp. While he has had all night to escape, unless he had contracted a private ship in advance, he cannot have traveled far. A pay box would need to be carried in a cart, restricting his speed."

With the tribune and his centurion dismissed, Cato returned to his tent with Longinus following. He dropped himself into his chair behind the desk, and Longinus took up his position at attention, looking like a marble statue back at the Senate.

"This is too far beyond him," Cato said.

"Sir? Do you mean Curio?" Longinus replied but remained at attention. Cato waved at him to relax. He did not need formality now, but someone to help clarify his thinking.

"I cannot accept that Curio sought to deceive me to such a degree that he would deny his friendship with Varro and Falco. He willingly gave up Flamininus's open secret about nearly losing the war indemnity to his conniving officers. I already knew it, of course, but Curio didn't realize it. So he passed my tests."

"He had me fooled, sir." Longinus's idea of relaxing was to let his head tilt forward, but he otherwise held firm as if ready to leap to his next order. "I knew he would still try to cover for his friends. That's only natural. But I'd ever expect this from him."

"It profits him nothing," Cato said, spreading his hands over the smoothness of his well-used desk. "He is already wealthy. If anything, a theft like this reverses his fortunes. I will have his wealth seized. Now all he will own is whatever he can carry away in that pay box, which must be less than the massive reward Flamininus granted him."

"Then it can't be for the money, sir. There must be a greater reward for him, like power."

"Money is power, Centurion. Money, reputation, and connections make the man. Curio and his friends have been building all three, making them dangerous for their uncertain allegiance. I cannot understand him, for in one stroke he has smashed all three pillars of power."

"Sir, are you certain Curio is behind this?"

"Who else vanished last night?" Cato felt a twist of anger at questioning his conclusion. But he valued Longinus's ideas and so listened.

"No one else, sir. Other than Varro and Falco and the command group. Maybe the theft is intended to pay off those who helped them escape. In which case, the pay box will be headed wherever Varro and Falco are going."

"That must be the reason." Cato rubbed his face hard, feeling his eyelids slide under his palms. "But they could've easily paid out of their own purses."

"Not while in country, sir. They'd have to get back to Rome to do that. Seeing how greedy Lars was, I'd expect all of those traitors would want coin in hand sooner."

"Greed is a harsh master," Cato agreed. "So let us suppose this was Curio's motive. It still goes far beyond what I believe are the limits of his capabilities. I selected Curio to break off from the three exactly because I considered him the least imaginative of the group."

"I thought Falco was simpler, sir."

Cato shook his head. "His mind takes longer to heat up, but when it does he can match Varro's cunning. Curio is always happy to follow another's lead. But in this matter, I cannot see how he coordinated with the two of them. Nor can I understand how he would've predicted things to work out exactly as they had. Could I have played into a trap? Did they want me to do this? To make me believe I was in control only to reveal I never was?"

"Sir, I don't believe we are dealing with those sorts of men." Longinus drew a long breath. "They are resourceful, but so far as I've seen they react rather than plan. You describe something too devious for their simple ways."

"Exactly!" Cato rapped the desk. "And all my self-doubt will avail me nothing. The answer is that we must recapture all three of them and immediately try them for desertion and theft. I will have them executed on the spot with no chance of escape. I have learned my lesson when it comes to them."

"But if it is not them, sir, then who is it?"

"Flamininus, of course. And Scipio. This theft of the silver sounds like something he would love for me to explain before the Senate."

Longinus raised his brows and Cato realized he mentioned old rivalries before Longinus's time.

"When I was much younger, I served with Scipio against Hannibal. I questioned his financial dealings and unusual accounting, which were evidently corrupt. I wanted him to be held to the same standard as any other man. But he felt himself above the law since he was leading the greatest war Rome has ever known. He got away with his corruption, and I fulfilled my duty. But Scipio has never forgiven me for it. Now, wouldn't it be grand revenge if he could call my accounting into question before the Senate?"

Longinus shrugged. "It still seems like a lot of effort to give you a black eye, sir. But I know nothing of politics."

"Be grateful for it." Cato folded his hands on the desk. "I wonder at this poison, though. How did Curio create it while carrying out his duties? How did he even know to make it? Perhaps he learned from the desert folk of Numidia. That's all I can think of. In any case, I shall have all my answers when Curio is returned to me."

"Should I go for him first, sir?"

Cato studied his First Spear for a moment. "No, I need you to go to the Ilegertes and impress my power and desire upon them. Their loyalties have slipped before, and I do not want to risk anything while I am on the edge of victory. You will await Varro and Falco there, or until I recall you. It is possible Iberia will devour them, and we'll never hear from them again."

"Yes, sir!" Longinus snapped to attention, but Cato knew he was dissatisfied with the task.

"By now, you've heard of Servus Capax often enough. With Varro and the rest gone, it may be time to consider your name for that roster. When you return, I will explain it to you. It's not as bad as Varro and the others make it seem. It could be especially lucrative for you as well. Now, select your men and prepare for travel. But before you do, have that treasury centurion sent to me."

"Thank you, sir! I will be back with Varro and Falco in chains."

During the interlude between Longinus departing and the payroll centurion arriving, Cato stewed on Curio's deceit. He underestimated no one, but yet he had Curio. Even if he was operating on another's orders, he had fooled him enough that he looked away. In that instant, he struck like a viper.

The guards announced Centurion Barbatus.

He ducked into the tent and stood at attention before Cato. The centurion was much like Longinus in build, only his face was cool and dispassionate, unlike Longinus's open and likable expression. He saluted and stood at attention.

"Centurion, I have new orders for you. Orders I believe you will enjoy. I know who poisoned your men and shamed them with a theft right under their noses."

Barbatus made no expression, but a feral gleam came to his eyes.

Cato knew he selected the right man for the task.

"What would you say to hunting down Centurion Curio and returning him and his men to me for a harsh interrogation and execution?"

"Sir, I only ask to be given a chance to take part in his death. I would gladly drag him and his traitors across Iberia for what they did to my men."

"Good, because that is exactly what I want you to do."

3

_____

Curio followed Centurion Lucian up the mountain trail. The old centurion, his commander in Servus Capax, leaped like a mountain goat from one rock to the next. His gray cloak caught the cool wind that flowed through these mountains and set the treetops waving. Curio doubted he looked half as heroic as the centurion surveying their path from atop ancient, lichen-spattered boulders. He remained with his men, straining to get the mules to haul their supplies and the heavy pay box up the narrow path.

"Come on," Curio shouted in frustration as he pushed from the back with two of his other men pressed to either side.

"They won't budge, sir!" Sextus groaned as he pulled on the mules. Curio couldn't see from the rear of the cart but imagined the wiry runner straining to move the stubborn mules.

They pushed until the wagon wheels creaked over a stone and then thumped to the opposite side. The cart rattled as it settled while Curio and the others stepped back in defeat. The cart held in place, and relieved the stress on the animals.

"All right," Curio called forward. "Just let the beasts rest. They must be tired."

"Like we aren't."

The muttered complaint came from Curio's former tubicen, Quintus. He was a swarthy man with dark circles around his eyes, often given to mumbled complaints. Curio glared at him and he straightened up.

"Sorry, sir. It's all been a bit much."

His eyes drifted to Curio's shins, where his hairs still carried the dried and clotted blood splatter from the scout he and Centurion Lucian had killed while still in the forest.

"I know," Curio said softly, then steeled his voice. "But whatever it may seem like to you, we're still in the legion. I'm still your officer. So keep your shitty complaints behind your teeth, or I'll make you regret it."

Curio never considered his height a disadvantage to intimidating others. He might look like an older teenager to some, but he knew his own strength. Unlike the men of his command group, he had been in continuous service for two campaigns. Physically and mentally, he towered over the others, no matter his actual height.

"Sorry, sir." Quintus lowered his eyes.

"Take a breather," Curio announced formally to his men. They staggered to nearby rocks and sank down, sloughing off their packs.

Curio settled across from them, removing his helmet and scratching his head. He missed his optio, whom he regretted keeping in the dark. But Curio felt a sense of duty to his century. His optio was a competent leader and at least tolerated by the century. So he had knocked him out and left him tied up when he and the others left. The century would be in excellent hands for the upcoming battle.

He chuckled at how his optio had tried to spy covertly on his doings. That was another reason Curio had excluded him. He was about as circumspect as a rabid boar with a javelin through its side. Taking him along would have surely jeopardized the entire mission. If anything, by leaving him behind, he could provide basic information to Varro and Falco.

If either of them lived to meet him.

He looked up to the flat gray sky and smelled rain. The glare caused him to squint, but he did not see a bird anywhere. This high into the mountains, he supposed there would be fewer birds to see. But the lack of anything in the air showed a storm might be coming. He had held that belief since childhood, and so far it seemed accurate half the time. Birds knew when to find shelter ahead of bad weather.

"What's going on down there?"

Centurion Lucien called from high on his rock. He looked like a statue of a Roman hero overlooking the Forum from this distance. His billowing cloak pressed to his side as the wind picked up. He waved at Curio.

"He will not let us rest." The complaint came from Fabius, the signifier and the largest man among all of them. He had a jaw chiseled from marble, with a brain to match. Curio lauded him for his fierceness in battle and not for his wit. He sat dejectedly on a low rock between the other two. His head still came level with the others.

Curio returned the wave. Let the centurion issue the direct order. Of course, he understood Lucian wanted them to move. But the mules did not want to. In fact, they swished their tails and flicked their ears at the centurion's voice, like it was a fly to chase away.

Lucian waved again, and Curio returned it. This time he pointed to the mules as if he should speak with them. Lucian appeared to sigh and shake his head. He jumped down from the boulder and vanished.

23

Curio maintained their moment of peace while Lucian retraced his steps. He yanked out clotted blood from the hairs on his shins. Today, two men who had just been doing their duty died by his hands. He wished that had never happened. He looked at the cart. A dirty white tarp covered it, nailed down on all sides. It rippled and cracked with the wind that swished through the thin trees and mountain paths. Then the wind would press it flat, revealing crates of supplies and the innocuous shape of the pay box.

That box was one-half proof of Cato's treachery. Curio held the other half against his body under his armor. Both had to be carried free of Cato's reach so he could send them to Rome. From there, Curio hoped he could help Varro and Falco. Certainly, they would escape. They had aid, even if they did not yet realize it.

Then they would all meet back in Rome, heroes once more, and free of Cato's corrupting grasp.

"What's going on here?"

Centurion Lucian emerged from the steep path ahead, face red from his efforts but glowing with an almost crazed enthusiasm.

After explaining about the mules and the near impossibility of the path for this kind of cart, Lucian shook his head.

Centurion Lucian had an uncanny ability to appear as anything, or so Curio felt. When the centurion had first approached him, he appeared little more than an old triarius with a missing front tooth. He seemed simple, almost daft. But then he transformed himself after revealing the gold owl's head on his pugio. He at once became a strong and fatherly figure to Curio. Now that their subterfuge was nearly complete, Lucian once again transformed into a visionary hero. He had easily persuaded Curio's command group to join them. They fawned over his descriptions of the future and what lay ahead for all of them. In fact, even Curio forgot his friends and his future when caught in the visions Lucian spun.

But now he shifted again, turning into something like a wise, old farmhand as he approached the two mules yoked to the cart.

"You can't whip mules into action," he said to no one in particular. "You just need to speak so they understand why they should cooperate."

He stroked their necks and heads and seemed to whisper things that Curio could not hear. He and the others of his command group simply sat watching, milking the last moments of their rest before resuming the path forward.

For Centurion Lucian gave a gentle tug on the bridle of one mule, and both started forward.

"That's all it takes," he said with a satisfied smile. "Now, we want to reach the other side of that crest where we can camp for the night. You men." He waved at the three sitting dejectedly on their rocks. "Get the cart rolling. Centurion Curio and I are going to view the way ahead."

Lucian had placed himself in natural command over everyone. Given his experience, no one questioned this. But Curio still felt he should be the one to give orders to his men. Yet he let Lucian guide him ahead by the shoulder.

"How are you holding up?" he asked as they climbed into the narrower path. "You're not still worried about Varro and Falco? I told you that Aulus will get them away from danger. Cato won't know which way to turn once they run."

"I can't help but worry, sir. I've seen plenty of grand plans go to shit."

They climbed in silence, Curio always a few steps behind Lucian's sure and energetic steps. The wind grew stronger, or so it felt as he clambered up rocks after Lucian.

"There's a storm coming, sir."

Lucian gave a crisp nod, but did not look skyward. Instead, he put both hands on his hips and nodded toward the crest.

"It'll take all we've got to mount that ridge. But from there, it will be like we carry no burdens. I promise you, Curio, we will all be far and away from Cato after that ridge. He'll never find this path, and even if he could, he'd never catch up with us."

"Sir, we still need to reach the shore and signal your ship. Cato's scouts might see it, or local people might investigate. Perhaps we should see about hiring local mercenaries for extra defense."

"Mercenaries!" Lucian put both hands on his head. "We can't pay them enough, and if they ever learned how much silver we have with us, they'd gut us where we stood. No, as we planned, it's all on us. Servus Capax will bring justice to Cato's betrayal and ensure we succeed here in Iberia."

Curio frowned behind Lucian's back.

The entire plan had overtaken him like a flash flood. It moved with such speed and precision, as if Lucian had been planning it for months in advance. They had knocked out the treasury guards with a sweet-tasting concoction Lucian had prepared. Then they simply walked out with proof of Cato's betrayal. A whole pay box of coins not from Roman mints, but Carthaginian ones. Alone, it was not proof the Carthaginian's had bribed Cato to hold back in his campaign.

That was the written agreement Curio secreted against his body, proof of Cato's dishonesty. He had snatched it himself from Cato's tent, a document carelessly hidden under the ever-present stack of wax tablets on his desk.

With all of this evidence suddenly acquired with Lucian's aid, he had no time to think through the plan. They had to get away. Lucian constantly agitated for escaping with evidence. But now he wondered as he surveyed this ridge and the approaching storm.

How were they going to get out of Iberia and into Rome before Cato intercepted them? He could easily catch them at sea or his agents could nab them in Rome itself.

Curio trusted Servus Capax and its hidden operatives to

ensure he got away with all of this proof. Lucian seemed supremely confident that the other side of the ridge was all safe territory.

Yet in Iberia there could be no such thing.

So they plotted their way forward then returned to the others. The mules indeed worked hard for Lucian and it drew sharp and enviable sighs from the others. As promised, that steep ridge nearly destroyed their cart with all the rocks, ridges, and drops, but in the end it held together.

The top of the ridge spilled gently down into the valley below, where dark trees crawled out to the hazy horizon. Everyone gasped at this, since Lucian's promises proved genuine. He gave a gap-toothed laugh.

"I told you it would be easy from here. We only need to make camp tonight and be well rested for tomorrow."

"We'll be in Rome soon," Fabius said, rubbing his hands together.

Curio broke into their cheerful mood, warning them about the storm and setting them to creating a camp for the night.

"How did you know to take these paths?" Curio asked after he had ordered the others to fetch firewood and collect water.

"I've lived in Iberia a long time," he said, his voice becoming wistful. "The land keeps no secrets from me, Centurion. I know it like no other Roman does. It speaks to me, and I listen."

"Sir, if I heard the land speaking to me I'd shit myself."

Lucian tipped his head back and laughed. He then grabbed a flat rock and moved it toward the location of the eventual cooking fire. Curio did the same, creating a small circle of seats to use to rest while cooking. They did not fear discovery so high in the mountains.

"It's just a manner of speech," Lucian said as he grunted while hauling over another suitable rock. "It's just my natural affinity for the land. Just like you have a knack for hiding and going unseen. The land speaks to me the way shadows speak to you."

Curio shrugged. He was just small and fast and had an eye for a good hiding spot. The skill came from having mean older brothers who used to enjoy thumping him when he was a child. Even after all his brothers died of fever, he never forgot how to make himself unseen.

They completed a ring of five rocks for seats. They tethered their mules to a tree, feedbags attached. Curio sat on one of the rock seats and regarded the animals, wondering if they would go aboard their escape ship or if they would be cut free. It seemed foolish to wonder about the fate of two dumb mules when he had two friends that were probably running for their lives right now.

Lucian cleared his throat, drawing Curio's attention back.

"You're getting that distant look again, Centurion. They're fine. Aulus has a plan, I am sure. Look, while you are in Servus Capax, accept that you may not always be with them. You could be called elsewhere. Happened to me enough. I wanted to stay with Aulus and raise him like my son. But it couldn't be. You understand sacrifice, don't you?"

"Of course, sir." Curio looked up the slope to the ridge they had crested. Somewhere beyond it, Varro and Falco were having adventures without him. It felt wrong to be separated.

Lucian coughed, then stretched his powerful legs. He wore the mail and gear of a triarius, but to Curio he looked far more commanding, like a tribune or even a consul. Other than an incredible sense of presence radiating from the centurion, Curio did not understand why. He was naturally a man to lead others.

"Centurion Curio, you have sacrificed much already. How much more are you willing to give in service to Rome?"

"I'd give my life, sir." He meant it and spoke without hesitation.

Lucian gave a warm smile. "I don't doubt it. You envision what Rome might be one day. That's good. I too have a vision. I see a future you cannot imagine and a greatness you cannot understand. A future that I'd give my life for, as well."

Curio tilted his head, not understanding Lucian's exact meaning. But in that moment, the others returned, with Quintus leading the group. He had two buckets of fresh water carried on a heavy spar over his shoulders.

They all prepared their rations and completed camp. The wind had picked up and a storm seemed likely to move in during the night. So they had no time to waste and had to reinforce their tent against the weather. When they finished, the sun had set, and they crawled into the tent. Lucian was so confident in the secret pass that he did not set any watches, claiming the rain would keep animals in their dens and that no one lived in these mountains.

Curio settled in that night to listen to rain pattering softly against the animal hide tent. The darkness was full of the rhythmic breathing of the others, and their bodies heated the interior. It was comforting, and he imagined the dark humps nearby were Varro and Falco. Though Falco was given to violent snoring, and no one here filled that role. He soon drifted into slumber.

He awakened with a start. A brilliant flash lit the tent and a loud crack followed. The rain fell harder now, and the tent leaned with the blowing wind. A thunderstorm raged outside. But they had done their work well, both in staking the tent and in selecting an area that sheltered it from the worst of the wind.

Once he realized lightning had awakened him, he relaxed. His dreamy brain had him expecting an enemy attack. He did not know the hour, but it had to be the middle of the night. The rest of his command group continued to sleep. To his mild chagrin, he heard marble-jawed Fabius snoring next to him. The other two rolled over or shifted, yet remained firmly asleep. Soldiers learned to sleep through anything, Curio mused.

Another lightning strike lit up the tent in a stark white light, but the ensuing thunder was less intense and more distant.

Yet the brilliance revealed that Centurion Lucian's bedroll was empty.

Now Curio sat up and ran his hand over the centurion's blanket. It was cool under his hands. He hadn't just awakened to the lightning, as Curio had.

He crawled forward and thought to awaken the others, then reconsidered. Maybe Lucian had gone to relieve himself and now waited for a break in the storm to return. Curio's mind was still fuzzy, and his body wanted to hide under the blanket and let the rain send him back to his dreams.

Instead, he pulled on his gray cloak over his tunic and yanked the hood up. He reached for his pugio and fitted the belt around his waist. Before he left, he removed the papyrus with Cato's seal and tucked it into his bedroll. He could not risk getting it wet in the rain. Then he slipped outside.

The tent stood amid a small clearing in the trees that shaded down the long slope of the mountain. They were high up so that rainwater ran in streams around the tent. The flashing lightning reflected in these thin streamers of water. Curio clutched his cloak to his neck and searched for signs of Centurion Lucian. But with the steady rain, no tracks remained.

Lightning struck nearby, a terrible boom that jolted Curio forward. Its brilliance blinded him a moment, and he looked to the tent. Yet none of his men peeked outside.

He chuckled at how well they slept, then decided to walk the perimeter of the camp to find Centurion Lucian.

The sky flashed with lightning and thunder followed in deep rolling waves. It made searching easier, for in the distance he saw a pale gray figure.

Instinctively, he ducked and sped forward bent at the waist. His hand clasped over his pugio. He fell behind a cold and rough tree trunk to better view the pale shape.

It was Centurion Lucian.

He was naked and dancing in a small clearing among the trees. Rain pelted his flesh, turning his extremities red from the cold. His hair was matted to his head and his skin gleamed.

Lightning flashed again, and when the thunder boomed, Lucian howled.

He danced like a madman in great, leaping arcs like a deer. Wherever he alighted, he sprang up again to land in a new place. He threw his arms wide and tilted his head back to accept the rain. He called out in a language Curio could not understand. But the wind and rain garbled the sound of it. Whenever thunder broke, Lucian paused his dance to howl.

Curio stared in wide-eyed fascination. Lucian seemed possessed with something. Maybe spirits had overtaken him while he slept.

Rain flowed off his hood into his face, making it hard to see details. It seemed the centurion was enacting some sort of mock hunt with his dancing. Lucian never paused in his mad dance, and Curio could not move from watching it. It mystified him how Lucian had the energy for this after a day that had exhausted men half his age.

Lightning again struck too close and somewhere he heard a tree shatter, drowned out by the ground-shaking boom of thunder.

He fell back from the tree trunk into the mud.

Looking up, Curio saw Lucian continue his mad dance undisturbed by the nearby lightning strike. His feet and legs were splattered with mud and what even might be speckles of blood.

It also seemed Lucian looked right at him as he sprang from one end of the clearing to the other in his graceful, powerful dance.

Curio scrabbled back, then ran to the tent, hoping Lucian had not seen him.

4

Curio led the cart down the muddy slope. The thunderstorm had abated in the predawn hours, leaving the sparse woods of the high mountains soggy and dripping. It felt as if it still rained whenever he passed under trees. The men complained of the treacherous footing. They had all been up with the dawn to break camp and begin the journey downslope to reach the shore eventually and signal the ship waiting to carry them to Rome.

Centurion Lucian scouted ahead of them and showed no signs of fatigue after his night of crazed dancing in a thunderstorm. Last night Curio had hidden under his blankets, dripping rainwater, and prayed Lucian would not expose him. But he had succumbed to sleep before he ever returned. If Lucian had noticed him, he said nothing when they awakened this morning other than the usual commands issued to get them underway.

He now called back with new instructions on the best paths for the cart to follow.

Leading the mules along with Curio was Sextus, his thin and

wiry runner. Both Fabius and Quintus guarded the rear of the cart and helped stabilize it over some of the rockier terrain.

What he had seen last night troubled him, and he wanted to tell someone. But he couldn't speak to his men. What if they confronted Lucian? Curio was not sure what it all meant. Perhaps Lucian had spent too much time in Iberia, and maybe the land spoke to him too often.

But this was the man who had changed Curio's life. He also felt it was his right to understand Lucian's actions. While he had done nothing overtly dangerous, and might only be indulging in a peculiar exercise, Curio still felt it portended something worse.

Normal people do not dance like naked madmen in thunderstorms.

He was no scholar, but couldn't think of a single Roman custom where people danced as Lucian had. Therefore, he reasoned Lucian had picked up something from the Iberians. He did not like it, not when he entrusted his life and future to the man. Who was he, really?

Such thoughts carried him through the morning until at last Lucian paused them.

"Hold!" Centurion Lucian called back. "Take a rest period."

The order surprised Curio, as they were now on a ledge. They would have to navigate around to reach a long slope that would at last dump them into the cover of a forest and level ground. Normally, Lucian seemed eager to clear those obstacles before allowing a break.

But the others did not question it and fell out into the shade of trees. As Lucian marched back to meet them, his face turned red and his eyes appeared glassy. Perhaps the prior night had affected him more than he let on.

"A word, Centurion Curio." He called him aside from the others to the shade of trees. Curio patted the neck of a mule, hoping they could remain on friendly terms long enough to reach the shore, then followed Lucian.

The summons made his stomach tighten, expecting Lucian would accuse him of spying last night. As he followed, he rehearsed a dozen retorts and barbed questions of his own. In his mind, at least, he got the better of Lucian and had him admit he was overly fond of Iberian ways. Yet his imagination ran out after this, and soon he drew up to Lucian far from the others.

"I have to be honest with you," Lucian said, his expression suddenly grim.

Curio's stomach burned. "You don't need to explain, sir. We all have habits others might consider strange."

Lucian tilted his head and frowned, but continued.

"I've found tracks of natives passing through here. There shouldn't be anyone in these mountains. I picked this way specifi- cally because it is remote, with no game to speak of or anything other than rocks and trees. But there might be a significant number of Iberians nearby."

"How many is that, sir?" Curio's face heated and the tension in his belly released.

Rather than answer, Lucian waved him forward. They side- stepped down a sharp decline, feet sliding in the mud, and into a sparsely wooded dell. Curio did not need Lucian to point out the fresh tracks impressed in the earth. Lucian crouched beside them.

"These were made after the rain, probably a few hours ago judging how the mud is filling in some tracks." He stood again and pointed. "And they're headed east toward the coast."

Curio stared at the tracks, estimating more than a dozen people had passed this way.

"What would they be doing here, sir? This is not a hunting or foraging party. The tracks seem ordered, like men marching in a file."

Lucian nodded. "My thoughts exactly, Centurion. I don't like the odds of at least two to one, especially when we have a cart of silver with us. We need to protect that at all costs and ensure it reaches the ship."

"And this document." Curio patted his side where the incriminating agreement between Carthage and Cato pressed to his flesh.

Lucian seemed confused a moment, then his expression brightened. "Yes, of course, that as well."

"Sir, it seems they have passed us. We could continue on behind them. With you scouting ahead, it should be easy to avoid running into them."

But Lucian was already shaking his head.

"There are a hundred reasons they would be out here, and they might suddenly reverse along their path at any moment. We couldn't turn the cart fast enough in that case."

"Sir, the cart has slowed our progress considerably. If we had to face these Iberians, we could just surrender the silver to them. That should distract them and let us escape. It is not the most important evidence we have against Cato. That would be the document I carry."

Again Lucian shook his head even more fiercely.

"I know how things work back in Rome, Centurion. If it wasn't important evidence, I would not have taken the risks we did to get it in the first place. No, we must show the Carthaginian coins in a numbered pay box issued from Rome. Cato was going to clean up his dirty coins by mixing it into the soldiers' pay and replacing his bribe with Roman coins. We will have the coins as proof and the sworn witness of you and your men, and probably his paymasters as well. When the interrogator's fire starts to blaze, they'll be certain to support us. Combined with the agreement you carry, Cato will have no way to escape justice."

Curio stared at the muddy tracks and hoped these Iberians were simply joining the battle against Cato in the northwest. While they traveled in the wrong direction, they might link up with other rebels before turning to cross the mountains. He at least hoped this was true.

"Then we will have to skirt around them, sir."

"We've no time to make a detour," Lucian said. "Our ship might wait a day out of respect for my relationship with the captain. But that would test its limits. We should get the cart down from that ledge, then encamp for the day. I can scout out these Iberians in the meantime and determine the next step based on what I learn. Once we're sure of a clear path, we can reach the coast from here on time. It's a straight shot to our meeting point. We'll march on the double."

"That depends on the mules, sir."

Again Lucian seemed confused, but his expression soon brightened. "Ah, I know how to speak to them. They'll work hard for me. Don't worry about it, Centurion."

Curio stared at Centurion Lucian. His Servus Capax pugio remained strapped to his left hip, the golden owl's head winking in the dappled light of the dell. He wore the mail shirt and bronze helmet of a triarius. His smile showed genuine enthusiasm, and he remained unashamed of the missing tooth that showed black against his yellow teeth. He was Rome's finest and most loyal servant, having made sacrifices few other citizens would ever consider.

Yet Curio wondered at him. His eyes were red-rimmed and glassy. He did not seem tired. Yet he did not seem well.

"What is it, Centurion Cato? You doubt I can get the mules to move on the double?"

"It seems unlikely, sir. But you've surprised me all along." His stomach tightened again, but he set it aside. "Sir, do you feel all right?"

"Never better."

Lucian clapped Curio's shoulder in a firm grip, then started back up the slope. As Curio followed, he noted the energy in

Lucian's stride. Given he had been up all night in the rain, his stamina surpassed even the hardiest veteran. Curio wondered if he used some sort of secret concoction to grant him this strength. After all, he had brewed a sweet poison to mix with the treasury guards' wine that had knocked them out. Perhaps he knew other secrets as well.

They rejoined the men and shared the new and revised plan. The three of them expressed both disappointment and pleasure. They were glad to spend the afternoon idling, but all were eager to escape Iberia to the assumed safety of Rome and their eventual rewards.

Guiding the cart down slippery mud and rough terrain consumed most of the morning. The mules did not respond well to the challenge, ignoring even Lucian's persuasions. Yet they at last reached the bottom and found an elevated position near to the dell where they made camp. Curio insisted on entrenching and staking their small area, even though Lucian claimed it was unnecessary. But Curio was adamant and started trenching on his own. The others followed his lead and called him Consul Curio. It was a jibe aimed at Cato, who often made token participation in menial duties to strengthen his personal mythology of being just one of the common soldiers.

For his part, Lucian stripped off his mail and helmet and set his pack down. He took only his spear, sword, and pugio.

"Anything more will load me down. I can't sneak around with a shield on my back. When I return, I'll have revised plans. In the meantime, you all can rest. Just stay vigilant for any others passing this way."

Once he had gone, Curio dismissed his three men to do whatever they wanted. Swarthy Quintus napped in the tent. Wiry Sextus went to rub down and feed the mules, while marble-jawed Fabius sat in the shade and pried mud and stones from the soles of his caligae.

Curio went to the cart and sat in the bed to rest. It was in the shade, its wheels set with stones to keep it in place. He passed a few hours wondering how Varro and Falco were. Would he feel it in his bones if they died, he wondered. Would the gods send him a sign?

He had few friends growing up. When it came time to join the legions, his mother begged him to hide. He was the only child left of a large family. But his father would not endure the shame, and indeed the criminal offense, of Curio remaining at home. So he enlisted as a velite, and soon got promoted to join Varro and Falco.

Both of them had mistrusted him at different times over the years. But by now, and especially after nearly dying together at Sparta, he had proved his trust. He hoped this small deceit would not ruin things between them. It hurt him to do this. But Centurion Lucian was his senior officer in Servus Capax, and this mission was of the utmost importance. Lucian commanded him to deceive the others, and so Curio obeyed. Besides, he had a higher duty to Rome, and if it cost his friendships, then so be it. He would make amends. But surely they would understand once he explained everything.

He had seen Cato's treachery himself. When called to Far Iberia, he did not even fight, and abandoned his army to the praetors, lesser men who could not wield the legions the way Cato could have. It all seemed to make sense on the surface. But Curio knew better. Cato was letting the rebellion continue, especially in the south where Carthage still had the potential to make gains. That was all detailed in the papyrus he carried.

He had been moving so fast since acquiring that document. After gaining Cato's trust, he was able to excuse his presence near the command tent to inquiring guards. He had worked with Lucian one morning while Cato was with his tribunes in a planning session. Lucian was certain he had spotted the document on Cato's desk. Curio could lift it away without issue.

Now, as he rested in the cart, the day progressed and the sun climbed higher into the sky. He wondered at this stroke of incredible luck. Curio never liked to think too much. His father had always chided him for it, claiming he wasted the intelligences the gods had gifted him. He did prefer physical action over mental exertions. But today his mind went to work on all that had happened over the last few days.

He started to think about things differently.

Just how did Lucian know where Cato's document was? He claimed to have glimpsed a suspicious papyrus buried under the consul's wax tablets while doing some spying of his own. Curio had never doubted Lucian's abilities as a spy. He had been in Servus Capax doing it for decades. But if he had seen it, why hadn't he snatched it himself? Why did Lucian leave it for him to steal?

And why was such an incriminating document left on his table to begin with? From his experiences with Cato, that was completely unlike him. Yet Curio had accepted it, so glad was he to be at last catching the man who had given him and his friends so much trouble.

His arm rested over the pay box. Shortly after stealing it, Lucian had opened it and pulled out the Carthaginian coins to prove his accusations. Combined with the document, Curio accepted everything. He hid the box in the tent until Lucian came to help them escape. But he never opened it to see for himself.

Suddenly, the pay box felt as if it burned under his arm. His hands itched to pull open the lid. But if the others saw this, they might think he was trying to steal coins for himself.

He stared hard at it. What if there were no Carthaginian coins in there?

Then Lucian would have deceived him.

Now the document pressed to his side itched his flesh.

He pulled it out and carefully unfolded it. The papyrus was

fresh and the ink lettering clear. Curio had only just learned to read, and so many of the phrases made no sense to him. Still, he puzzled out the sentences which Lucian had helped read to him and the rest of the command group. He didn't think the others were literate either, but they still looked at the papyrus as if they understood.

His fingers traced the words as his mouth silently formed the sounds he knew. This was all formal language and too much for him. Even so, it outlined a payment from agents of Carthage for Cato to hold back in Iberia as much as possible and to leave the southern tribes undisturbed. For this he would be paid a talent of silver in installments. The first payment was the chest Curio leaned on as he read the document.

He let it drop to his lap. Here was proof of Cato's betrayal, solidified by his actions in the Far Iberia. But why did he still feel something was wrong?

Once his mind engaged with that question, it became obvious. Why put all this in writing in the first place? That seemed incredibly foolish, because Curio now held proof that anyone could use against the consul. Here was the document with Cato's seal.

At least, what he assumed was Cato's seal. He had never seen it before.

Now his heart beat faster. What if this wasn't Cato's seal?

He studied the hastily made mark. It looked official enough. But he noticed that the so-called Carthaginian seals looked similar. In fact, they looked the same only pressed at different angles to appear as something different.

But he couldn't be sure. What did he know about things like this? He had seen few formal communications, and never anything from the consul.

He stared at the papyrus as if he might discover something new. The longer he stared, the stranger he felt until he at last found something he had not noticed before.

The top and sides of the papyrus had been cut to size. But the bottom had been torn. It was done carefully, but the edge was uneven and ragged, with the papyrus fibers hanging in small strips. That seemed out of place given the other edges were cut. An image of Centurion Lucian tearing the papyrus came to mind.

"No, you didn't." Curio spoke to himself as he leaped out of the cart.

He looked at the others. They had moved around, but all were resting in silence. So Curio calmly walked to where Centurion Lucian had left his pack. He kneeled over it as if he had every right to investigate. No one even looked up as he pulled aside standard kit issue items. But as he dug to the bottom of the pack, he found other nonstandard items.

Including a folded wad of papyrus.

He lifted it out and unfolded the square. It was not a large amount, and the folds had damaged its usefulness. It was dented and torn from being jostled under all the other gear.

One edge of the papyrus was torn.

Curio's hands trembled as he matched the torn edge of Cato's document to this papyrus sheet.

They meshed in a seamless match so perfect that if Curio knew how to make papyrus, he might rejoin both sheets into one.

"You forged this agreement." He whispered the accusation to Lucian wherever he had gone. "You put it on the desk for me to find, you bastard, so I'd believe it was true."

Stuffing the papyrus and the forged agreement into his tunic, he stalked back to the cart. Only swarthy Quintus looked up quizzically from his nap. Curio didn't care. His entire body was trembling as he tore away the cover to reveal the pay box.

The lid had been pried off after they captured it and now was held only by rope, which he untied. He slid the wooden lid back to reveal a glimmering sheet of denarii.

He scooped out coins into his palms. All Roman coins, with an image of Luna driving her two-horse chariot. The other side showed someone the mint magister probably wanted to honor. Curio didn't recognize who, but the letters ROMA were clearly stamped at the bottom.

These were not the Carthaginian coins Lucian had displayed to them. Those had been his own coins, Curio decided, and he had held them in his palm before he reached in to withdraw proof for the others to see.

"Sir, what are you doing?"

Quintus squinted with his black-rimmed eyes at the coins Curio held in his palm.

"Look, Roman coins." He extended his hand forward. "Lucian has played us for fools to help him steal from the treasury. This, the document, all of it are lies."

Quintus shook his head, eyes flicking wide.

Then wiry young Sextus began shouting.

"Iberians! We're surrounded!"

5

Standing up from the bed of the cart, Curio looked to where Sextus shouted his warning. Quintus also whirled around, and the pay box loaded with enough denarii to last a man's lifetime three times over was forgotten. The coins in Curio's hand chimed as they fell back into the chest.

Emerging from the thin woods and running up the slope came at least a score of Iberian warriors. They converged on the camp from all directions, round shields held forward and spears poised overhead. Their war cries gusted through the trees like the howling of hungry wolves.

Curio drew his gladius but had left his shield leaning against the cart. One glance at the closing enemy and he knew they couldn't survive the attack.

"Scatter! We'll find each other later. Just get away!"

Marble-jawed Fabius snapped up from his nap, immediately answering with his own war cry as he grabbed his sword.

The first spears came sailing over the spiked trench. One plummeted down into the cart bed, the shaft shuddering through the wood planks. Curio leaped down beside Quintus, who drew his own gladius but had taken Curio's shield for his own.

"This way!" Curio tugged his shield arm, indicating they should head west where it seemed fewer enemies approached.

Sextus screamed as a spear impaled him. Curio only glimpsed it. Poor Sextus caught it in his back, the bronze point exploding out of his chest to spray his lifeblood before him.

Iberian war cries filled Curio's ears as he and Quintus fled toward the mules. The cart offered cover from the fate Sextus had suffered. He heard Fabius bellow. The damn fool loved fighting and probably ran at the first enemy he spotted. Curio couldn't help him now.

Quintus fell. Curio wasn't sure why, but he heard him curse as he crunched into the dirt. Ahead, the mules strained against their tether, panicked by the attack and the stench of Sextus's spilled innards.

Iberian shields covered their companions working at the stakes. It was just the delay Curio needed to escape. But Quintus remained prone on his face, pawing and cursing at his ankle.

"By Jupiter's balls! I broke my fucking ankle!"

Curio turned, then lifted him up. He glanced at Quintus's ankle and the foot twisted at a terrible angle.

"Serves you for stealing my scutum. I'll drag you to hiding. I can't carry you and escape."

He would've liked Quintus to tell him just save yourself, but he locked his arm over Curio's shoulder and they hobbled forward.

The Iberians had now pulled up the stakes and were laughing as they entered the small camp, heading for the cart. The mules bucked and more spears flew overhead. One arced down into a mule's neck killing it instantly and sending it thudding to its side. A geyser of blood shot a dozen feet into the air as it kicked in its death throes. The other mule's eyes rolled as it pulled on its tether until blood flowed down its neck. It broke away, or the Iberians cut it away.

Curio staggered toward the dead mule as two Iberians walked through the stakes. Their urgency had ended and they laughed at Curio's pathetic attempt to drag Quintus away.

"Forget me, sir. Throw me at them and run."

"We're getting out, Quintus!"

But his swarthy tubicen shoved away and flung himself at the two men who had just been laughing at him. They stepped back and braced their spears. The last Curio saw, Quintus hopped on his good foot with his sword readied to strike.

More Iberians combed the trees ahead. There had to be twenty or more of them, and they did not seem concerned with capturing the camp. They had encircled it, making escape impossible even for Curio.

For the moment, it seemed no one watched him. So he threw his helmet aside, then dived under the dead mule. He wasn't certain of his plan, but he thought to hide there long enough until most of the Iberians came to claim their spoils. After that, he could shimmy out of hiding and slip into the forest.

The gap under the mule would never have covered a man the size of Fabius, whose cries and the thud of combat still echoed across the camp. But Curio was small and the mule strong. The tangy scent of blood filled his nose along with the musky scents of animal fear and mud. But he pulled under it enough that he felt the warmth of the beast cover him.

With luck, even if his foot or arm hung out, they would overlook him.

He immediately understood the flaw in his hasty plan. It limited vision to the immediate area around him. He pulled his knees to his chest with some struggle, hoping it would raise the mule enough for him to see out. But he remained mostly blind to his surroundings.

When Fabius died, he let out a death knell that carried to the summit of Mount Olympus. Curio could not smile but was glad his signifier died fighting the enemy. It was how he wanted to leave the world. The Iberians let out a cheer, for they had captured the silver and easily overran the camp.

Curio heard excited voices passing over him and saw the shadows of their feet passing. Blood dribbled down into the collar of his mail shirt. The weight of the mule made his breathing difficult. Getting out from under it without alerting others would be harder than he expected. He closed his eyes at his foolish plan, wishing that he had tried to run the gauntlet of enemies instead.

The Iberians shouted happily in their strange language, likely complimenting each other for a job well done. He heard them clomping up the shallow slope, their merry banter becoming louder before shading off as they passed him, seeing only a dead mule.

Of course, Lucian was behind this. He had gone ahead to fetch his mercenaries and guide them back to slaughter the four fools he had duped into helping him rob the treasury. He would notice Curio's absence from the body count.

He had to flee while the Iberians were still flush with an easy victory.

Shimmying to the side, he slid easily through the muddy gore. He felt fresh air on his legs as these escaped the press of the dead mule. Next, he pushed out his left arm and felt around for something to grip. He found the rope tether and yanked it to find it still held to the tree. So he used it to drag himself from the mule. When he at last popped out, fresh air assaulted him and glare from the sky struck his eyes in shafts that fell through the lattice-like canopy. He held his breath and remained still.

No one had seen him.

He carefully rolled over so he could crawl through the grass at the edge of camp. The voices were louder now without the mule's body muffling them. They were much closer than he estimated, and someone spoke in low, deep tones to his right.

Like a snake, he crawled on his belly until he had slithered into the grass. The voices were close, and he doubted he could pass them undiscovered. The grass hardly rose higher than his body and became patchy as it grew into the woods where light did not reach it.

He came to the trench, finding the sharpened stakes pulled up and discarded in it. With gladius in his right hand, he gathered a sharpened stake into his left.

The voices were louder now, and someone called from the center of camp as if gathering everyone together.

They would have to step on Curio, but would see him long before.

He sprung up with a shout. Two Iberians leaned on their spears and let their shields rest against their legs. They were wild-looking men, with matted hair and dirty skin covered in swirling blue tattoos. They wore only soiled, plain tunics.

Curio raced at the first, plunging his gladius into his hip and sending him falling back with a scream. The man beside him snatched up his shield and tried to bring his spear around.

But Curio was inside his guard. So he tripped the Iberian by hooking his foot behind his enemy's then driving all his weight into the shield presented to him. The Iberian cursed as he flopped onto his back.

Curio chirped with delight, then drove his gladius into the man's crotch before running ahead.

The way forward seemed clear. It was a sun-dappled slope leading down toward the dell. Curio hoped he could gain that relatively flat ground and run its length to lose pursuers. His legs pumped as he fled down the slope, carried by momentum and gravity.

An Iberian charged from behind a tree, unseen until the last moment. But Curio's nerves were tense and his survival instincts took over. He twisted sideways to present a narrower target for the spear and used the sharpened stake to parry it away.

The Iberian cursed, his gray hair flying wildly about his head and littered with twigs and dead leaves. Curio slid down the length of the spear and punched in with his gladius. It punctured the Iberian under his collarbone and spilled bright blood down his chest. Curio shoved him aside and continued to bound forward.

He was going to make it. The dell lay ahead and all the other Iberians were behind him now.

"Centurion Curio! Halt!"

The command struck as brilliant as the lightning from last night and rolled through the forest with the power of thunder.

Despite knowing better, he could not fight his conditioning. He had only been a centurion for a short time and was still used to taking orders.

Besides, an eerie sensation rippled along his spine as if warning him the enemy would soon lay it open if he did not obey.

So he slowed and skidded to a halt, turning with both stake and gladius readied.

Centurion Lucian stood atop the slope, surrounded by the bulky shadows of his Iberian bandits. Their hair was all unkempt, flowing over their shoulders and making them look like lion manes from this distance.

The centurion stood poised like a Roman tribune commanding his troops, and beside him a young boy, naked but for a loincloth, stood with an arrow nocked to a hunting bow. A quiver of arrows hung from his hip. He drew the arrow to his chin and Curio could trace the line of the bronze head to the center of his throat.

"He can shoot a sprinting hare's eye out at fifty paces," Lucian said. "You don't want to run. I don't want to have him kill you."

"You dog shit!" Curio brandished his gladius. "You don't have the fucking guts to face me. Instead, your boy lover does your work."

Lucian laughed, the gap in his teeth still visible at a distance.

"Come on, I know all the tricks you do and then some. He's a sturdy boy, but he can't hold the arrow forever. Throw down your weapons and come up here. We've got to talk."

"Talk?" Curio's voice cracked with emotion. "Everything you say is lies. You fucking thief!"

"That's fair," Lucian said. "But now I want to talk about the truth. Listen, put down your weapons. If you don't, you'll get an archery demonstration that will ruin your sword hand for life. You're caught, Centurion Curio. Be practical."

The boy made the slightest adjustment to his aim and Curio accepted he was done. He was not faster than an aimed arrow.

The sound of his gladius thudding into the dirt filled him with anger. He flung the wood stake up-slope at the Iberians. It struck a tree with a wooden thud and spun away.

Yet the arrow remained pointed at him. With reluctance, he unbuckled his harness holding his Servus Capax pugio and dropped that at his feet.

At last, the boy lowered the bow and the spearmen started down the slope for him. Curio thought about running now, but although the bow was lowered, the arrow remained nocked. Besides, he figured the boy would only need to reposition to get a better shot if he fled, not to mention all the Iberians would give chase.

He was captured. This was not new to him. But to be captured by a Roman, particularly one who claimed to serve the same goals as himself, was an entirely new experience of shame and hurt.

He scowled at the wild-haired, dirty Iberians who came to collect him. Others went to the gray-haired madman he had

49

stabbed. No one said anything, but collected his weapons and herded him up the slope to Lucian.

When they came face to face, Curio found he could not stand to look at Lucian and so studied his feet. The centurion represented the worst kind of treachery and highlighted Curio's own foolishness. He should never have done this on his own. If he had spoken to Varro and Falco, they would have seen through the deception.

"Good work, Centurion," Lucian said. "Even outnumbered you killed one of my men and wounded two others. Fabius accounted for two more killed."

"I will hack you to pieces one day," Curio said, at last meeting Lucian's gaze. "I swear it."

But Lucian simply laughed.

"I know you are angry. I had to deceive you or otherwise you would never go along with me. But there is a purpose to it all, I promise."

"You killed my men. No matter what you say, I'll never cooperate."

Before Lucian could answer, one of his savages—for Curio could not see them in any other light—presented his captured weapons. They spoke in their native tongue, which Lucian used to answer. It made Curio's stomach burn to hear him speak it. When finished, Lucian nodded to Curio.

"Remove your mail shirt," he said, falling into his centurion voice. "If you do that, we'll let you move freely. No need for bindings or other restrictions."

"Such generosity," Curio muttered. But he knew he could not keep the mail. It was an expensive piece, certain to become spoils for one of Lucian's favored savages. After several awkward moments, he had worked off his chain shirt and dropped it into the dirt with a metallic crunch, hoping it tangled into uselessness.

But Lucian did not seem to care. He had already handed off

Curio's gladius to another but tucked his Servus Capax pugio into his own belt beside his own.

"You don't deserve that pugio."

Lucian paused while speaking to his warriors and raised his brow.

"I don't? You do not know what you're talking about. Anyway, let's bury your men and mine."

"Do not put them together," Curio said. "I would not insult their bravery."

To his surprise, Lucian dipped his head in acceptance.

"I will let you arrange your men as you wish. They were brave."

"And they were betrayed."

But Curio's quips had no effect on Lucian. He no longer seemed Roman to him, dressed only in his tunic now. Even though he lacked the myriad tattoos of warriors, he seemed to belong to them now. Speaking their language so fluently only enhanced that feeling.

Curio found all three of his men. Swarthy Quintus lay face down in a wide puddle of blood. Sextus's wiry body twisted around the spear that had broken through his chest. Finally, marble-jawed Fabius lay on his back, his blank eyes staring into the sun and a terrible puncture through his stomach had exploded his entrails in a sickening streak across the camp.

He would let none of the savages touch his men, though he showed Lucian where he wanted to bury them. The savages dug the graves at Lucian's command while Curio gathered them to their resting places.

The Iberians did the same for their own fallen, but Curio did not care. They started wailing and dancing once their bodies were in the graves. But Lucian only watched in silence, instead standing guard over Curio.

"How can you watch me do this?" Curio asked. "How can you

pretend to act saddened by these dead men? We all trusted you, and from the start you planned to kill us."

"All life ends in death," Lucian said. "Will these three not go on to the Elysian Fields for their bravery? They died fighting their enemies. They did not live long enough to make the mistakes that send a soul to the darkness of Hades."

"You fucking prick. You're calling this a favor to them? Do no not make me vomit here, not on their graves."

Lucian remained silent as Curio set their helmets on stakes next to the stones he had used to mark their resting places. He had nothing to carve their names. Perhaps they would never be found in this remote place. After whispering his apologies for leading them to their deaths and promising to avenge them, he shoveled dirt into the holes.

"My men can do that," Lucian said. "You should rest."

But Curio continued to shovel. "Your concern overwhelms me. But this is my duty. Let me bury them."

When finished, Curio's back ran with sweat. His arms and legs trembled both from emotion and all his exertions. He could not stop thinking of how foolish he had been, and with every iteration of self-pity, he wished for his own death. He deserved nothing less. But it seemed Lucian wanted him alive a little longer.

Lucian now joined with the Iberians, and Curio seemed forgotten. But whenever he thought of fleeing, he would notice they were not so careless of his doings. They watched him, particularly the boy archer. He had unstrung his bow, but Curio did not doubt he could restring it and shoot before he could escape.

Besides, he realized now he had nowhere to run. He was lost in the southern reaches of Iberia. He had at least a passing familiarity with the north, but not so here. Furthermore, he was a traitor. Neither Roman nor Iberian would welcome him. He had no home and nowhere to escape.

Lucian at last approached him, seeming to sense Curio's resignation. He gave him a knowing nod.

"I know how you feel, like there is no hope for you now. But it's not true. You can join me in my great purpose." He gestured to his men. "These are but a handful of my tribe. You can find a new family in them, as I did. Come. We must travel while the sun is up. Like you, I've no desire to linger in this place. I will show you a new light in the darkness."

Curio looked back at the three graves. Bronze helmets set on the sharpened stakes that had surrounded their camp leaned at different angles. For an instant, Curio thought he saw the faces of his men in the shadows of the helmets they wore in life. They scowled, silently cursing him for their deaths.

"I will never see light again," he said as he followed Lucian out of the camp.

6

Lucian set a pace for his warriors as relentless as he would have for Romans on the march. The chaos of Curio's emotions exhausted him. Yet the day had been full of physical stress that also took its toll. His thighs and back burned as he marched in the middle of the column with Lucian at his side.

To the rear, small horses the Iberians had in reserve were hitched to the wagon carrying the silver. These were far more tractable beasts than mules and kept pace as the column passed through the dell eventually regaining a path back into the mountains. Curio smelled rain in the air but had no desire to raise his head to check the sky. Nothing mattered to him now.

His freedom was illusory, for even though he moved among these dirty, wild-haired savages, their hands were ever ready to lower spears at him. They surrounded him even when they rested by streams. During the march on that day of betrayal, Curio had no desire to run. He simply moved forward without care for where he traveled, his mind dwelling on all that had happened.

That night, they made camp and erected hide tents. Curio was allowed to sit by their fire and fed rations from his own pack. Such was his worry that it lacked any taste at all. Lucian at last showed his true feelings that night, for he had Curio tied to a tree, though allowed him to sit.

"If it does rain," he said, "then we will provide you cover. You understand we must take these precautions while your mind is full of confusion."

Curio accepted his fate as Iberians that smelled like raw onions wound a scratchy rope around him. He shook his head at Lucian.

"If it rains, will you entertain me with that mad dance again? I hope you impale your foot on a branch while leaping about like some sort of animal."

But Lucian acted as if he had not heard and abandoned him to the tree.

Despite his condition and all his fears, exhaustion pulled him into a fast slumber. Later, he awakened in the depth of night to cool sprinkles of rain pattering on his face.

The Iberian camp was dark but for the red embers of their campfires. The drizzle did not develop into more, and he soon drifted back to sleep.

But then he heard a distant howl, and he feared wolves were near. Except as he listened, he realized it was a human imitation, and not howling. Though the sound was thin, it resolved into some sort of crazed, warbling song. More than one voice produced these eerie notes. Tied as he was, Curio could do nothing. He looked once more at the camp, but no one stirred. Even if guards were on watch, they gave no reaction.

"They're all mad," he said to himself. "Maybe I will become as mad as them."

He smiled at the thought of himself prancing under the rain and howling like a wolf. Maybe Lucian had the right idea. What could he do now other than join with these madmen? He let that thought lull him back to sleep.

Curio awakened the next morning, having slept yet feeling sodden and tired. The rope itched his skin and left his fingers cold and tingling. The Iberians came to untie him. For once, he could study them up close. The two who approached had sunken eyes in sockets so black Curio wondered if they had daubed coal around their jaundiced eyes. Their tattoos made no sense to him other than strange swirls and patterns that made him dizzy. Both were dirty with matted hair, and one wore a necklace of what seemed like finger bones.

They were unlike any Iberians he had seen and they made the barbarians he had fought before seem like civilized men. Further, they had a look of illness despite their sharp, animated movements.

After untying the rope, they helped him up. One looked over his shoulder toward the tents, then turned back to Curio with a vicious snarl. He slapped him hard across the face. The crack of the open palm striking his face echoed through the camp. The sting of the blow spread out on Curio's cheek. But he smiled, then spit in his assailant's face.

"Thanks. I needed to remember that I must live long enough to kill all of you."

Both Iberians balled their fists as if to strike him and Curio shifted into a fighting stance.

Then a sharp call from the camp brought both Iberians to heel, but Curio remained ready to fight.

"At ease, Curio!"

Lucian strode across the camp, rushing to intervene before the fight escalated. Curio considered whether he should strike anyway. Not only would it feel good, but it might create enough chaos for him to flee.

That idea vanished as both Lucian and the other Iberians came rushing from camp. The savages were all babbling in their own language, and the two assailants seemed to defend themselves against accusations. Lucian deftly inserted himself before Curio, dusting off his shoulders.

"I hope the night was not too harsh."

Curio pushed Lucian's hands away. "Fuck your concern. You're a liar in every way."

Lucian remained undaunted, his smile embossed on his face. Indeed, Curio wondered if Lucian heard only what he wanted to hear. Insults just seemed to rebound from him.

He led Curio to his tent where the young archer was kindling a cooking fire before it. He spared Curio a disdainful glance.

"Without his bow, that boy is nothing. I'd cut his head off in a stroke."

At first, Lucian seemed confused, then laughed. "I don't doubt it. That's one reason I want you by my side for what is coming. I told you, Curio, you underestimate yourself. Of the three Servus Capax members I met during my brief return to the legion, you were the best."

"It is impossible for you to flatter me. You are worse than dog shit between my hobnails."

Lucian at last frowned, assuaging Curio's doubts that he heard only what he wanted.

"Once, I doubted as you do. It will take time to understand how you fit into the purpose. But once you see it with your own eyes, you will know that I am taking you home."

"My home is far from here. All you've done is make me a traitor and deserter."

Clicking his tongue, Lucian gestured for Curio to sit beside him. Though he had sat all night on hard earth, making his backside ache, he hoped to conserve his strength. They sat on logs dragged from nearby trees. The wood was cool and damp from the night's drizzle.

The boy archer now had the cooking fire lit and erected a black iron trestle over it while other savages waited beside him with a cast-iron pot filled with water. Curio and Lucian watched as they prepared a breakfast of some sort of meat. It looked as if it would be a bland, unseasoned broth.

Lucian drew a long breath and shifted to face Curio.

"I volunteered to join Servus Capax years ago when Carthage ravaged these lands. I dedicated myself to the ideals of Roman civilization. I gave more than you can ever understand. Whatever you think you suffered, Curio, I assure you I have suffered more. That is why I still possess this."

His powerful hand slapped the pugio at his waist. Curio gave a disdainful glance, noticing his own Servus Capax pugio tucked into the belt beside Lucian's.

"Whatever else has happened since, I still carry this pugio with pride."

"You shouldn't," Curio said. "You're a traitor and murderer. That's really what you're about, isn't it? You're happy to see me become like you and lead other loyal soldiers to their deaths."

"Servus Capax eventually makes everyone see the world as negatively as you do." Lucian shook his head. "It is unfortunate the others died. But they did not have the mind to see what you and I see. They fulfilled their purpose and go to the gods as heroes. But we remain here to serve the gods still."

Curio squelched his arguments. Lucian was mad and therefore beyond any logic or persuasion. Instead, he let him speak and used the time to think of a way back to his old life. There had to be an escape from this nightmare other than death. He resolved to find it.

"You saw me dancing. I knew you were there, but only because you chose to expose yourself to me. Why do that, Curio? Were you moved by what you saw?"

"I moved from a crouch to falling flat on my backside in horror."

Again, Lucian appeared not to hear the sarcasm. Instead, his eyes took on a dreamy cast.

"It is a dance sacred to Bandua. He is like Jupiter and Mars in one mighty form."

"I see." Curio watched the boy ladle soup and bits of meat into a wooden bowl that he then presented to Lucian. It seemed he might be a personal servant of some sort. All around the camp, savages squatted around similar fires and ate while others broke down the camp.

"Bandua guides our people," Lucian said, his voice dreamy. He seemed to search his imagination. "He has selected me for a noble purpose. The shaman has proclaimed it and the tribe understands."

The boy now handed Curio a bowl. He did not seem to hold any ill will but seemed overly proud of himself. Taking the bowl, Curio stared into a murky broth with bits of gray meat floating in it. It smelled like rabbit. He ignored Lucian, who continued to speak, and chewed on the stringy meat to find it gamey and hard. The barest hint of salt bloomed on his tongue. But it was likely all the food he would have for a while. In the meantime, Lucian ate as well.

"So, this noble purpose of yours includes stealing from Rome? Your god Bandua can't earn his own silver? He acts just like all Iberians. Complain and fight against Rome, but take whatever they can from it. The people learn from their gods, I suppose."

Lucian set his bowl aside, unperturbed at the insult.

"The gods do not need silver coins, but the people do." He wiped his mouth with his forearm, then issued orders to his followers, including the boy. Even when spoken in a foreign language, Curio could identify an order. The boy and other savages set down their own bowls and left to carry out Lucian's commands.

"People like you," Curio said. "You need silver coins. But you're not satisfied with what you have. So you steal, and shamelessly at that."

"I did steal the silver, but only what I needed. We had laid the treasury open, you'll remember. We could've taken more, but I only acted as Bandua directed."

"How noble. And to think, you not only ruined my life and scores of others, but you also led trusting men to their deaths. Truly, Lucian, you are a holy man. You only murder who you must."

"That is so."

Curio now stared hard at this maniac.

"Do you not understand an insult? You are a madman, and these sick savages have twisted your mind. What are these grubby barbarians going to do with silver coins? I can't imagine. For that matter, what are you going to do with so much wealth? You can buy yourself a lifetime of whores and wine and still have coin left to keep a small villa in the countryside. But out here? Gods, looking at the state of your men, I would want their whores to pay me."

Lucian lowered his head and waved away Curio's words.

"Wine and whores. I do understand an insult, and that is one. No, Curio, that coin will go toward Bandua's noble purpose."

"Which is what, then?" Curio gulped the rest of the broth and chewed down the last bits of stringy meat. "You're going to build a bath for the tribe?"

"I will raise a city to rival Rome."

Curio dropped his bowl to the dirt. Lucian continued, staring up as if admiring the lofty towers of his imaginary city.

"Bandua has willed it, and has led me to his people. The shaman has proclaimed it so and confirmed my visions. It has been long spoken around the fires that a hero would come from afar to raise the tribe above all others and to build the mightiest city ever known on the foundations of our homes."

"You can't be serious?" Curio looked across the camp at the dirty, uncivilized men working to break down their animal hide tents. They hitched their small horses to the cart where the pay box sat hidden under the yellowed tarp Curio himself had nailed down.

"It will not be a simple thing." Lucian continued to stare up at a tower only he could see. "We tried to gather the other Lusitani tribes, but they are too proud. Each tribe agrees that the vision is true, but the location is wrong. It should be their tribe. But Bandua is clear. Still, men are stubborn. My tribe is small, but dedicated to me and the vision. We can only achieve so much, and have sought help from other tribes to build our city. That is why we need the silver. To pay for their labor and skill and for the materials we will need."

Curio narrowed his eyes at Lucian and wondered how he had not seen this madness before. The old bastard was truly a master of masquerading as whatever he needed to be. Now he dropped all his disguises to reveal the crazed man beneath.

At least he had learned these were Lusitani tribesmen. It meant they were far from their home on the western shores of Iberia. He was no expert in tribal territories, but he had heard them mentioned often as western barbarian tribes who were also fierce cavalrymen.

"I don't understand it," Curio said. "If you're living so far west, wrapped up in Bandua's plans, why did you come back to the legions?"

"I could never get close to the treasury any other way." Lucian snapped out of his reveries and leaned back as if shocked. "Rome had to be my target. I could not steal from fellow tribesmen or any other tribe. How then would Bandua's city grow?

"But once I heard of the great rebellion and so many tribes rallying to it, I knew Rome would come. I spoke to the shamans, and to Bandua."

"You spoke to a god?"

"I did, and he agreed that the silver must come from Rome. The shaman confirmed my vision. So I traveled east and met my adopted son, Aulus. What a joyous reunion it was. Though it pained me to lie to him as well. Bandua's work demanded it of me. He has become more Roman than I like and seems he has become lost to that way of life. That at least made it easier to deceive him."

Curio narrowed his eyes in disgust. Yet learning that Aulus was dedicated to Rome gave him hope Varro and Falco had a reliable ally to help the escape. But to call Aulus a son and then use him like a tool revealed how hollow Lucian was. He continued, oblivious to Curio's revulsion.

"Aulus arranged for us to both join the arriving legions. He was already part of the local garrison, and it was an easy transfer for him. I've kept my old skills sharp enough to get assigned to the triarii. There was some confusion at first, but no one tries to join the legion when a war's on. More often, they're expecting soldiers to desert. So, I was back in the ranks after more than a decade away."

Curio had to nod in agreement. Officers wouldn't doubt a soldier with forged transfer orders from the garrison. No one wanted to leave garrison duty to fight on the line.

"I had different plans on how to get that silver, but then you three showed up." He gave Curio a jovial punch on his shoulder, as if they were old friends. "Cato fooled with the treasury, making it impossible to take any action. Soon I found out you three were the reason for it. It shocked me to learn you were all Servus Capax. Things must have changed since I served. I never heard of more than one member operating at once on the same mission. So I had Aulus get close to you while I watched. Later I found out how talented you are, Curio. You know the rest."

"The rest of that story is a tragedy," Curio said. "You're stealing from Rome so you won't upset any tribes and probably end up looking like a hero. Given the rebellion, that sounds reasonable. But Cato won't let you build a rival city. Even if he never learns, when Rome does, then Bandua and Jupiter and Mars are going to have a fight. And I'm certain Rome's gods will win."

"You can be part of it all," Lucian said, his eyes once more dreamy. "We will be as Romulus and Remus, founding a city whose glory will fill the world."

"Well, we're not twins," Curio said, leaning away. "And I have no skill for building glorious cities."

"We shall see." Now Lucian's dreamy demeanor faded, and his eyes widened with anticipation. "Tonight, we will climb to the summit of these mountains and there we will ask Bandua. You will speak to him yourself. I will take you to him."

Curio blinked. His throat constricted as he imagined how this meeting with Bandua might take place. He looked to the sickly warriors now lining up to begin the march, then back to Lucian who apparently never slept. His voice trembled.

"How will you take me to your god?"

"Tonight, I will show you the way." Then he tapped Curio's head. "A way out of this body to where gods and mortals may meet for a short time. Then, Centurion Curio, you will no longer doubt me or the purpose. Instead, you will join us with joy in your heart."

Curio swallowed hard. Something would be in his heart, he agreed, but it would not be joy. "What if Bandua doesn't want me?"

Lucian did not answer immediately but seemed dumbfounded by the question.

"If Bandua does not want you to aid in his glorious task, then he will state what he wants from you. Perhaps all he will ask for is Roman blood sacrificed in his honor."

7

The peak of the mountain was not especially high, nor was it the actual peak. Curio decided Lucian had a penchant for exaggeration. This so-called summit sat high in the mountains as a wide ledge amid craggy terrain. The night sky overflowed with uncountable stars gleaming white in a velvety black swath. Below, treetops protruded from a bowl of darkness.

He could not observe more of the surroundings while Lucian led him firmly by his shoulder along with a dozen spear and shield warriors to the center of the stony ledge. The summit was like a blank scar in the brilliance of the stars, and a stiff wind fluttered through his stained tunic.

His throat was tight and dry and he tasted stale bile at its back. He had fretted all day about what this meeting with Bandua would entail. Given the amount of weapons surrounding him, he expected violence would have a role. He was tired from a long march and the arduous climb to this ledge. But now that the moment was at hand, fear drove trembling energy into his limbs once more.

His sight grew sharp and focused, just like the moments before clashing with a line of waiting enemies. Only now he had no shield to hide behind and no armor to protect him. He wore only his caligae and an unbelted tunic that hung loose over him, the hem and sleeves torn from days of hard travel. The exposure to the cool night left his body tingling with the expectation of a pike or sword laying open his bones. He couldn't prevent the feeling, not after so many years of battle.

Yet that same tension aided him now. Lucian's muttering to his warriors, though unintelligible to Curio, was still clear. The outlines of the shaggy bulk of his men were crisp even against the shadows. His entire body was tuned up to seize any opportunity presented.

After speaking to his men, Lucian accepted something from the boy archer. It was a human skull, sawed away at the top and filled with a cup. The hollow eyes seemed to stare at Curio as it passed into Lucian's hands. Something liquid shimmered reflections of the stars.

If the boy had carried a filled skull up to this place, Curio had to credit him. He had seen nothing dispensed into it, but then he was absorbing whatever details of his surroundings that he could. Lucian cupped the skull in both hands so that the face seemed to look upon Curio. Twine woven through gaps between crooked yellow teeth held the jaw shut.

One warrior now positioned Curio while Lucian spoke quietly in the Iberian tongue. The man seemed intent on aligning Curio to something in the sky, as he continued to look up and reposition him until he stepped away, at last satisfied.

This would not be a disaster, Curio decided. He did not want to see any gods other than Roman ones, and even then he would be happy to never meet one in either life or death. What good could come from a mortal meeting gods? In every story he knew of, mortals always ended up worse for having encountered one. How much worse would it be to meet a barbarian god?

But now warriors encircled him, including the boy archer. Lucian's voice suddenly rose, and Curio startled at it. It seemed the signal for the barbarians to begin a dance. They danced in a circle, raising spears and pulling up their shields as they chanted in their language. The warriors seemed to enact a mock battle, with some mimicking spear thrusts and others taking wounds. They also sang in time with their steps, their deep voices and strange phrasings rattling Curio's resolve.

Lucian held the skull up as he chanted, and the warriors increased their pace. A chill wind swept along the ledge and Curio wanted to fold over and die from fright. This was not a human enemy to fight, but spirits and evil magic. They were cursing him; he was certain.

Lucian seemed enthralled with his ritual and Curio felt like an insect under the stars, where the dark gods of Iberia gathered, called by this terrible dance and song.

But as he stood in mortal terror, he noticed the two pugiones tucked into Lucian's belt, now loosened and sticking forward.

Curio knew what he had to do.

"Jupiter best and greatest. Drive away these foreign gods and their wicked spirits."

"Roman gods cannot reach you here, not where Bandua and Nabia hold court." Lucian now lowered the skull level with Curio's head. "Drink this, then lie on the ground."

The warriors continued their wild dance as Lucian proffered the skull in both hands.

Curio needed a distraction, something to break Lucian's iron focus.

"Whose skull is this? Your great enemy's?"

"No, it is my wife's skull."

The answer nearly sent Curio to his knees. This monster used his wife's skull for evil magic? Was there no end to his madness?

When he recovered from his momentary swoon, Lucian pressed the skull cup towards Curio's mouth, so that he smelled a vile, moldy scent wafting up from it. Were it not for the wind, the stench might have overwhelmed him.

"Drink now, beneath the stars where the eyes of gods see you."

Curio swallowed hard, peering down into a brown fluid that swirled with the reflected stars.

"Will drinking this really take me to the gods?"

"Yes," Lucian said with breathless reverence. "I carry the ingredients with me always, so that when Bandua summons me, I may journey to his court. Now drink and discover what few men might ever glimpse."

"Certainly," Curio said, raising both hands. "Tell your gods to get fucked."

He slapped the bottom of the skull, splashing the fluid into Lucian's face and sending his wife's skull spinning away.

Fast as a striking viper, Curio snatched one of the pugiones from Lucian's belt as he covered his face and howled.

The dancing warriors continued to spin wildly, caught up in whatever frenzy gripped them. But Curio knew it wouldn't last.

He turned on his heels and plunged ahead, the naked bronze of a white-edge pugio streaking in his wake.

He crashed into the archer boy, purposely targeting him for his size, which made him the weakest link in the circle of burly warriors dancing around him. They both crashed out of the circle, and Curio plunged the bronze blade into the boy's throat. He gasped and stiffened as Curio yanked out the blade then scrambled to his feet and fled into the purple darkness.

Lucian howled in rage behind him, clear above the throaty songs of his men. A foul taste like spoiled mushrooms suddenly spread into Curio's mouth and he spit in reflex as he ran. What-ever that concoction was, some of it had splashed on his face and now flowed between his lips.

Curio staggered down the slope they had taken to reach this place. But he could not follow a known path.

"Jupiter best and greatest." He labored to repeat this as he scurried into the crowded spaces off the path. His small body easily slipped into gaps that larger men could not fit. This slowed his progress but also hid him from the bigger men certain to pursue him. Curio smiled at having eliminated the only one among the savages who might have been able to follow.

In the distance, Lucian's raging seemed to have ended. Curio fervently hoped whatever potion he was about to consume now sent Lucian to see his gods. The manic singing of his warriors had also fallen silent. For the time, he heard only the crunch of his hobnails on the dirt and the scratch of his tunic against rock as he slipped deeper into the maze of crevices.

Then he heard a dozen cries of anger and he knew the chase was on. He redoubled his efforts to get away, seizing upon every wide gap to double up his pace. Rocks and scrubby bushes sawed at his exposed flesh, but he continued to put distance between himself and the others. All the while, he tried to head down the slope.

The foothills would remain dangerous since most of Lucian's deranged warriors were still in the camp there. Curio lacked any coherent plan other than to put distance between himself and danger.

As he continued downward, he stepped off a ledge onto a slope hidden by shadow. He had only starlight for illumination, and being deep in the mountains it rarely touched the ground. Now he slid forward on scree, and then suddenly swept into a flow of rock and dirt.

He bit down on the cry of surprise as he slammed to his

back and rode the slide to its thankfully abrupt conclusion. The brief fall dumped him onto hard dirt with enough stones to bruise him. More scree followed to cover his head and back. But when it ended, he remained still, both to prevent dislodging something worse than scree and to hear if he had given away his position.

But other than distant shouting, he heard nothing more.

"Of course, they're not as desperate as me," he chuckled to himself. "They'll come looking in the daylight."

As he lay flat on his stomach, the smell of earthy dust clogging his nostrils, he realized he was now looking into a deep cleft under the ledge he had just slid down. It was pitch dark under it and seemed just high enough that he might shimmy beneath it.

His first thought was snakes or foxes might hide in it. But nothing investigated his crash landing. He patted around himself and grabbed a dry stick, then swished it through the crack. It raked back and forth through emptiness. Satisfied he wouldn't be pushing himself into danger, he remained on his stomach and slid into the crack.

He shimmied as far back as he could, the rock here cold but somehow comforting. It was like a giant hand pressing his back, assuring nothing would hurt him. Better still, he had reached the rear wall and had only to watch the entrance.

"So this is what a roach feels like," he said. It wasn't so bad, he judged, since no one would ever find him here unless they fell down the same slope and got on their bellies to peer into a space most men would assume no one could fit.

No more sounds came as he rested. Only now did he realize his heart pounded, and squeezed as he was in his rock enclosure, his chest hurt for the wild beating. But slowly his breathing and pulse calmed. He realized he felt dizzy even though he lay still. Could that be from tasting the drop of whatever Lucian wanted to feed him? He smiled in the utter darkness of his hiding place. No wonder Lucian stopped howling. He must be meeting his gods by now.

So he rested in peace, confident that at least until dawn he was safe. He shoved his hand under his face pressed to the rocky ground to serve as a pillow. Then, like a true soldier, he drifted into sleep.

The moment of his awakening was less decisive than when he had dropped into slumber. His eyes fluttered open to the white light as a long, thin line striking his face. But he went through several cycles of seeing the light and falling asleep again. Such was his exhaustion that he couldn't rouse himself.

It was only when he realized something made noise nearby that he awakened. He heard rocks crunching and some dirt drizzled from the ledge.

He tried to sit up but found that comforting stone hand on his back now kept him flattened. If the sound came from Lucian or his savages, he had to maintain strict silence. While he was more than an arm's length back from the narrow opening, spears would have no trouble reaching him here. Also, his back was to the rear wall of the cleft, preventing escape.

The pugio had fallen out of his grip while he slept, but now he wrapped his hand around it. In such a restricted space, he could not fight but wanted to be ready if an enemy flushed him out.

Something dark flitted across the light and Curio jerked in answer, thumping his head on the stone ceiling. Fortunately, only a mouse peeked inside before darting off when Curio stirred. He rested a while longer, hearing nothing.

His stomach growled, and his throat was dry. He could go without food, but not without water. Lucian would know this as well, and likely watch local streams.

"Come on," he said as he shimmied out of the cleft. "You can be thirsty until nightfall. Better to go hungry than die with a full stomach."

Pulling himself out of the cleft, he lay stiff beneath an afternoon sun. He had been asleep longer than expected. He rubbed his limbs and face to warm up before he stood and looked at the pugio.

The pommel had a stylized owl's head in silver. He kissed the blade and laughed.

"What's mine is mine!"

He ensured he hadn't ruined the edge during his crazed flight. It lacked the sheath, dropped or else still stuck in Lucian's belt. In any case, he would keep it in hand until he was safe.

Since he had heard nothing but a mouse, he wondered if he should remain in place or move on. There were advantages to both, as well as downsides. He did not want to deliver himself to Lucian but stuck amid deep crevices and towering rocks, he could be easily cornered if discovered.

The need for water drove his decision. He would have to reach the foothills and retrace his steps. He was in Far Iberia now. If he could locate a Roman garrison, he might try to pass himself off as an escaped prisoner. He had the rope burns on his arms from being bound to a tree all night as proof.

The trail downward was difficult to find, and he climbed up nearly as often as down. The effort spent only stoked his thirst and he reconsidered his path. But he could not have been traveling more than an hour when he heard his name shouted in the distance.

"Curio! I know you can hear me! Your trail is close!"

Lucian's booming centurion voice echoed through the mountains behind Curio. Even with the distance between them, he still crouched behind a rock as if he had been spotted. The echoing shouts continued.

"You've made a terrible mistake. You could've had a new life. But you've chosen death. I will not follow you, Centurion Curio.

You have offended the gods. Flee, if you will. The land will consume you."

He waited, shrinking into the shadow of a rock until the echoes died away. When he thought Lucian had finished, he began anew.

"You were a good soldier, Centurion! I bear you no malice. I will pray the gods grant you a swift death. Good bye, Centurion Curio."

It had to be a ruse, he guessed. This was Lucian's way of lowering his guard. Every word he spoke was a lie. So Curio hunkered down into hiding, certain he would soon hear those crazed warriors scurrying through the crevices and defiles.

Yet an hour passed and all he heard was the wind shaking needles from pine trees that grew thicker at the base of the mountains. His knees stiffened and at last he had to stand when cramps in his hamstrings drove him out of hiding.

He had not sat idle during the hour, but fashioned a makeshift sheath out of bark and strips of his tunic. It would not survive heavy use, but would prevent an accidental cut. Without a belt, he still had to carry it in hand.

So he filed out of the mountains and located the path Lucian's men left when they first passed this way. He traced it back to their old campsite, where he found a stream to refresh himself and enough pine nuts and berries to stop the growling in his gut. He did not expect meat for a long while yet. Curio was no hunter, and in any case, his goal was to push south toward the coast where he was certain to find civilization and a Roman garrison.

Over the next days, he followed the trail Lucian had left for him. But one night of heavy rains erased what remained of a trail already petering out. He picked a southern route that led up into low tree-covered hills and counted his luck with both forage and water. In fact, as evening fell some six days after escaping Lucian, he had the temerity to mock his threat of the land rising against him.

"So much for curses. The land loves me," he said as he cooked a squirrel he struck with a thrown rock. He had been working out frustration, never expecting to actually strike and break the creature's skull. So he skinned what he could and now roasted it on a spit. What more proof did he need to show the gods had forgotten him?

Yet Curio had forgotten his situation. He realized it only when his sharp ears picked up the crack of branches from the surrounding trees. He sat now in a small clearing, campfire burning and roasting squirrel turning on the makeshift spit.

He was still in enemy territory. Lucian and his mad followers had become so large in his mind that he forgot any other threat. It was as if he merely had to walk away from them to remain safe.

Only now, he felt the threat drawing closer. Attracted by his fire and the scents on the wind, opportunistic men lurked behind him. He stiffened, but then relaxed as if he were unaware. While he carried nothing of value, he would fetch a good price as a slave. He imagined the hungry look in the eyes of the men creeping up to him.

A loud snap gave one away, and a curse followed. Curio sprang to his feet, grabbing both pugio and smoking spit of roasted squirrel. He plunged forward and heard shouting behind.

Fear lent him strength as he fled, biting off what he could of the bony flesh. It burned his tongue and tasted horrible, but he gulped a mouthful before flinging the spit away when he reached the tree cover. Only then did he glance back to see four men in heavy furs converging on him.

He raced like a deer, leaping fallen logs and protruding rocks, dancing between trees with a speed only mortal fear could inspire. Whoever pursued him was long on curses, but short on speed.

Curio realized they likely knew the land better than he did, and might somehow cut him off.

Still, he was light and driven to escape. After a headlong pitch that left him scratched up and breathless, he doubled over and listened for his enemies. Their shouts were far behind and moving in the wrong direction.

Looking down, Curio discovered his caligae had driven hard prints into the soft ground, and his heedless flight left a path of trampled bushes and broken twigs. His enemies would soon correct their path and easily follow. So now he took a more deliberate path, removing his sandals to leave a lighter print.

The ground was cold and wet, and root and rock were merciless on his soles. But he padded down into a ravine where mud from recent rain filled in his tracks. He followed it to the end, then climbed out and continued into the night. All the while he listened for sounds of his clumsy enemies.

His pursuers had given up.

From now on, he decided to be more careful. That night, he slept under a carpet of leaves and branches. Wolves howled in the distance, and Curio regretted his haughtiness. The gods were indeed still watching him.

The next two days he traveled with greater care. He paused less frequently, except to forage and drink from streams. His belly was never full and his thirst was never satisfied. His beard had grown past the point of itching. He had been heading south for over a week now, and on the late evening well into the second week, he spotted white smoke above the trees. Not a campfire, but smoke from a settlement, something bigger than a few houses. Perhaps it was a town.

A wave of relief filled him. For he had made the long journey back to civilization. The gods had not risen against him, and the land had not devoured him. He increased his pace, jogging through an ever-thinning forest toward the milky light beyond it.

And voices called behind him.

Four figures emerged out of the woods, their hunched and shaggy forms pointing at him.

"Not you four again?"

Whether it was the same four still on his trail or a new group of Iberians, he had no choice but to flee. He sprinted ahead, again trusting fear and dexterity to lead him to safety.

The four men cursed and chased, leading Curio to believe they wanted him alive. Otherwise, he felt a target on his back ripe for a javelin or spear.

Now he burst out of the thinning woods into a cleared field.

His heart soared.

Ahead were the high stockade walls of a Roman garrison, the source of the smoke. He saw two bored guards by the opened gate and more leaning over the parapets.

He screamed, waving hands overhead.

"I'm a Roman citizen! Help!"

The four Iberians ran close behind. Curio dared a glance, seeing red faces with gnashing teeth. They were more like rabid hounds than humans to him. The glimpse afforded him no other details, not even what they wore.

His feet slammed over the ground as he sped for the opened gate, waving hands and screaming for help.

The two guards heard him, lifting shields and grabbing their light pila. The guards on the wall stood straighter as well.

And the two guards began to close the gates.

"No! I'm a citizen!" Curio's voice cracked with urgency. The Iberians were right behind. "I'm a sol—"

He crashed to his face, the dirt driving into his teeth and nose as if the Iberian gods themselves sought to humble him.

A roar of victory followed behind, but Curio was so terrified he did not remember getting to his feet again. He waved both hands, one holding his drawn pugio so that it flashed in the late-day sun.

Now he drew closer and the gate slammed shut. The two guards had vanished behind it, leaving Curio alone with his enemies. But Roman soldiers stood on the wall, watching the drama below while resting their heads in their hands.

Behind, the four pursuers jogged to a halt, then leaned on their knees. Curio looked long enough to see one wild-haired man enduring the punches and curses of his companions. They all wore heavy furs, and so they must be the same men he had recently evaded. He had escaped them now that he was in javelin range of the garrison. His pursuers had lost their potential slave after days of what must have been patient tracking.

Curio looked up to his saviors, his fellow Romans.

"I am a centurion! Open the gates!"

A dark face in a bronze helmet glared down from the walls, surrounded by three others.

"What's the password?" Then he laughed with his companions as he added in a mocking tone, "Sir."

"What? I'm not from this garrison. I can prove my rank. Just open the fucking gates!"

Curio looked back and the four Iberians had noted his dilemma. They stopped arguing and walked forward with heavy clubs, while one shook out a net in both hands.

"What's the password, sir?" The soldier spoke through his nose as if addressing some vagrant scum. "If you're one of us, you know the rules."

"I know the fucking rules! The password is open this fucking gate or I'll cut your balls off and stuff the tiny things down your fucking throat! Open up, now!"

The Iberians continued their cautious approach, sneering at Curio for being spurned by his own kind. He turned back to the gate. It remained shut and still.

"They'll kill me! Open the gate!"

"Sorry, sir. That ain't the password." The haughty soldier and the others beside him lifted their pila over the side so the iron points glinted as if in anticipation of a bloodletting. "Get back from the gate now. Or we'll fix you where you stand."

Curio growled. Behind him, the Iberians stopped but fanned out to catch him no matter which direction he ran.

Above him, he heard the order shouted.

"Ready pila!"

8

_____

V arro set down the silver cup with a soft puff against the wood table, staring at a deep red reflection of himself. Ripples spread across the strong wine, distorting his hard face. How appropriate, he thought, a reflection as scrambled as the real man.

"What's wrong?" Falco asked. "A fly land in your wine?"

"No, but one may as well have." Varro swirled the wine, then gulped the last of it. He again looked into the cup, watching the dregs settle before extending it to a servant.

He and Falco both reclined beside a table where the tangles of grape stems rested on trays holding crumbs of bread and cheeses. Both wore clean tunics of white cloth and functional sandals. Their grass crowns lay atop their beds, though Falco often wore his when he wanted to remind Varro of their past glories.

"The wine is good, but it's tasteless to me," he said. Yet he waited as the servant refilled his cup.

Falco sighed as well, staring into his own cup. His face had healed from the terrible beatings he had suffered in Iberia. But green bruises still lingered under both eyes and a fresh scar parted the heavy brow over his left eye.

They sat in silence, the pleasant trickle of wine flowing into Varro's silver cup the only sound in their lushly appointed apartment.

"Consul Flamininus sure knows how to treat a guest," Falco said as he finished his own cup.

"He's not a consul. How many times do I have to correct you? He's a senator."

Falco shrugged. "Sorry, old habits."

With his cup refilled, Varro waved the young servant back into a corner. He was a young boy taken as a slave from Macedonia among Flamininus's uncountable spoils. He hadn't learned to speak much Latin yet but understood how to pour wine and fetch food. That was all they needed since they had nothing else to do.

"Are we really guests here?" Varro asked, sweeping his hand across the room they shared. "Yes, we have a servant and we have a beautiful room."

"I am in love with my bed," Falco said. "I'm going to buy it along with ten slaves to carry it for me on campaign."

"On campaign?" Varro's hand slapped down to the table. "Are we even in the legion anymore? What are we but prisoners in a beautifully appointed cell?"

"You sound ungrateful."

"We'll, I'm not happy about never leaving this room. Are you? We can walk to the latrine and back, and not without our young slave. He probably understands more than he lets on and tells Flamininus everything we discuss."

"Then the senator," Falco nearly yelled the word, "must be bored to tears, since all we talk about is how we're going to find Curio and make everything right again. By the gods, Curio made his own choice. It's been over a month now. If he showed up anywhere, we'd know."

"Does Mercury deliver you news?" Varro blinked in astonishment. "If Cato found him, it might be months before a report reached us, if he bothered to report anything at all."

Falco sat up from reclining beside the table, then sat on his bed before letting out a long sigh.

"Mercury doesn't have to tell me what'll happen when Cato finds Curio. He's a deserter, just like us. That's why we can't leave this room except to shit. You know that. So, how many times do I have to correct you?"

Varro remained reclining on his side, staring at a thin line of red streaking down the side of his cup.

When they had arrived back in Rome, they were two desperate fugitives from Cato's wrath. They had recently killed his henchman, Centurion Longinus. He wondered if Cato would ever learn his fate, or if Prince Albus of the Ilegertes tribe had covered his disappearance with a probable story. The only others to know of the death were the merchant ship crew, who couldn't tell one Roman officer from another, and Varro's treacherous slave, Servius. He would probably die at sea. Therefore, Longinus went to an unmarked grave with no one to remember his passing. It served him right, in Varro's opinion.

He and Falco had slipped into Rome disguised as part of the merchant crew, but shortly after sought to meet Flamininus at his home. They had expected to be rebuffed by servants and given a runaround. Yet he and Falco had to only state their names and display their pugiones. Senator Flamininus saw them that night.

Life away from the battlefield had softened his body. He was still a young man compared to other former consuls, with soulfully sad eyes that grew sadder as Varro and Falco recounted what had brought them back to Rome.

He welcomed them, embracing each like a brother. That night, he assigned them a room on the grounds of his own home, and the luxury of the place amazed both Varro and Falco. But regarding Curio, Flamininus was less charitable.

"I am not so certain Curio has found anything of substance regarding Consul Cato. As much as I am opposed to his narrow views, and as much as he dislikes me personally, I cannot believe he has betrayed the republic. But Curio, perhaps he and his men have begun a new life in Iberia."

Varro argued it made no sense, and that Curio had more in Rome than he would ever hold in Iberia. Something else was going on, but Varro did not know specifically what it was. His arguments only succeeded in drawing a noncommittal agreement from Flamininus.

"We shall see what time reveals. I fervently hope Curio has a good explanation for his actions, which will be hard to explain even so. But for now, there is the matter of your so-called desertions. You've admitted some serious crimes to me, including killing soldiers and officers of the legion. Fear not, for I support you both. Unlike what Cato promised, I am not plotting to dispose of you. Besides, he already knows what happened with the war indemnity. I've nothing to hide.

"For now, you will have all that you need. Take a well-earned rest after your labors. But I ask you to confine yourselves to your room. I will assign you a slave to care for all your needs. Do not leave your room without him, and only for your basic needs. I will summon you again when I have sorted out your situation, which will require some time."

So it had been nearly a month, and Flamininus had only spoken to them through messengers. They had a window in the room that looked out on a space of garden where only servants passed. Were it not for Flamininus's vague messages assuring them he had not forgotten them, they might have believed he was not even at home.

But by now, so much idleness with nothing but worry to

occupy his thoughts drove Varro mad for action. Falco, however, seemed born for a life of idleness. When he wasn't sleeping or eating, he was content to do little more than stare out the window. Varro found it disturbing, since this was not the man he had known since birth. Falco should be mad to escape by now, and probably would have made an attempt at it were he acting himself.

Yet somehow luxury and comfort had lulled both of them. Inaction led to indolence. Each day that passed in a haze of food and wine, dice games and chess, and afternoon dozing created chains heavier than Varro ever experienced in any prison cell.

"I'm going to see the senator," he announced. He stood up from reclining beside the table and looked to the slave in the shadows, sitting on a stool made for a child.

"Did you hear that, spy? I'm going to your master now."

The young boy had a mop of thick black hair in a bowl cut. He looked at Varro with eyes wide and mouth agape, head tilted in incomprehension.

"What are you saying?" Falco asked, still sitting on the edge of his beloved bed. "We're not supposed to leave our rooms."

"For fuck's sake, Falco! Who are you? Are you a mouse hiding in a pretty garden, or are you a centurion of the Tenth Hastati, with balls of bronze and a heart of stone?"

The shouting caused Falco to lean back and the slave to shove into his corner as if he were about to be beaten.

"Hold on, Varro. I think you're drunk. We're not supposed to leave these rooms on order from the consul."

"He's a senator!" Varro felt his head throbbing at the temples. "Gods, I cannot stand it anymore. How long are we to sit here with no news? How long to decide if we should be executed as deserters or assigned new duties? What about Curio? What about Servus Capax? I demand answers, and I'll have them. Not in a tomorrow that never comes, but now!"

He glared at Falco, daring his opposition. His friend glared back, heavy brows drawn into a thick line. They remained locked until Falco rose to his full, imposing height.

"I guess it is time that we get answers. We deserve them after all we've been through."

"That's right." Varro thumped Falco's chest. "Come with me. It's time we take matters into our own hands."

"All right," Falco said, adjusting his white tunic. "And to be clear, Lily, my balls are made of bronze and they're twice as big as yours."

"Then prove it," Varro said with a conspiratorial grin. "Let's go right to his room and get our answers."

They both made for the door and the slave followed, speaking in broken Latin.

"Where, masters? Please, stay here. Sit. More wine?"

But they both charged into the hall, the most familiar area in the entire place. Flamininus called this his house, but it was more like a compound that the senator kept locked and guarded against the mob of Rome. Former soldiers, many who had campaigned with him, guarded his house. Ostensibly, they were forbidden weapons in the city, but Varro was certain they carried pugiones and had access to other weapons if needed. He hoped they would draw none against him. He carried nothing but indignation and frustration.

Shoulder to shoulder they strode down the hall with the slave following, repeating his same offers for food and wine.

"Maybe he's not a spy," Varro admitted as they reached the end of the hall and familiar territory.

"What's the plan?" Falco asked. "Do you remember where his office is?"

"Vaguely. The plan is to walk with confidence, and to correct our mistakes."

"Mistakes?" But Falco's confused expression melted away and he turned with Varro to face the slave.

"Please, go back, masters. More wine?"

"Yes, more wine," Falco said.

After returning to their room, they tied up the slave in their fine blankets and gagged him with a hand towel from the table.

"Can't believe we missed this," Falco said as they both stood over the horrified slave lying on Falco's bed.

"We're out of condition," Varro said. "In mind and body. We've been in a stupor of idleness. No more, my friend."

Now they reentered the hall with less drama. Both walked confidently and easily, as if they should be in these hallways. Varro did not expect to go unchallenged, but hoped that his relaxed manner would not draw attention from anyone in the distance.

Mostly, the plan succeeded. He and Falco strode to the end of the hall and turned right to cross the central garden area. Servants at the edges did not notice them, likely mistaking them for guards or messengers. They only met trouble upon reaching the other side of the garden and passing under the awning to where Varro remembered Flamininus's office to be.

A muscular man in a plain brown tunic sat on a stool by the deep red door. He fanned flies away from his face as he stared after a young female servant in the distance. There was no way around him, and Varro knew he would do his duty. The guard still looked like a soldier, even out of armor. He sat erect like he might spring to attention. His face carried the deep lines of a man who had stood before enemy pikes for too long. His forearm also had a tattoo of his legion and unit numbers.

"Hello," Varro said brightly as he strode up to the guard. He had been intent on the woman at the far end of the garden and jumped up at Varro's bright voice.

"We're here to see the senator. He has called for us."

The guard stood almost equal height to Varro, and his smile broadened.

"Of course he did." His voice was dry and rough, as if he had just been screaming in the faces of raw recruits. "But he didn't inform me of that. Also, where's your slave?"

"He making our beds," Falco said. "Listen, friend, I know we're not in the legions anymore, but I think we've got rank on you. We're both centurions. Now, go announce us to the senator."

"Oh my, centurions," he said, his smile growing wider. "Guess what, boys, so was I. The last one of all the others I served with. Now, I know I look stupid. But you must think I left my wits on the battlefield. I know who you both are. Everyone here does. It's not like being in legion camp where you see fresh faces every day. Now, turn around and go back to your rooms. I hope you did nothing to that slave. He's one of the senator's favorites."

"We're going to meet the senator," Varro said, putting an edge to his voice. "You can step aside or we will move you aside."

"Is that so?" The guard shook his head and fished out a wooden whistle, probably the same one he used on campaign. "When I blow on this, you're going to have to move an extra dozen men as well. And we're all in better condition than you two are. You both look puffy, a shame for men touting themselves as centurions."

Falco stepped forward. "Right, then. Let's get to the fight."

He threw a strong but wildly aimed punch. The guard side-stepped it and landed a hard blow to Falco's kidney. At the same time, he slipped a foot behind Falco's, sending him sprawling.

Varro didn't move to aid his friend, who cursed as he fell backwards into the garden shrubs by the gate. Instead, he nodded to the whistle dangling from the guard's neck.

"Are you going to sound the alarm?"

The guard snorted a laugh. "I think I've got you boys both in hand."

"Ah, yes," Varro looked to Falco, who struggled to get out of the bushes. "That was a shameful display. You're out of shape from eating and drinking all day."

"Like you'd do better! Help me up. Why does the senator plant brambles in his garden?"

The guard inserted himself between Varro and Falco, addressing them like they were his troops.

"Stop this nonsense and go back to your room. I'll forget about everything if you behave."

The guard extended his hand to Falco. In that moment, Varro struck.

His hand whipped out, snatching the whistle that swung forward when the guard bent forward. He snapped the twine cord and stepped back, putting the whistle to his mouth.

He blasted on it as if he were sounding an alarm for a thousand enemies appearing out of the fog. The guard had his hand on his neck where the whistle had been, and his face paled.

"Are you fucking mad?" Then he grabbed for Varro, who was already backing up to the door while blowing the whistle.

The servants in the garden all spun around, and doors around it all opened up.

Including the freshly painted, deep red door beside them.

Flamininus stood in the doorway, his hair tousled as if he had just gotten out of bed. But his eyes were full of anger. When he saw Varro sounding the alarm, he shook his head.

"Stop that!"

"Sorry, sir!" The guard came forward, face glistening with sweat, and bowed before Flamininus. "I didn't think they'd go for the alarm."

Pinching the bridge of his nose, he sighed then waved away his guard's fear. "Don't fret about it. They're a resourceful pair. They've only been in their room as long as they have out of obedience. I see now that obedience has reached its limits. What have you done to my slave?"

Falco, who had at last won his battle with the bushes and stood, stepped forward.

"He's tied up, sir. A good lad, really, but he would've given us away."

"That was the point." Flamininus seemed to bend under an unseen weight. He then pointed to Varro, then to his door guard. "Return his whistle, and you go untie my slave and see that they didn't damage him."

"Doubt it, sir," Falco said. "Those are some fine bedsheets he's wrapped in. Plus, the rag in his mouth has a bit of wine on it. I'm sure he'll be in great spirits."

The look of disgust on Flamininus's face was outmatched by his guard's same expression, who snatched back the whistle, then stomped away on his new duty.

They followed the senator back to his office, which was off the hallway where Varro remembered. Once inside, Flamininus dropped into the chair behind his desk, where papyrus letters curled under a silver figure of a kicking bull. But Varro's attention drifted to a plush couch against the frescoed wall. Two wine cups, one spilled, rested on a small divan along with plates of oysters and prawns. The couch seemed askew along with the divan, as if knocked aside from a sudden motion. The scent of flowers hung in the air, suggesting the senator might have been with a woman.

Varro gulped at the implication. He had probably just interrupted Flamininus in the middle of a tryst.

The senator gave a long sigh and spread his hands out on the table.

"I'm surprised it took you so long to come to this point."

Varro and Falco exchanged confused looks, both standing at attention. But then Flamininus gave a tired smile and gestured they pull up stools. Once they sat, the senator raised his brow. Varro cleared his throat.

"Sorry for the commotion, sir. We're not ungrateful for your hospitality."

'No, sir,' Falco agreed. "That bed would please the gods, sir. And I've never drank or eaten better in my life."

A brief smile passed over Flamininus's face, but he let Varro continue.

"We need to know our status, and what news of Curio?"

Falco broke in. "And we need clear answers about what we're doing in Servus Capax. Who are we serving, really?"

Flamininus leaned back, both brows now raised along with both hands.

"Let me answer as I can. First, the easiest question to answer is Curio. I've heard nothing more from him, nor do I expect to."

Falco folded his arms and scowled, and Varro's own disappointment must have showed, for the senator turned a sympathetic eye to him.

"It sometimes happens that the pressures of long-term service can undo a man's will and skew his perspective. I mistook your youth and enthusiasm for a mental vigor that hasn't had time to develop. And honestly, given all you've experienced, even the most hardened veterans would buckle. I believe Curio has reached such a point, and for whatever his reasons he has left Rome altogether."

"That's not like Curio," Varro said, straining to keep his voice level. But Falco sighed and unfolded his arms.

"I agree with Senator Flamininus. First, he let Cato sway him over, then he realized nothing was going to change under him. So he took off with his men. Simple as that."

"You've spent more time with him than me," Varro said, his voice finally cracking. "Do you honestly believe what you just said?"

Falco stared back, and for once his expression was inscrutable. But he could not meet Varro's eyes when he answered.

"I believe what I saw. Curio cut us off, and then he left without a word. Why else would he do that? He knew we'd stop him."

Flamininus cleared his throat to draw them back.

"As for your situation, it is not so easily solved. Cato is well within his rights to declare you deserters. Hold on, I see you both disagree. Don't shout at me about it. It's delicate work. For now, Cato has sent nothing back to formally declare you as deserters. I've kept your arrival a secret. One reason I've confined you is to keep you hidden from my guests. If Cato learns you are here, then he will demand you face judgment."

Varro nodded, but the answer did not satisfy him. He looked to Falco for his reaction, but he only slouched in his chair. So he squared his shoulders and spoke for both of them.

"Sir, we cannot hide forever. Send us back to Iberia. We'll look for Curio and bring him back. I swear it, sir. I know he has not deserted but has another reason for what he did. He never once gave any sign that he was dissatisfied. If anything, he was proud to become a centurion and took pride in his century."

"I cannot send you to Iberia. Cato is the highest authority there and would find you immediately."

"Not as regular legionnaires, sir." Varro leaned forward on his stool. "Just as Servus Capax agents searching for one of their own. Sir, do you just allow your agents to go missing? If Falco and I were to vanish one day with no record of what happened, you'd do nothing to find us?"

Flamininus had heard enough, for his sympathetic countenance shifted to anger and he slapped his desk, reminiscent of the way Cato addressed them.

"I will not send you to Iberia to find him. If anything, we will send another agent to track him. Now, you asked to know who you really serve. Well, do you think you serve me?"

Falco and Varro checked with each other, then both nodded.

The senator hissed. "No, I give you orders on behalf of the Senate. But you serve Rome first."

Varro straightened up in the face of Flamininus's temper.

"That is good to know, sir. But Cato spoke of factions and of us being assassins and thieves."

"Assassins and thieves?" Flamininus leaned back from his desk. "Perhaps, if the need arose. But only against enemies of Rome, and only with the approval of the most senior senators. As for factions, wherever power gathers there are factions. Does this surprise you? But all factions in the senate, if you can even call them so, are united under the same purpose, which is to grow Rome's power and influence in the world."

He paused to study them. Varro listened intently, at last about to learn more of what he was involved with. The senator continued, less agitated now.

"Servus Capax may seem like a highly formal organization to you. But it began with spies who served during the first war with Carthage. Your great-grandfather was a founding member, Varro. He and his companions were spies, as well as assassins and thieves. They created a framework for Rome's future success, though their efforts may be unknown to the people."

"Thank you, sir," Varro said. "I knew he was involved, just not as a founder."

"Recruitment into this group is only by recommendation from an active consul or senior senator. That is how I brought you three in, with some help from others. Also, there are only thirteen members active at once, though we've struggled to keep that number in active service. That's why I had openings for you three."

"Back in Sparta," Varro said. "There was a man inside Nabis's palace and a woman."

"Yes, he had been in place for years and Sparta has ever been a troublesome land. When Nabis gave me cause to destroy him, I wanted you three to link up with your fellow member. While not all went to plan, Sparta surrendered on our terms. But the woman remains a mystery to me. Be glad that she aided you. That is all I can say for her."

Questions built up in Varro's mind, and he struggled to organize them. Falco seemed in the same shape, for he leaned forward with his mouth poised to form a question that he couldn't phrase.

Then a servant knocked on the door, claiming an urgent message. The interruption let Varro think while the senator accepted a papyrus scroll that had apparently been rushed from the docks to his estate.

But as Varro thought, he realized Flamininus had been silent too long.

When he looked up, he had his hand over his mouth as he held up the letter to study something at the bottom of the torn sheet.

Both he and Falco now awaited the senator's response, for his eyes shifted between the papyrus and them. At last, he let his hand slip from his mouth and set the letter face down on his desk.

"The gods are certainly listening in to us. The two of you have a new assignment. I'm sending you today, without delay. You're going back to Iberia. This is a letter from Curio."

9

As the ship rocked on gentle waves and the wind snapped the sail overhead, Varro pulled out the papyrus letter from his tunic and unfolded it. Falco, who stood beside him at the ship rail and under the flat glare of the wide ocean sun, scoffed when he saw this.

"Reading Curio's letter again? Haven't you memorized it?"

But Varro ignored him, turning his back to him and the wind. Cool ocean spray floated over the rails, and he shifted closer to the mast to avoid moisture disturbing the ink. Crewmen flowed around him, busy with tightening ropes, tying knots, and a score of other things sailors did to keep their ships moving.

They sailed upon a bireme headed to Iberia with supplies and fresh recruits. The sailors enjoyed a fair wind without the need to row. Flamininus had somehow gotten them on the ship without having to include their names in the roster of soldiers replenishing losses in Far Iberia. Such was the power of a senator and former consul.

Curio's writing was all skewed letters and trailed ink like spiderwebs as he moved his stylus over the papyrus. But it was proof the letter was created by his own hand. To Varro, it also proved everything he had suspected. He read it every day of their brief journey across the sea. Not to memorize it, though he had incidentally done so, but to see what else he could glean from it. Curio seemed to have written in haste and therefore might have omitted useful information. Varro wanted to garner as much as he could from between Curio's lines.

They did not know what awaited them in Iberia.

The letter was politely addressed to Senator Flamininus and had been sealed with wax and an impression of some sort of seal. Varro suspected it belonged to the garrison commander where he claimed to be recovering.

Once more, he examined the letter as Falco yawned behind him and complained about boredom while at sea. Varro wanted to ask how he had stared out a window for a month without complaint, but just shook his head as he began the letter.

The opening detailed how Curio had believed himself following Servus Capax's ranks when he first met a man claiming to be Placus. He carried a pugio with a gold symbol like Varro himself had inherited, which indicated a senior member. He then explained how he had been deceived and that this Placus character was in fact a former Centurion Lucian who was as mad as he was clever.

Apparently, Curio's men were all murdered, and they spared Curio to be recruited into Lucian's plans. Here's where the letter became less clear to Varro.

Lucian will use the silver to build a new city to rival Rome. He talks to his gods about it, and I was supposed to as well. But I escaped and fled here, where I was nearly killed by our own men. Fortunately, the commander took mercy on me and let me inside. I'm not sure how long I can stay before he sends for me. I might need to move again.

Do not underestimate Lucian. He is mad and his gods are with him. Please help me. I served who I thought was my better, but was fooled.

How could I know not to trust others from SC? Please get me out of Iberia. Also, you must help Varro and Falco. You must know their problem by now. We will all be indebted to you for the rest of our lives. I will watch for your sign. I am not sure how long I can hold out here. Please send help.

Varro sensed he might have written more had he not reached the end of the page. That someone had torn it seemed suspicious, but the message had arrived with the seal intact. Also, Curio had impressed the stylized owl's head at the end of his last sentence. The mark was crude but clear enough for those knowledgeable to understand the significance of it.

What did Curio mean about talking to Iberian gods? Perhaps he was about to be killed and escaped. The location of Curio's "here" must be the garrison from which he had sent the letter. But according to Flamininus, the message came by merchant ship and was not bundled with regular mail. Curio had somehow convinced a civilian to speed his message directly to Flamininus, which Varro considered amazing.

It had shocked the senator to learn of Centurion Lucian. After allowing both Varro and Falco to read the letter, he balled his fists and slammed them on the desk.

"This is the worst kind of traitor," he had said through gritted teeth. "I know that name and considered Lucian long dead. But all these years, he has cavorted with barbarians and gone mad. Even if he didn't think to challenge Rome, a laughable thought as it is, I would still want his head for the treachery he has wrought. You three will remove him from the game board. Use whatever means you think appropriate."

So, as only just spoken, they were to become assassins for Servus Capax. But on this point, Varro did not disagree. He had ruined Curio's life and led men who thought they risked their lives for the greater good to fruitless deaths. He also sullied their names and dishonored their families forever. Death was too kind for Lucian.

But there was a mischievous gleam in Flamininus's eyes as he handed the letter into Varro's keeping.

"Now Consul Cato has a problem. Is it not fitting that he has to explain the theft of silver to the quaestors after what he did to you? It will be a stain on his reputation and a terrible blow to his pride. There are those who would twist that thorn in Cato's side at every chance. However, if you recover that silver first, then I will have leverage over him. That is how we negotiate your situation. You spare Cato the agony of shame and preserve his reputation, and he will drop his false accusations against you. Though be certain you will have a lifelong enemy in Cato and those under his influence."

Varro had wondered if Cato could go back on his claims after publicly declaring them thieves and deserters, but Flamininus frowned and waved off his concern. "Anything is possible for him. He is a consul, after all."

So it was that Varro now found himself aboard a navy ship speeding to the same garrison where Curio awaited them. However, his letter indicated he might not be there. *I'm not sure how long I can stay before he sends for me.* Curio must have meant Cato, who would certainly search for him after he abandoned his post.

"Learn anything new?" Falco peered over his shoulder, glancing at the letter before Varro folded it and then stuffed it back into his tunic.

"Nothing. I can't help but wonder if Curio intended to say more. It feels as if he couldn't fit all he wanted to say on the page. Why didn't he just get another sheet and continue?"

"Varro, your mind has been idle too long and is now running everywhere like a puppy let out of a cage. Papyrus isn't cheap. They probably only have so much of it at a garrison outpost."

"You could be right. But I feel as though he wrote under pressure. Maybe he has fled the garrison ahead of Cato's men coming for him. It could be trouble for us if they are still present when we arrive. But I suppose we will find out soon enough. We will make land today?"

"It is according to what the captain said. I think the blue smear on the horizon is Iberia. Still seems far off. Can't say I'm excited to be going back to it."

Varro drew a long sniff of sea air and held it. Iberia was fraught with dangers on every side. Adding this madman Lucian into the mix only made it worse. He would be happy just to reunite with Curio and get the details of all that had happened. Falco had been promising to thump him for being a gullible fool, but Varro doubted he would. Both of them were excited to be made whole again.

They sailed for the rest of the morning. Varro watched as the blue smudge Falco mentioned changed into mountains and forests on the horizon. The bireme pulled in as close as it could before it risked its hull on the sea bottom. From there, fresh soldiers loaded into rowboats. Officers kept them in order, and some mistook Varro and Falco for one of their charges until a few sharp words set them straight.

Soon they were ashore and dressed in their finest gear, all requisitioned back in Rome and paid for out of their own purses. They had replenished their funds at a bank, a concept Varro still did not fully grasp. One of Flamininus's trusted servants had assisted with this. He was not pleased to let others handle his fortune, but had no time for the tedious process. The coins were still there when needed, and that had to be good enough for now.

"We'll travel with the column," Varro said. "You've got the documents?"

"No, I needed something to blow my nose with." Falco

thumped Varro's shining new helmet, then ruffled the black feathers in its crest. "Yes, I have them. Do you think I'm stupid?"

"Of course I do. Why else would I ask?" Varro fell in with the column lead, Falco trailing along and cursing him.

Flamininus's letter outlined the assignment and what he required of the garrison commander, including men and supplies. It was a large ask, Varro knew, but from what Curio described in his letter they would need excellent soldiers and local guides.

The senator also promised he would join them as soon as he could arrange a suitable excuse. He did not intend to travel with them but would await their return with Lucian's head or news of his death. His main purpose in going to Iberia was to negotiate with Cato.

They marched alongside the centurion leading the column of recruits. He and Falco had more experience than any of them. Their chain shirts were heavy with round bronze medals for bravery and their campaign seasons. Varro promised not to interfere with their leadership, but he saw the self-consciousness in the less-decorated men.

Falco tried to cheer him up. "A season in Iberia ought to earn you a few of your own. Plenty of barbarians around that want your head on a pole. You'll be knee-deep in fighting before long."

Yet his words seemed only to make those who heard them blanch, though a handful seemed eager for the fight, especially the centurion.

The tops of stockade walls and log towers poked above the dark pine tops that surrounded the track they followed. Blackbirds flitted over it and curls of white smoke from hearth fires rose into the late afternoon sky. The scent of the sea already faded from the air, overwhelmed with sweet pine and smoke.

They found the gates open, where Curio claimed his own side had nearly killed him. Varro squinted up at the men watching from the walls, teasing the new recruits from the parapets. Maybe these were the same men.

The garrison commander, his staff, and other centurions were waiting to receive their new troops, about forty men. For the time, Varro mixed in with the ordered column and he used the moment to study the commander whom he would present Flamininus's order to.

He was a solid man who seemed to have earned his rank rather than bought it. Ostensibly, he was just another centurion. But he was the highest authority on this border of Roman rule, unless a praetor or Cato himself decided otherwise. He was imposing, with wide shoulders and a ferocious scar on his left cheek. He wore a muscled bronze chest plate like a tribune would, but still held his vine cane behind his back like a centurion.

"Seems like a reasonable fellow," Falco said. "I wonder if he's Cato's man?"

"Why wouldn't he be?" Varro straightened his shoulders and drew a deep breath. "He's part of the legion, all under Cato's command. Let's just see how this goes."

The garrison commander finally deigned to look at them as they stepped away from the formation. They had been conspicuous enough in their armor alone that everyone but the commander had taken note. Now, Varro forced his acknowledgment, presenting himself with a salute.

"Well, seems I've acquired two new centurions?" The garrison commander curled his lip and his nostrils flared. He seemed like a man presented with a plate of spoiled meat. "The two of you look too glorious for this run-down garrison on the edge of nowhere. Did I fuck up? I suppose you've got orders?"

Varro looked to Falco, who produced the papyrus from within his tunic and presented it to the garrison commander. He took it in rough, calloused hands and then scanned its contents. His frown deepened until it became a display of bared teeth.

"Special orders from a senator?" The garrison commander held the papyrus back so that a ray of the late-day sun revealed the lettering in reverse, along with the senator's seal at the bottom. "What have I done to deserve the attention of a senator?"

"Sir, I am Centurion Marcus Varro and this is Centurion Caius Falco. I'm sure the senator's request is quite clear," Varro said. "We'll need a dozen men and at least three local guides, more if you can spare them. They'll need to be outfitted for an extended time in the field."

The commander's eyes pierced Varro from over the top of the letter.

"I just got forty new recruits, and it's not because we're idle out here. The fucking barbarians are still calling for Roman blood. Not a patrol comes back without someone taking a javelin wound, usually in his back. The native scum have learned not to stand up and fight. They're behind every fucking tree, cutting up my boys whenever they look away. I've got a score of sick and injured going back on the boat that dropped you here. So, do you think I have men to spare?"

The commander's eyes seemed to smolder in his deep sockets. Varro returned the same intense glare. There was a time when he would've withered under such hostility. He pointed to the letter crushed in the commander's hand.

"Sir, read the letter once more when you have a moment. I apologize for the poor timing, but we're not here on a trifle, either. Perhaps we can discuss this after you address the new arrivals? In the meantime, we will settle in."

The commander's face reddened, and a vein throbbed in the thin skin of his forehead. But he knew Varro and Falco both represented a greater authority.

"Strange that everyone is remembering me now, after I've been screaming for reinforcements ever since taking over this dirt pile.

Seems like we're suddenly popular with important men on critical missions."

The commander reviewed the orders again, narrowing his eyes as he focused on the words. His brows drew together as he studied the letter.

"This wouldn't be about that runt calling himself a centurion? Curio? Everyone wants to meet Centurion Curio."

"In fact, there is some connection," Varro said cooly, glancing to Falco, who thankfully remained expressionless.

"Well, go speak with Centurion Barbatus. We camped him and his men over there. They arrived two days ahead of you." The commander pointed behind Varro. "The consul wants Curio first. So if Senator Flamininus wants him too, you two can roll dice for him. Curio repaid my kindness by stealing supplies and vanishing in the middle of the night. I should've trusted my boys and let them stick him outside the gates."

Varro did not follow the pointing finger, but shook his head.

"We'll be needing appointments inside the main garrison, sir."

It seemed the commander would burst into a fit, but one of his staff dared whisper to him. He listened, nodding vigorously, then looking again to Varro.

"He'll take you to a place to rest. I'll call you when I'm ready. I'm only being so pleasant with you because of that."

He tapped Varro's Macedonia campaign medal, encircled by others awarded for bravery during the same war. The commander's frown softened just enough that he no longer looked sickened.

"My brother served with Consul Galba on the same campaign. He didn't survive it. You've got a nice set of medals from the consul. I respect that, but get out of my sight. You've delayed me long enough."

The adjutant that had rescued their situation now led them away from the parade ground. The commander already began shouting at his replacements. But Varro was more interested in Cato's men. As they crossed the trampled down grass toward the main building, he noted the standard camp layout. As this was a more permanent location than legion camp, the main buildings were all constructed from logs. The soldiers still slept in tents, but many sections were being replaced with permanent structures. Varro glanced to where Cato's men encamped, finding them easily.

They ruined the symmetry of the ordered tent lines, attaching themselves to the end of a row. He did not want to stare, but realized several of them watched their arrival. Varro hoped they mistook him and Falco for more replacements. It seemed Cato had sent about thirty men after Curio. He couldn't get a better estimate before they were inside the main building.

The adjutant set them up in a storage room.

"It's better than sleeping on cold dirt," Falco said. The adjutant agreed and left them to settle in.

"I like the commander," Falco said. "A proper soldier. It don't hurt that he noticed our medals. I think he likes us."

"He might like us, but he will not help us," Varro said as he dropped his pack. "And Curio isn't here, but he'll stay close. He's waiting for the senator to send aid. So we will need to get our own men and handle this Centurion Barbatus."

Falco was half crouched over a small chest, ready to sit. But he stood again.

"I don't think the commander is going to be helpful, either. Cato's men are a problem. How did they know to come here?"

Varro considered the question as he arranged his gear. The leather bag holding his scutum shield slid down the wall he leaned it against, and he caught it.

"It's easy to figure Curio robbed the treasury. So Cato sent trackers after him. He probably doesn't even know Lucian exists. Based on what Curio said, I don't think Lucian took care to hide their trail. Cato's men probably followed that trail and came to this garrison to resupply. They just got lucky. In any case, they are here now and I don't doubt they know we're also wanted men. We'd be a fat prize to bring back with Curio."

"We're not anywhere near where Cato thinks we should be," Falco said, at last sitting atop the chest. "They're not thinking about us, but are here for Curio."

"And so are we," Varro said. "As well as Lucian, and the silver. We can't have Cato's men getting all of three ahead of us, or we'll lose our chance to restore our names. They might already have an idea where Curio is. It won't surprise me if they have deployed trackers to search for him already. We need to take action."

Falco stared at him as he finally braced his scutum in place. The hard look made Varro chuckle.

"You look worried."

"Do I? I was only thinking how wonderful it is to be back in Iberia and remembering all the great times we had here."

Varro laughed again. "More great times are coming. The race is on. Now, stop sitting on your ass as if this is Flamininus's villa. We've got reconnaissance to do."

"We're just going to walk out of the garrison for a stroll in the forest?"

"Of course not." Varro removed his helmet and scratched his head. "We're going to spy on Cato's men. Now, start thinking like a fresh recruit and follow me."

10

Varro and Falco now wore only plain beige tunics and caligae as they walked down the row of tents leading to where Cato's men encamped. Both had their harnesses and weapons, so they would not be mistaken for servants or slaves. They blended in with the off-duty soldiers who rested in their tents. As they walked with purpose, the soldiers left them to their business. They moved with a familiarity that said they belonged here, not to mention forty new men had joined the garrison. They were as good as invisible. As they walked, Varro reviewed their plans.

"Remember, you're not Centurion Falco. You arrived with the recruits and you're lost. When they try to wave you off, just keep them tied up long enough for me to have a look inside Centurion Barbatus's tent."

"Fuck, Varro, this is risky. If we're caught, we're headed back to that bireme under guard."

"Well, Curio isn't here to do this sort of work. So, I'm the next best choice. You're better at acting like an oaf and distracting them. Besides, you look the part."

"Remind me to break your nose when we've got some free time. Fortuna be with you, Varro."

"She always is." He gave Falco a quick wink, and they separated before reaching the ad hoc encampment.

Falco looped back out to the main road and Varro ensured no one watched him from behind. He counted his luck that Cato's men had picked the end of a row that abutted the outer wall. Grass grew in the space between, leaving a safe zone against enemy projectiles coming over the wall. It also allowed Varro to duck behind the tents when the few men who might spot him looked away.

These were typical marching tents, weather-beaten hides that contained eight men each. The centurion would have his own tent with his command group, which might vary in number for a special assignment like his. Varro had marked the tent earlier and now crouched behind it. Soft voices murmured within, maybe three men at most.

Falco made his appearance, speaking loudly, so Varro knew the ruse had begun.

"Excuse me, sir! I am looking for the Eleventh Hastati. Where are they camped?"

A rough voice growled back. "The eleventh? There's never been an eleventh anything."

"Sorry, sir! That's what I was told. Eleventh Hastati. I'm in the command group, sir! The centurion said I'd be in charge of latrine duty for the rest of my life, sir! And I could start with cleaning his backside!"

The men outside the tents burst into laughter, but Falco persisted in his ludicrous story, drawing curses and ridicule. Varro listened for the reaction of the men inside the tent. They raised their voices but didn't leave. While waiting, he found the loose edge of the tent where he could easily pry up a stake. He had to take care or risk bringing it down on himself. All he needed was a quick search for written instructions, a map, or anything that might show what they had found so far.

Falco also knew the intended target and would continue with his antics until he drew out everyone in the centurion's tent. While his act had fooled the ordinary soldiers, he resorted to a secondary plan that would draw out even a centurion.

"Listen, boys, no one is expecting me for a bit. Centurion said I should stick my head in the latrine for a good long time so I get used to the smell of shit." After a few jibes at him, Falco continued more conspiratorially. "I just happen to have a hot hand at dice right now. I cleaned out everyone on the ship coming over here. Do you think you can beat me?"

Varro heard the jingle of silver coins, and, sure enough, the men inside the centurion's tent would not miss a chance to part a fool from his coins. They spoke excitedly as they joined Falco's dice game. Varro listened to be certain no one remained, then pulled up the stake and shimmied under the tent.

He pushed through bedrolls into the dim interior. Outside the open flap, he saw men crouching in a circle, excited for what they believed would be easy winnings. Scanning the interior, Varro dismissed items expected for soldiers on the march but discovered set on the floor of the tent a hide map.

Crudely drawn lines traced a route from Cato's camp to this garrison. Forage locations, campsites, fords, and passes were all clearly marked. Notes on enemies encountered were neatly written at the edges. Rough ink lines divided the area around the garrison into sectors, with most struck through. Only two forest sectors remained unmarked to the northwest. One abutted the foothills of steep mountains.

Satisfied that Curio hid in one of the two sectors, he slipped back under the tent wall, replaced the stake, then headed to where Barbatus's pack mules were tethered. Again, these stuck out from the regular garrison's stable as they picketed them close by. The mules rested beside their carts, looking at Varro as if hoping for a treat.

He only offered them a stroke on their necks, and they flicked their tails in answer. Drawing his pugio and checking his surroundings, he sawed at their harness belts. He pulled the straps away from the mule and cut just enough beneath the belt that it would snap under enough pressure. He repeated the same for the next mule.

When Barbatus set out in pursuit—which he would once he realized Curio was with them—having all their supplies dumped would slow them. Varro wagered they lacked tools and materials to repair these straps on the march, and would become weighted down with their own gear. He would need every advantage against so many men.

He left the mules, hoping to catch Falco's eyes as he did. But he was playing his role too well, with Barbatus's men shouting or laughing at every throw of the dice. Falco stood up, hands on his head as if he had lost more than he could afford. Varro snickered and returned to the garrison without him.

Across the field, the commander and his staff reviewed their new troops, all standing under the late day sun as centurions and optiones circled them. Again, Varro smiled as he remembered both being one of those sweating recruits and shouting in their faces as an officer. He longed to return to the simplicity of basic soldiering, having to only worry about an enemy's blade and not one from your own side.

He entered the log building as if he were the commander himself. Staffers busy with their own concerns simply glanced at him. Only one man asked in passing if he had business here, and Varro claimed he did. That seemed enough for the questioner, who continued with his task. Varro tilted his head at the lack of suspicion. Life in a garrison differed from the fighting line, he guessed.

So he jogged up the wooden stairs to where the command room would be. The stairs creaked as his hobnails thudded on the planks. The staffers downstairs scribbled on their vellum as they chatted.

Without even looking about, enhancing his illusion of belonging, he strode into the empty command room.

The garrison standard pole rested in the far corner, surrounded by freshly painted shields of red, green, and black. Vellum pages and more delicate papyrus sheets were stuffed into cubicles on shelves, or held under decorative weights. Varro imagined Curio scribbling out his letter in this very place.

On the table was a stack of hide sheets. These were various maps to mark forage and water sources, as well as skirmish sites and enemy camps. These were better produced than Centurion Barbatus's map, but he was not interested in these.

Instead, he peeled back the top layers to reveal the bottom map. This showed all of Far Iberia and sections of the interior still under native control. The map of those areas was incomplete, as the Romans had not penetrated far into these lands. Yet there was enough information to make the map useful. He would need this knowledge after linking up with Curio and beginning the pursuit of Lucian. If he was with the Lusitani tribe, then he would head into the incomplete regions of the map as he marched for the west coast. Varro's finger traced mountain passes, streams, lakes, and potential forage locations. The scouts who had created this map had done excellent work.

He tugged it out and rolled it up under his arm. Then he readjusted the maps to seem undisturbed as best he could. As he descended the stairs, he ran into another of the commander's adjutants.

Varro's expression must have marked his horror at being caught with a stolen map nonchalantly tucked under his arm. The adjutant blinked and stepped back, but recovered his professionalism and saluted.

"Sir, the commander will meet with you now. Where is the other centurion?"

"He went to the latrine," Varro said. "And probably fell in. He sometimes takes a while, if you understand."

The adjutant nodded, noticed the hide rolled under Varro's arm, but said nothing. "Will you follow me, sir?"

"Now? I was just looking for my quarters."

The adjutant blinked again. "Sir? The commander has summoned you. Now, follow me, please."

Seeing how the request had become a command delivered on the commander's behalf, Varro swallowed hard and followed the adjutant. He feared his armpit sweat would destroy the map. Fortunately, he had rolled it up so that the map was on the interior side.

As they crossed the field, he sorely wished Falco would join so he could pass off the stolen map and then send him off. But glancing toward the tents, it seemed Falco had become too absorbed in his own ruse. The crowd of their erstwhile enemies gambled alongside him. Falco dropped coins into one man's palm while another dropped coins into his other hand. He was not returning soon enough.

So they crossed to where the recruits and their centurions broke up and the commander waited. He had a look of utter disgust as he watched the new arrivals depart to their temporary campsite. The adjutant introduced Varro, and the commander's frown did not diminish. He glanced at the hide under Varro's arm. To him, it felt as if the commander would rip it out of his grip and reveal the theft with a dramatic flourish. But his eyes shifted back to Varro's with no hint of change.

"All right, Centurion Varro, I suppose I should consider your request, given you're here on Senator Flamininus's orders. Did you serve with him in Macedonia?"

"I did, sir. He led us to victory at Cynoscephalae. It was a battle I'll never forget."

"I'm sure. I wish I had been there instead of being sent to this backwater. I heard it was a tribune who turned that battle into our victory. Did you know him?"

"Only in passing, sir."

In fact, it had been Varro's own realization that they had bypassed the Macedonia rear on the flank and they were open to attack. But history would never bestow glory upon a plebeian soldier. Tribunes and consuls always took that credit, and he was happy to leave it alone.

The commander turned to walk, his vine cane held behind him. Varro pressed down on the stolen map and followed.

"You need men I cannot spare. But, there is Centurion Barbatus. Can't you work with him? You're both looking for the same man, though for different masters."

Varro glanced behind to see the commander's adjutant walking away on other business.

"It is an excellent idea, sir. In fact, Centurion Falco is discussing this possibility with them right now."

The commander stopped and turned to him. "Then it's settled. How long will you need to operate out of my garrison? The replacements have brought supplies as well. But thirty extra men that I can't order to go forage for themselves is a burden."

"I don't expect to be here long, sir." Varro shifted the hide from under his arm while the commander looked up at his gates closing for the oncoming night. He clasped it in both hands behind his back. "But I fear there is a bit of competition between me and Centurion Barbatus, sir. Nothing serious, of course. It's that there is a reward for Curio's arrest."

The commander shook his head. "It always comes down to the pay, doesn't it? Well, I can't support your greed, Centurion Varro. I know you've got a letter from a hero of Rome, but he's no longer consul. Senator Flamininus is far away, but Consul Cato is right here along with his legions. Not only is he my rightful commander, but displeasing him is more dangerous than irritating Senator Flamininus. I'm denying your request. Cato's men have all the guides I can spare. You're welcome to remain while you make plans. But if you're going to stay long, I'll put you all to work. This is no vacation villa."

Varro smiled and inclined his head. "Of course not, sir. I appreciate the thankless work you and your men perform out here. I would ask for provisions enough for Centurion Falco and me to take for a week in the field."

The commander frowned again. "I'll arrange for your provisions. Listen, this land is not like Macedonia. It's a wild place of bloodthirsty tribesmen and their dark gods. I've been here long enough to know two Romans will not survive seven days in the Iberian wilderness. Not here, where even my garrison struggles to hang on. Past those mountains to the northwest, you enter a world where even Carthage dared not go. One day we'll conquer it all. But that's not in our lifetimes. Maybe it's better if you let Centurion Barbatus deal with Curio. He has enough men for the task."

"I have my orders, sir. It's unfortunate you cannot help, but it does not change what I must do."

"I see how you earned those medals, Centurion. Fortuna go with you." The commander now shifted away, as if ready to dismiss Varro and move on. But he looked to Varro's hands hidden behind his back. "What is that you carry?"

"This, sir?" Varro produced the stolen map, hoping there was nothing on the back of it to reveal what it was. He extended it to the commander, trying to smile while he steadied the tremble in his arm. "This is a map of the area where I've marked Curio's likely hiding places. I was preparing it when you summoned me and brought it in case you wanted to review it."

The commander seemed about to accept the map, then leaned away. "Perhaps later. To be honest, Centurion, there are too many places for him to hide. And if he possessed a shred of sense, he'd have headed to the coast where Rome keeps the peace. If he fled into these forests, then you'll just be bringing back his bones. If wolves haven't eaten him first."

"I've said as much to Senator Flamininus, sir. But you know how it is." He tucked the map underarm once more and waited for his dismissal, which the commander granted. Varro held his breath as the commander headed for the gates, then let it go in a rush once he was out of hearing. His underarms dripped sweat down his sides and his legs trembled as he returned to the storeroom that served as his temporary quarters. He hid the map in his pack and withdrew his own vellum and ink. While he waited for Falco to return, he recreated Centurion Barbatus's map from memory. If the commander asked for Varro's map, he would have one prepared as a plausible cover for this theft.

Falco returned about an hour later, his expression sour.

"Just lost my entire purse to those cheating bastards."

"Seems fair, given how badly you cheat others."

"Is that what you say after all my good work?" Falco settled to the floor and leaned against a crate. "Tell me you found something worthwhile, please."

Varro looked up from drawing his map and explained all he had done. When finished, Falco was pinching the bridge of his nose.

"You stole a map from the commander? You know that is going to come back to us, and maybe he needs it."

"He'll need it if he intends to send men after us," Varro said. "And he might after what we're doing tonight."

Falco now folded his hands in his lap and set his head back

against the wood wall. "Don't tell me what we're doing. Just tell me if I should get some sleep first."

"You should. We'll either be up all night or we'll be running for our lives."

"So a typical mission. Right, I'll be napping then. Wake me up when you're ready to gamble my life away." Falco reached for his bedroll, then stopped. "Scratch that. No more gambling today. My luck is cold."

Varro set the map aside to dry, then cleaned his stylus of ink.

"The entire mission is a gamble, Falco. Better you run out your bad luck on dice games. From now on, only good luck will suffice."

Falco groaned and unrolled his bedding.

"Like I said, typical mission. Let me sleep, Varro. It's probably the last good rest I'll have for a long time."

Varro nodded, silently agreeing.

11

Varro peered through the crack in the garrison door, having carefully slid the bolt aside. The first watch of the night had taken positions on the wall, marked by fluttering torches. The main garrison buildings were now empty and dark. Staffers had organized and cleaned their desks at the end of their day. Only the commander and his servants remained in the building along with Varro and Falco. He stood watch at the top of the stairs, holding their shields and pila and ready to rush back to their room.

The garrison commander had invited them to dine with him and his officers. They declined, claiming fatigue from long days at sea. The commander hadn't seemed too eager for his acceptance, making the offer out of courtesy rather than desire. But he sent a servant to them with a spicy soup of local vegetables and goat meat.

Varro estimated they only had tonight to act before Barbatus knew they were here. He had to be away long before that time.

Varro and Falco exited the garrison building, satisfied the garrison commander slept, and his men followed their routines.

They headed for the line of newly pitched tents where the recruits had settled until they could be integrated with existing units. They did not conceal themselves, but Varro watched the dark tents where Centurion Barbatus and his men slept. If anyone might suspect them, the centurion would.

"This is complete madness," Falco muttered. "But I like it better than some of your ideas."

"Just believe the lie," Varro said. "I'm afraid we're both getting too good at it. As long as you act the part and don't give these men time to think, it'll go our way. Remember, the legion conditions soldiers to obey orders. We're going to twist that to our ends tonight."

"Twist? More like tie it up in a fucking knot. All right, I'll follow your lead."

Varro nodded, keeping his shoulders square and alert to activity in the garrison. They stayed wide of the regular tent rows until heading for the tent where the centurion and optio slept.

"The centurion was eager for glory?" Varro asked in a whisper. Falco nodded, searching about like someone would stab him in the darkness. "All right, stop looking nervous. Look irritated instead, please."

So Varro began the boldest ruse he had ever planned.

He leaned down and slapped open the tent flap.

"What the fuck is this?" He kicked the foot of one of the two snoring under their blankets. The sleeper recoiled in shock, reaching for his gladius resting against the tent pole.

"It's me, you fool," Varro said. "Why the fuck are you not ready?"

"What?" The weary man sat up, and now so did his companion. Varro wasn't certain if he addressed the centurion or the optio, but had to figure out their ranks immediately. So he backed out of the tent and growled.

"Get out here, Centurion. We need an explanation."

"Who are you?" One man crawled out of his tent, presumably the centurion. When he stood up in the dim light he seemed amazed at Varro and Falco in their chain shirts and bronze helmets. He looked to their pila and shields, then to their packs. Falco rested on his shield, shaking his head in disgust.

"Who am I?" Varro repeated the question. "I know it's dark, but who else would come for you tonight? Where are the men, Centurion? Why is everyone asleep? I thought you were a veteran?"

"I am. Now, wait, you're the centurions that sailed over with us."

Falco laughed. "And so he finally wakes up. Of course we are. And you'll address us as sir, or we'll have you on a charge."

"What? Wait, what the fuck is going on?"

The centurion folded his arms, and his optio now followed him out of the tent. Varro pointed to him.

"Do you know the mission? Please tell me at least one of you got the brief?"

But the optio looked to his leader, plainly afraid to admit he hadn't. The centurion waved him off.

"Listen, sir, I want an explanation. We were together on the transport ship for days, and you never as much looked at me. Now you're kicking my leg in the middle of the night like you have some authority. Where's the garrison commander? He should be out here."

"Keep your voice down, man," Varro hissed, genuinely looking around for others. "The commander is the last one we need to alert. Look, you clearly weren't briefed. This mission is already a mess."

He gave a suffering look to Falco, who shook his head again. "Typical army fuck up. If these two don't know, then none of them do."

Varro raised his hands. "It doesn't matter who knows, it only matters that they support us."

The centurion sighed. "Explain this to me. I'm running out of patience."

"All right, Senator Flamininus didn't brief you, it seems. I'll try to explain."

The mention of Rome's most recent and famous hero eased the centurion's furious glare. Varro produced Flamininus's letter. He had carefully splashed it with water to blur out sections that did not agree with the story he would tell the centurion and added new sentences to bolster his lie. The centurion accepted it and held it close to his face.

"It's too dark to read," the centurion said as he scanned the papyrus.

"Then light a lamp and give it a review. In the meantime, Optio, you fetch me sixteen of your best men and we'll need local guides."

"Guides, sir?" The optio looked at his centurion again, who struggled to read in the dim light.

"If you don't have guides like you should have," Varro said, "then we just pick the men with a talent for tracking and scouting."

By now, the centurion had studied the papyrus letter and handed it back.

"It got wet, sir. I couldn't read parts of it."

Varro glared at Falco as if it had been his fault. He stared a moment with a blank face, then shrugged. "Everyone makes mistakes."

"Well, it's still clear enough, and that's Flamininus's name and seal at the bottom. This is a covert night mission, Centurion. We chose you for your bravery and talent. But if you never got the brief, then who did?"

"I don't know, sir. But if you need men for the job, then I'm ready."

Varro now rubbed his chin as if hesitating. "This isn't some march around the camp, Centurion. We're linking up with one of our scouts and heading into enemy territory. It's dangerous work and I need men I can depend on."

"Sir, I didn't reach this rank because I'm afraid to fight."

The centurion's eyes glanced over Varro's medals.

"It's more than fighting, Centurion. We're heading deep into enemy territory, and we'll have to fend for ourselves. A medal at the end of all of it might not feel as gratifying as you believe. Not even the goodwill of Senator Flamininus will make up for losing a limb or worse. Can you handle that pressure?"

"Of course, sir, and I've got the men to do it, too." The centurion now straightened his shoulders, then tilted his head. "But why the secrecy, sir?"

"It isn't obvious?" Varro looked around. "You see the state of this garrison? The commander is losing men faster than he can replace them. Senator Flamininus realized he would want to hold on to all of us, just like he's doing with that other group the consul sent."

Both of them looked to Centurion Barbatus's tent row.

"But I don't feel bad for them," Varro said with a chuckle. "Consul Cato is offering them a reward as well. I fear they might give us trouble and try to bag our prize first. But if we can bring back proof that we eliminated the Lusitani chief before them, then we get the reward. You read it yourself. That kind of wealth turns men against each other, if you understand."

"I do, sir. Seen it myself, actually."

"Then you know why all the secrecy and the haste. Get your men ready, Centurion, and keep it quiet."

Varro had added lines to Flamininus's notes promising rewards big enough for a man to live out his days in comfort. They would get nothing of the sort at the end of all their troubles, though Varro promised himself he would find some way to reward the centurion and his men. While he disliked the deceit, he hated how easily it came to him even more.

So the centurion and his optio set about rousing sixteen men to join their mission. It was half of what Varro wanted, and he feared not having a local guide, even if they would not know Lusitani territory.

"That was the simple part," Falco whispered. "Getting the gates opened will be harder."

Varro looked to the barred gate and the square log tower beside it. The guards on watch would be there, along with the soldiers normally assigned the tower as their barracks.

"You unbar the gates," Varro said. "And I'll make sure the men inside let us pass."

Once more, Falco shrugged and offered a twisted smirk.

"You've become a better liar than when we were just boys."

"I was a better person then. Now, I'm forced to be practical. Have the centurion form up his men and meet us at the gates. Quietly, of course."

Varro strode into the night, crossing the parade ground while Falco organized the men. He counted on the garrison being sound asleep. At least in the legion, a typical soldier ended each day so exhausted that even a thunderclap by his bed could not wake him. Garrison life appeared easier in comparison. The clatter and thump of the preparing troops behind him would've awakened all of Cato's legions. But the garrison remained dark except for the men watching the wilds beyond the walls.

The tower guards had set the bar on the entrance door. Varro rapped on it until someone opened the peephole window. Two bleary eyes glared out at him.

Varro provided the password for the day and asked to be let inside.

"I've orders from the commander."

The window snapped shut and he heard the bar rattle. As he

waited, Varro reached under his mail coat. He tugged out a wad of vellum he had used to forge documents during the afternoon. He counted on the rank and file's lack of experience with official documents to realize nothing official would be written on vellum.

The soldier now framed in the dim light of the first-floor room had clearly been awakened. Varro would not have to fake his anger, as his laxness endangered everyone depending on his vigilance. Yet it served Varro's purposes.

"Did I wake you?" Varro pushed inside, closing the door enough to reduce the dim lamp light from spilling out to alert others. "It's a quiet night, easy to doze off."

Though Varro was new to the garrison, the soldier took in his medals and his centurion's crest and immediately stiffened to attention. His mouth moved with voiceless panic. Varro waved him down.

"I know how it is," he said, as if revealing a dark secret in confidence. "I came up through the line, too. Had plenty of long and boring nights on a fort wall. I'd be lying if I claimed I never nodded off. We'll forget this incident."

The soldier, being surprised and flustered, did not even defend against the accusation. "Thank you, sir. It was only for a moment before you knocked."

"Of course," Varro gave a blithe smile, then extended the vellum to the soldier. "Do you read?"

The soldier's face seemed to grow white even in the golden glow of the clay lamp sitting on a trestle table. He took the offered vellum.

"Only a little, sir."

"Well, read what you can, but you recognize the commander's seal at the bottom?" Varro had used his own pugio's pommel to fake a seal, inspired by Curio's message earlier.

"I'm not really familiar with it. This says something about a mission, sir?"

"Correct. If you have an optio or someone here who can read, you can wake him up and verify the letter."

"I can't leave my post and I don't think anyone here reads, sir."

"Then give it to your officers tomorrow morning if they question you. I'm leading a night operation. With all the losses this garrison has experienced, we suspect spies have infiltrated us. Therefore, knowledge of the mission has been kept in strict secrecy. We're leaving tonight. I expect you to inform the others on watch here and to bar the gate behind us."

The soldier nodded again, staring at the vellum in hand as if it had come from another world.

Varro heard his force arriving outside, certain to draw attention from those on watch.

"Hurry, soldier, we're ready and I don't want any problems. Don't stare at me. Move!"

The unwitting soldier scrambled up the ladder, calling to his companions above. "Hold on, we're to let them out."

With a smile, Varro emerged from the tower to find Falco along with the centurion and sixteen men in a column.

Varro joined them. "Any louder and you might as well sing."

Falco rolled his eyes. Then the centurion ordered two men to lift the bar aside and open the gates.

"This is going to gain us some attention," Falco whispered.

"Move out," Varro said to the centurion, following a chain of command with himself as the senior commander. "We'll meet our contact, then we will push for the first objective. Maintain strict silence, Centurion."

The short column marched out of the open gates into the starlit darkness of Iberia. Once the gate closed behind them and the bar thumped into place, Varro experienced both relief and dread, like cold water pouring down his back.

"Congratulations," Falco whispered as they marched at the head of the column. "We've somehow stolen sixteen soldiers.

Centurion Pilatus left his optio in charge back at the fort. I imagine the garrison commander is going to have a few stern words for him tomorrow morning."

"You got his name," Varro said, turning back to see the centurion in the rear where his optio would traditionally march. "Good work. I was afraid he'd ask why I never used his name."

"That's the least of what you'll have to explain to him. Got any more brilliant ideas about keeping them loyal once they realized we've duped them?"

"We're doing exactly what I told them, just without the garrison commander's authorization. We are going after an enemy deep in Iberia. I just didn't say he was a former citizen."

"When glory-seeking Pilatus finally wakes up from his dream, he's going to realize a lot of shit doesn't add up. What then?"

"One problem at a time, Falco. By tomorrow, we all cannot return without the silver and Lucian's head. When we do, Pilatus and his men will all have the glory they seek. But until that time I'll have to keep their trust, which will be all the harder for having starting with deceit. I have done no better than Lucian did in his deceit of Curio. I will one day have to answer for it."

He gave Falco a hard stare, feeling his face heat.

"This is different," Falco said. "We're saving Curio and putting an end to a fucking madman. The bastard deserves death a hundred times over for what he did. He marked Curio and his boys to be killed from the start. Don't think you have anything in common with that shitbag Lucian. Besides, Flamininus will cover for all when we get back. He'll hand out medals for everyone. Bronze isn't that expensive, especially for what we're doing."

"I hope you're right about Senator Flamininus. Certainly, he did not authorize me to mislead troops intended for the garrison."

"Well, it ought to wake him up to his actual power. He's not consul anymore and soldiers don't jump to his commands. Just fools like us do." Falco sniffed and scanned the dark trees that loomed higher as they left the track to find their way into the hills. "What's the plan now? How are we going to find Curio?"

"That's my least concern," Varro said. "He will find us. Just as he said in his letter, he's watching for a sign. I agree with the commander that Curio watched the harbors for signs of help. When he saw our bireme arrive, he would've certainly seen who arrived. He couldn't have missed forty disembarking soldiers and the two of us in all our medals. I'm certain he is watching even now."

"If he's not asleep. It's dark out. Even sixteen men in full gear could probably march right by him without being seen."

Varro did not disagree, yet he had the highest faith in Curio. After all that he had endured, he would be cautious in approaching any legion force, even one led by his friends. He would watch and wait and only reveal himself when he was certain.

But Varro worried as they pushed deeper into the trees and slowed as the terrain fell into darkness. The column still maintained silence, but it grew so loud that Varro could hear their questioning in it. Even Falco, marching beside him, was so quiet that it grated.

Yet at the moment Varro was ready to halt their march, he heard a sound.

It came from the rear, and when he turned he found Centurion Pilatus and his sixteen men had already faced the same noise. He recognized the clomp of hobnailed caligae on the ground and saw the orange points of torches.

"Looks like the garrison sent reinforcements, sir." Centurion Pilatus was a dark outline beside the jumbled shadows of his men. "Should we try to link up with them?"

"No," Varro said. "Those are our competitors. Apparently, they're determined to reach our contact first."

Pilatus turned back again to the few points of orange light on their trail. The column also turned to face Varro.

"Who is it?" Falco whispered. "If the garrison commander was after us, there'd be more."

"You can't guess?" Varro narrowed his eyes. "Those are Cato's men, with Centurion Barbatus in the lead. We've got to move faster or all our efforts will be for nothing, or worse."

12

The breeze rushing through the dark trees surrounding Varro and his column carried the sounds of the closing enemy. Had it just been himself and Falco, he would simply flee into hiding. But his freshly duped men were still within marching distance of their garrison. If Centurion Barbatus caught up with them, he might turn his own men against him. He had to only reveal the flimsy deceit Varro had constructed in one afternoon. If his men had time to consider the facts, they might easily see through the ruse.

They all stood among the trees, silently watching the long column snaking up into the forested hills.

"How did they do it?" Falco pressed against a tree, whispering to Varro at his side. "They just walked out?"

"I don't know what they did. If they're Cato's picked men, then they are capable of anything. Maybe they killed everyone in their way. No matter, we have to keep them off us."

Varro looked to Centurion Pilatus, his feathered crest jutting above the heads of his men. He stared back, plainly confused but still obedient.

"Falco, you continue the march to the top of this hill. Take all the men with you. I'm going to lead off Barbatus and hopefully get him distracted enough that I can meet you up there. We'll camp there for a short rest and move out in the daylight. Curio will have to find us along the way."

"All right," Falco said, his disagreement plain in his growling tone. "But move out to where? Curio didn't show up."

"He'll find us eventually," Varro said. "Once we get Barbatus off our trail, we'll think of a way to locate him. But otherwise, we head west after Lucian. His silver and his head are our primary mission. Finding Curio is our own choice."

Varro left Falco and the others while he raced back the way he had come. If he could get Barbatus to follow him away and then set them in the wrong direction, then Varro would've bought time to permanently evade them. He could not figure how Barbatus knew his plans, other than he had seen Varro and his group leaving and investigated. Once he heard the lies Varro left behind, he would understand enough to realize he had competition to find Curio.

Their marching path was simple enough to follow in the daylight, but now it remained obscured. About halfway back, he heard his name called from the right. He stopped in mid-stride, gently setting his foot down in case what he took for his name was only the sound of his own passage between the trees and underbrush.

"Varro, over here!"

He could see the torches now, close enough to reveal the orange flames twisting over the heads of Barbatus's lead scouts. But he still could not find the voice.

Curio emerged from hiding. Varro recognized his outline in the darkness, short and hunched as if afraid to stand straight.

Both men stood frozen in disbelief. But Varro was the first to move, opening his arms to his friend and hoping it was not a vengeful forest spirit repaying him for his own deceits.

But Curio accepted the bear hug and clapped Varro's back.

"I couldn't believe it was you and Falco. I saw you get off the ship with all those other soldiers. I thought you were up north?"

Varro pushed back, clasping Curio by both his shoulders. The brush of silver starlight revealed sunken cheeks and haunted eyes set into emaciated sockets. His tunic was torn and smeared with dirt and dried blood. A simple leather belt clenched a waist that had become too thin. But his smile was bright even in the darkness.

"It's a story for later. Did you see us leave the garrison?"

"I was following until you were far enough away. You're about to enter enemy territory. Did you realize that?"

"Everything beyond the garrison walls is enemy ground in my mind."

"I've been searching the area while waiting for Senator Flamininus to send help. There are Iberian war parties all around. They don't cooperate, and the garrison is lucky for that."

Varro looked back to Barbatus approaching from the rear. Their shapes flickered through the trees like star-lit ghosts. A bright orb of golden light encircled the lead elements. The echo of a clipped command bounced off tree trunks.

"Those are Cato's men, sent to hunt you."

"I know," Curio said. "Centurion Barbatus and his treasury guards. They have good reason to hate me. They're why I had to flee the garrison."

"Is there an Iberian war party close by?"

"That way, on the other side of that slope is a camp of about fifty. They prey on garrison foragers and harass the wall guards, or so I've been told. But they have been sitting in place and getting drunk since I've been watching them."

"All right, we're going to lead Barbatus and his men to a fight.

That will weaken them and keep them occupied for our escape. Then we're going after Lucian."

Curio paused as he turned, and Varro saw dark fear pass across his face. Then he resumed his step.

"I'll show the way. Come on."

Curio glided into the verdant dark moving with startling familiarity through the trees and around rocks and ruts. His time hiding in the forest had taught him how to flow through it without giving himself away. In contrast, Varro felt like a war elephant tramping after him.

"First to get Barbatus's attention," Curio said. "I'm the best bait and a faster runner than you in all that armor. Guard me while I get their attention."

Varro nodded, fearing to answer while so close to their enemy. Curio led him to a clump of bushes and fallen trees. They both crouched behind it as the first of Barbatus's men trod up the gentle slope. They studied the ground ahead of them, following the shadowy footsteps Varro's column had left to discover.

"Here it goes." Curio's voice quivered with excitement, and he seemed like a rabbit tensing before a sprint. "Let's introduce Barbatus to the natives."

He fit a stone into a makeshift sling, probably crafted from the ruins of his tunic. Stepping out from their hiding spot, he whirled the rock overhead and started forward.

"Barbatus, have you come looking for me? I'm innocent, you know. It wasn't me that fed your men poison."

Curio continued ahead, but the forest seemed to shelter him from the enemy's sight. He twirled the sling overhead, whistling like a breeze through the forest. The column halted at Barbatus's shout.

"You humiliated my men. One died and others still can't speak. Show yourself, traitor."

"Sorry, Barbatus. But I'm about to humiliate your men again."

He let the slingshot fly, striking the lead scout carrying a torch square in his shoulder. Sparks flew as the torch crashed to the forest floor and then Curio sprinted off, laughing as he went.

Varro stepped to run after him. But his foot caught on a root, and he stumbled to land on his backside. He squelched a curse, but fortunately Barbatus shouted orders to pursue Curio that concealed his crash.

When he leaped to his feet, the column had already broken up and the leading force already peeled away. The men at the rear and the wagons for their gear and provisions lumbered upslope.

Rather than directly pursue Curio, Varro tried to parallel him. But his small friend remained out of sight, only calling out taunts to keep Barbatus and his men following. So Varro fought through underbrush, ducked under fallen timbers, leaped ditches, and kept pace as Curio led everyone up the slope.

Barbatus grew more infuriated as the heavy infantry plodded after him.

"Cato wants you alive!" he shouted. "But he's not here, Curio!"

"My grandmother could run faster than you, and she had bad knees!" Curio's taunt sounded like something Falco might have said. It heartened Varro as he shoved pine tree branches aside to keep up. Curio's voice was thin and distant from atop the slope. Varro had only kept pace with the rear of Barbatus's column.

Yet he persisted and noticed some of the enemy looked in his direction as he forced his way alongside them. But Barbatus's exhortations drew their attention to the fore. Curio had been leading them up a relatively clear path. The mules struggled with their supply wagons and soon were protesting the rapid climb. Their guards left the drivers to handle the beasts and surged ahead to join their companions.

The lead forces had crested the ridge and now vanished from sight. Varro could not see far in the darkness, and the trees blocked what little else he could see. Yet the vengeful pace set by the column made enough noise to trail them even in the dark.

At last, he reached the top himself. Huffing and sweating, he turned a sympathetic eye toward the mules being driven up with their loads in tow. But then he heard the shouting from the opposite side of the ridge.

The trees on that side of the ridge thinned as they swept toward a flat grassland. Red dots of campfire embers marked where the Iberians had encamped, and shadows flitted before them.

Varro loved nothing better than to see an enemy fighting another enemy. He leaned against a pine tree, setting his arms over a low branch to relax as he awaited Curio's return.

Barbatus's hateful shouting now turned into panicked orders to form ranks. But the alerted Iberians drowned out his voice with their own wild cries. In the night's dark, with only watery starlight to guide their swords, Iberians and Romans clashed together in battle.

The column had strung out during the pursuit, leaving Barbatus to face the massed Iberians without his full strength. Varro watched as both sides attacked with no preliminary skirmishing. He heard the thunder of shields and swords clashing together, and the desperate war cries from both sides. Barbatus even carried a standard, which his signifier now rose at the center of their line.

Seeing the outmatched Romans struggle, Varro felt a twinge of guilt. Barbatus might want to see Curio dead, but his desire for revenge was understandable. Furthermore, all his men obeyed orders and had no choice in what they did. He almost hoped for Barbatus's victory. But seeing the dark swarm of barbarians lapping his front ranks, he realized the stragglers of his column would never form a cohesive force.

Worse still, Varro would not allow Barbatus's bad luck to improve.

The mules and their drivers had halted behind the crest. Barbatus's men called for help, so that even the drivers had to join the fight. They tethered their mules loosely to whatever they could find, then sprinted over the crest.

Varro approached the two mules crouching low. He drew his pugio and approached the beasts. With a wicked grin, he finished what he had started in the garrison. He cut their harness so that the mules were now free of their burden. Stepping back, he snatched up stones and hurled them at the mules. They kicked and brayed, then sped away from Varro's attack.

Now he turned to the wagons and shoved them down the slope until they rolled on their own. One crashed and flipped while the other thudded against a tree. He raced down to steal whatever supplies he could, mostly rations and wine, which he set aside. Whatever else he left, he then scattered and ruined.

All the while, the crash of battle echoed over the ridge. The shrill notes of a bucina signaled a retreat, and Varro knew he had to flee. The smell of burning wood was heavy in the air, and he could imagine what the scene was like on the battlefield.

Then he straightened up after dumping the last cask of wine onto the ground.

Why was there smoke?

Down the slope, a fire now climbed into the trees at the base.

"The torch!" Varro shouted with the sudden memory of Curio's target being hit with slingshot and dropping his torch. It had smoldered in the forest debris of dead leaves and dried branches to eventually start a fire.

"They're coming!" Curio shouted while mounting the crest, but then stopped at the trees now burning up.

"Grab what you can of this." Varro scooped up the bundled rations in both arms. His pack was filled with his own gear, but he had stuffed more looted rations into it. Had he not carried his shield on his back, he could have fit more.

Curio raced down the hill, scooped up what he could into both arms, then looked to Varro.

"Where are we going?"

"Follow me." Varro had no more time to elaborate. Barbatus's men came over the ridge. The orange blaze framed him and Curio, and it spread with every minute.

"He's attacked the baggage! Kill him!"

Varro did not remain to hear the other threats shouted at him. The breeze was strong enough to encourage the fire and spread it to other trees. The garrison would see the flames and send a force to combat either fire or Iberians. Barbatus's remaining men also pressed from behind, but were scattered from both their lost battle and the fire.

So Varro and Curio both sped toward the prominent ridge, heedless of the ground beneath their feet. When Varro at last joined Falco and Pilatus, he forced through his breathlessness.

"Got Curio here. Captured some supplies. There are about forty Iberians, the remnants of Barbatus's force, and a forest fire behind us."

The blaze reflected two orange dots in Falco's wide eyes.

"Do you know what a covert mission means?"

Breathless, he shoved his armful of dried meats and bread at Falco. Curio did the same.

"No time for joyous reunions," Falco said, taking what he could.

"Correct." Varro was glad to be relieved of the burden. He had dropped enough on the way up to leave a fine trail for pursuers. "That fire is going to bring the garrison and all the Iberians within ten miles of here. We've got to push deeper. Curio, can you lead us to Lucian's last known position?"

"We're not going home?"

Varro turned toward the orange glow below and heard the echoes of enraged and panicked men rising in the distance. He could not turn back to face Curio, but remained looking out across the destruction he had left behind.

"No, we can't go back until we recover both Lucian and the silver. Until then, we're stuck in Iberia."

"Excuse me, sir." Pilatus stepped up to Varro, his arms filled with supplies Falco had dumped off on him. "Who is Lucian? Is this part of the mission?"

"He is the entire mission," Varro said. "But we can't hesitate to explain now."

He looked at the centurion, his face hidden in shadow like the sixteen men standing in formation behind him. He owed them the truth, but it would have to wait until they reached safety.

"Share out those supplies," he said. "They'll last us a good while if we stick to half rations. We are heading out. Centurion Curio here will guide us."

Curio stared at his feet, not reacting to his name. It did not seem to encourage Varro's freshly acquired troops, who began to murmur.

To his credit, Pilatus commanded their silence with a glare, then handed out rations as commanded. Falco gladly offloaded his armful of supplies.

"I've been dreaming of home," Curio said. "I don't want to be here anymore. This land belongs to other gods who hate us. We don't have enough men to face Lucian. He's got an entire tribe thinking he's their god's chosen."

"Enough," Varro said with a force that surprised even himself. Although Centurion Pilatus and his men were occupied, they listened to Curio. Varro couldn't lose them now. "We have a duty to perform. Don't talk about Iberian gods. They've been piss poor at keeping Rome out of their lands. And when we're ready to take all of it, these gods will roll over as they always have."

He spoke for the benefit of those listening in. Curio's thin body hunched in defeated acceptance. Falco now took him under his arm.

"The three of us are together again. Don't let this Lucian character get into your head. He's never had to deal with us before. But we're going to show him he can't run far enough. Remember, we brought down Sparta. What is this Lucian prick going to do to us that we haven't already beaten?"

With the men settled and Curio persuaded, they marched away from the growing blaze. Tendrils of smoke now reached them on the high ground, meaning anyone below would be driven to their position if only to escape the fire. So they marched at the fastest pace possible in near-total darkness.

Curio led them as a loose group that flowed around the thickening trees and increasingly rocky ground. Soon they enjoyed fresh air again as they left the fire and their enemies behind. Their curses became dim echoes that faded with every step forward. But Varro felt the weariness of a long night and knew his men would suffer as badly. He needed them fresh to keep pressing into unknown land.

He called a halt for the night, found a place for a rough encampment, and set a short rotation of watches before bedding down. Curio shared a tent with Falco and Varro. When he crawled inside, Varro was immediately aware of the pungent odors of sweat and dirt. Rather than say anything, he rolled away from him. Before long, they would all be as ragged and smelly as Curio.

"Good to see you again, Curio," Falco said. "You've got some explaining to do tomorrow."

"You do, too." He seemed about to say more but fell silent. Before long, Varro felt heavy and his mind flooded with random thoughts. Falco snored. But then Curio spoke again in a hoarse whisper, drawing Varro's mind back from the nonsensical world of his dreams.

"The gods will see the fire we started. Bandua will come for revenge like Lucian promised. We have to go home now, or we never will."

Curio spoke to two men he thought were asleep. But Varro heard, and a shiver rattled his body. He hated forests for their confusing darkness and the vengeful lost souls trapped within. Yet all of Iberia was mountains and forests. He closed his eyes to Curio's prediction and struggled for hours before he found sleep.

13

A t dawn, Varro found the campsite and the forest seemed less secure than it had in the darkness. Steep cliffs on their west side overlooked the treetops, leaving them exposed to enemy observation. The trees were less dense here, with wide gaps for easy approach. He stood with hands on his hips, scanning the brightening surrounding. All around him, his new recruits and their centurion went about their morning routine.

Varro appreciated the simple acceptance these soldiers demonstrated. Centurion Pilatus stood with two of the recruits, adjusting their straps and packs. As far as centurions went, he seemed more patient than most.

It comforted Varro to watch the soldiers' routine. Yet it was an illusory comfort, for he had to explain their actual situation which would require anything but routine soldiering. Therefore, he had set his medals on his armor to enhance his air of authority. But medals would not serve him in the days ahead. He would pack them before they marched out in search of Lucian.

He sniffed hard at the air and smelled nothing but the sweet notes of pine. The guards who had stood the last watch reported nothing more than animals moving in the night. It seemed both fire and pursuit had petered out. But they had left a trail that would certainly be discovered and followed. Starting today, they would take care to conceal their path.

He returned to his tent, where Curio and Falco sat outside and chewed on cold, dried meats looted last night.

"Cato sent them along with some tasty stuff." Falco braced the hard meat with both hands, then tore at it with his teeth.

"They're too far south for it to be Cato's provisions," Varro said, settling on the ground with them. "Those must have come from the garrison."

Falco chewed, then shook his head. "We had to dance on the head of a needle to get out, but they just followed us like it was nothing to them."

"Barbatus must've seen us leaving," Varro smiled as he accepted the black bread from Curio. He held it as he considered last night. "He probably woke the garrison commander and told him what we did, and got permission to leave in pursuit of us."

Falco raised a bronze cup of watered-down wine and let it hover before his lips. "How badly did the Iberians hurt him last night?"

Curio now stretched out and explained how he watched the fight from the rear until someone tried to push him into the line, mistaking him for their own troops. He fled before that happened.

"Barbatus's men were completely disordered." He used his fingers to imitate running. "The Iberians were faster to react and had slightly better numbers. So they were set to win the fight. I think Barbatus lived, but I'm not sure of their other losses."

Varro nodded. "They pulled back before the Iberians could get at them. I'm sure most of them survived but are spending the morning looking for each other. We can use this time to put the final distance between us. Once we're in the mountains, we should be able to hide our trail."

Falco finished drinking and set his cup on his knee. "Well, they came for Curio, who had vanished as far as they knew. So that means they'll have expert trackers. You know, men who don't give a fuck where we went and will find us anyway."

"That's true." Varro let out a long sigh. "At least they don't know about the silver and Lucian. They won't know where we're headed. So we just have to confuse our trail as best we can. Maybe we can make part of the journey by river. I've seen some marked on the map I took from the garrison, though I don't know how navigable they are."

Curio made a strange noise in his throat and started rubbing his feet. Varro noted the ragged condition of his caligae, and the centurion in him wanted to shout a reprimand.

"Remember when you asked me how I got a letter out to Flamininus?" Curio's face reddened as both Varro and Falco started at him. "So, there's a story about that. I think Barbatus knows about Lucian and the stolen silver or will know soon enough."

Varro took a bite of the hard black bread, knowing after he heard Curio's story he would lose his appetite. "How could Barbatus learn the contents of your letter? It arrived sealed, according to the senator."

"I needed to get the letter to the port. I had met a merchant who had traded with the garrison. We agreed on a price for my letter. So, I had to steal from the commander. He hid battle spoils in a chest inside his quarters. He mostly left me alone while he thought I was recovering. I grabbed a thick silver chain to give to the merchant to carry my letter with all haste. I promised him Flamininus would reward him too."

"Thieves and assassins," Varro said, repeating Cato's slurs. "Maybe Cato wasn't wrong about us."

Falco shook his head and sipped again from his bronze cup. Behind them, Centurion Pilatus reviewed his men, offering clipped criticism or praise. Curio watched them as he described his adventure.

"Stealing it wasn't hard, since he didn't expect a thief in his garrison. I thought about using his desk to write my letter. But I wasn't sure if he would notice that I had done so. I went to his command room and found some blank vellum there. I only had the papyrus sheet I stole from Lucian. I wrote a practice letter on the vellum first, so I could just copy it over to my papyrus."

"You left that copy letter behind," Varro said, looking between Curio and Falco.

"I had stuffed the copy in my tunic. But I remember it falling out when I returned to the barracks they had assigned me to. I just shoved it into my bedding. When Barbatus arrived that day, I had to flee immediately and left that copy behind."

Varro nodded. "He would've gone right to your barracks and searched it for clues, finding your copy. So he knows he has found more here than he ever hoped. He'll be Cato's hero for life if he can capture all three prizes."

"Gods, Curio!" Falco slapped his palm to his forehead. "Why did you make a copy?"

"I only had the one sheet of papyrus," he said, extending his palms in exasperation. "I just learned how to write, and it was an important letter. So I wanted to practice what I would say first. You told me to do that!"

"Not with secrets like that!"

"It doesn't matter now," Varro said. "After last night, he'll certainly want revenge on all of us."

"But he wouldn't chase us across Iberia if he didn't have Curio's letter," Falco said. "I hope those barbarians will keep him occupied."

"We knocked over the beehive last night," Varro said. "I'm glad to be leaving that all behind. If the area holds as many Iberian war parties as Curio says, then they will swarm the garrison during the confusion. With luck, Barbatus will be caught in the middle."

They then agreed to update each other on their time apart while they marched. Before they set out, Varro had to ensure Pilatus and his men were committed. It was not the best moment to reveal their situation, but his conscience grated on him. This was their last chance to turn back, though he had made it a risky choice.

He led Centurion Pilatus away to speak privately.

"I want you to have the full details of what we're doing and the actual risks we face." The centurion regarded him with a flat expression, giving no hint of his mood. So Varro continued. "I cannot have anyone who isn't committed following me into danger."

When Pilatus said nothing, Varro explained how he had contrived to get them out of the garrison after the commander rejected his request. He withheld nothing about the background leading up to this and the reality of Cato's wrath. All the while Pilatus remained inscrutable with only his eyes squinting as the morning sun skimmed over the treetops to strike his face.

"The truth is, our mission cannot succeed without you and your men. I am serious about the medals for bravery. I know Senator Flamininus will award one to every man here. And no matter what Consul Cato feels about our tactics, if he is made whole again he will be grateful as well. You will have earned a name with two influential men."

"I don't like it," Pilatus said, his expression never shifting from the tight flatness of indifference. "You deceived me and my men and made us abandon our posts. We're fucking deserters now."

"That depends on who you ask," Varro said. "I suffer the same accusation, but Senator Flamininus has assured me that can be handled. I served him in the Macedonia campaign, and I know he is good on his word. You're free to return to the garrison and take your chances. Maybe you'll be forgiven, especially if they're under attack and you can break it up from the outside. But that's the best you can hope for. If you go with me, and we return alive, we will all become heroes."

"Why are you telling me this now?" At last, Pilatus titled his head and frowned. "I wouldn't have known otherwise. I just thought Barbatus was competing for the same prize."

"The stakes are higher than that. You are all tied to me now. Eventually, you'd realize my story didn't add up. So what is your choice?"

Pilatus folded his arms and frowned.

"My choice? There isn't any for me or the men you tricked. If we go back, even if we're forgiven, we'll be branded as fools. I'll certainly lose my rank. You haven't left any choice. In fact, I resent you telling me all this. It's so you can feel better about yourself. Well, you're still a liar no matter what I choose. So fuck you and your choices."

Varro drew a sharp breath at the rebuke. His face warmed and he bit back on the excuses ready to gush out. Pilatus was right. He offered the truth to ease his own guilt, and it felt horrible to face up to it. But he held his composure.

"All right, so you'll stick with us."

"Of course." Pilatus looked past Varro toward the men standing in loose formation. "But don't say a fucking word to those boys. Let them believe the lie you created for them. Don't let them die thinking they're no better than traitors."

"None of us are traitors," Varro said, the heat on his face flaring and his stomach tightening. "We are caught between two rival senators. But we do our duty to Rome. Lucian murdered Roman soldiers and stole from their pay chests to fund a barbarian army. Does killing him and returning stolen pay to our fellow soldiers sound like the acts of a traitor?"

Pilatus held his gaze but looked aside first. "It doesn't change what you did. We were needed to strengthen the garrison. Does cheating an outpost already understrength sound like the act of a hero? I'll play along since there's no other choice now. But I want my reward by the end. I want to be free of charges and given a medal. Same for all of them that make it back."

"You have my word, and I know you cannot trust it now. But you will before long."

"I doubt I will ever believe anything you say again, or anyone else. This whole thing is a mountain of shit with you standing on top of it."

Varro slapped Pilatus's shoulder as if they were old brothers in arms. "You're a good centurion and a better man than me. Do your job and you will never regret this. And another thing."

Varro paused, then wrapped his fingers into Pilatus's chain shirt, tugging him closer.

"While we're on this mission, I'm the senior officer. If you can't respect me, then you'll respect my position. If you don't, you'll find out I'm unstinting in my punishment. Maybe I'm a shit liar, but, by the gods, I don't tolerate disrespect and foolishness on a mission. Anyone who wants to test that had best make peace with losing all the skin off his back, including you. If you believe nothing else I say, believe that."

He released his grip and patted out the wrinkle in the mail. Centurion Pilatus blinked in astonishment, but a grudging smile came to his thin lips.

"Am I dismissed, sir? I've got to get the boys ready for a hard march ahead."

Varro dismissed him, and a bitter smile tugged at his mouth as well. He had picked a good leader, one the garrison might've benefited from. His criticism had been hard to hear, but on point. Yet Varro recognized the shame in the centurion's voice. Pilatus realized he had also been a dupe and had his own desire for glory used against him.

When he returned to Falco and Curio, both looked quizzically between him and the men lining up for the march. One of Falco's heavy brows lifted in question, and Varro lowered his head.

"He's with us, and his men don't need to know any better. They'll follow orders."

"Good," Falco said. "So why do you look like you just wet your tunic?"

"Do I? It's nothing. Pilatus just taught me a lesson for the future. Next time I deceive someone, I should have the balls to deceive them all the way."

Falco inclined his head. "A wise man, that one. But he could do with a bit of self-reflection. His prick got hard just mentioning medals and glory. You got to watch where you're going. Can't blame no one but yourself if you step in shit."

"I've had all the wisdom I can stand this morning." Varro held out his palms. "Let's get ourselves ready to march. While we do, we can share stories about where we've been these months. I want to hear every detail about Lucian. We'll need to understand his tricks before we can challenge him."

Curio shuddered. "There's nothing to understand about him. He's mad and he's sick. All his barbarians are sick, like they're rotting from the inside."

Falco gathered up his pack before hoisting his shield. "You mean they have the plague? Fuck, that could be bad for us. How do you feel, Curio?"

"It's not the plague. It's something else like there is nothing in their heads. They follow Lucian but are in a dream. Even Lucian acted like that by the end."

"But he once acted as whatever he needed to be," Varro said. "So maybe he just acts that way in front of his men."

Falco laughed. "Yeah, the barbarians here are strange. The northern tribes seem civilized in comparison."

"It's not an act," Curio said. "He drinks a strange brew that takes him to his gods. But it also seems to leave him weakened. He doesn't sleep either."

"Then he will be easily overcome," Varro said, trying to recapture their momentum from the prior night. "All we need to do is pin him down."

"And defeat an entire tribe of Lusitani with twenty men." Falco slung his shield bag across his back. "This is too easy."

Falco had hit on Varro's genuine concern. Lucian himself might have once been a skilled fighter. However, now he was old and either sick or else poisoned by whatever he consumed to seek his gods. His sole strengths had been in deceit and secrecy, as well as using others for his own ends. Now that he had been dragged into the light, his defeat was inevitable. But if he surrounded himself with hundreds of fanatical tribesmen, Varro would need a matching force to defeat him and not sixteen recruits led by a disillusioned centurion.

They set out as the sun reached over the treetops and lit their path. In the distance, black smoke lingered in the air. The forest fire had died out. The trees and ground were too moist from recent rainfalls to truly create an uncontrollable blaze, but Varro hoped it had caught Barbatus up in the confusion it created. He was aware of the irony of his being pursued while pursuing Lucian. With luck, he wouldn't face the centurion until he returned with Lucian and his stolen silver. But then, Senator Flamininus would be present to put an end to this long nightmare.

Yet soon these fears faded behind the practical challenges of marching through unfamiliar territory. Varro had his stolen map, which proved invaluable to tracing their way to where Curio had last seen Lucian. They skirted the worst of the mountains and followed an alternate route through a narrow pass.

It took two days of travel through the rugged terrain to reach Lucian's last known position. The signs of an old encampment had already faded back into the earth. But they found remains of a funeral pyre and the ghastly blackened bones left there. Animals had pawed through it, probably drawn to whatever bones hadn't been completely blackened.

Curio used his light pilum to fish out a small skull from the black ash. A strange smile crossed his face, but Varro did not ask for the details. He let the skull drop off the iron point and turned away from the pyre.

During the two days of travel, they had shared all their stories. Curio had been truly duped, and his unquestioning obedience had led to his downfall. Varro described their harrowing escape, the death of Centurion Longinus, and their boring confinement to Senator Flamininus's estate. He glossed over that part, since Curio had been suffering in the wilderness during this time.

By the end, they set aside all the confusion and misunderstanding in the name of friendship. They vowed to never keep secrets from each other again, no matter who gave the orders.

"We're forming our own secret organization," Falco said, joking. But Varro took it to heart.

"It could be time to change how Servus Capax works," he said. "Until today, it's been secretive and anonymous. But has that really served anyone? Look at Lucian or my great-grandfather, for that matter. In both cases, I think it drove them mad. Now look at us, caught up in the vanity of two senators who distract us from our greater cause to bring Roman prosperity to the entire world. There would be less of this in a more open organization, at least open with itself."

His speculation died when neither Curio nor Falco took it up. It was a concern for another time, but Varro determined to think more about this. Perhaps with the three of them cooperating, they might have more power against a secretive and isolated organization. They could make genuine changes. If they ever returned from Iberia.

They broke up to scout the area and determine if the area remained a viable campsite. It seemed undisturbed since its last use, and Varro gave the command to settle for the night. While Pilatus and his men created the ditch and stake defenses for their small party, Varro used the remaining sunlight to plot their route.

"It seems our best opportunity is to reach this river and at least follow it into Lusitani territory. It's the best signpost we have to be sure of our path." His finger traced the thin lines, circling the areas where scouts had indicated forage and game opportunities and signs of native activity. He followed it out to the river, which then spread into empty space on the vellum.

Both Curio and Falco hovered over him, staring wordlessly at a map that charted a path into the unknown. Varro's finger tapped on the empty space.

"Once we're in their territory, it should be simple enough to find out where Lucian's tribe is. We'll have to question some of his neighbors."

"I hope they speak our language," Falco said.

"We can make our point known through other means," Varro said. "And based on Curio's observations, I believe Lucian's neighbors don't care for him or his tribe. So it might be easier to get a local to show us the way."

Curio sighed and traced the same path to emptiness on the map.

"And what will we do when we find him?"

Varro remained fixed on the blank spot where Curio's dirt-encrusted finger tapped.

"We will have to make plans based on what we discover there."

Curio's finger stopped tapping but remained on the blank area of the map.

"No Roman has gone so far. We're creating the map as we go. But will anyone else ever see it?"

Varro tugged the hide map from beneath Curio's finger and rolled it up.

"No one else will need it. We're going to finish Lucian and end the madness that consumes the tribe following him."

With a sad smile, Curio turned away.

"Or the madness will consume us first."

14

Varro led his column through the gloomy forest. While above the canopy the sun might shine, the forest floor did not receive its light. It was twilight or night while trapped in its confines. The column paralleled a stream that he expected to join with the river he sought. Now out of the mountains, the air grew warmer and more humid. The earthy scents of dirt, rotting debris, and pine hung in the still air. Varro felt as if the forest directed his path, forcing him to skirt trunks too tight to allow a man to pass. Wherever he sought to place his foot, a rock or root would threaten to upend him. The forest never allowed him to choose his own way. It dictated even where he could set his feet.

Falco marched beside him and struggled even more because of his height. It seemed the trees extended their branches to bar his path. It was an eerie coincidence when it happened, for in the forest's heart most branches did not grow close to the floor, but high overhead. Falco would inevitably catch his pack or shield bag on the limb as if the tree were trying to grab him up into its maw of leaves. Fortunately, he always pulled free, though with a growled curse and glare backward at the offending branch.

"A rest soon?" His whisper still sounded a normal volume to Varro.

"We'll need to check the map again," he said. "These damned trees go on forever. I'll have someone climb one to get our bearings. The river should not be far but I just can't tell from the ground."

He also wanted to add that the air felt thick with menace and he expected disaster behind every moss-covered trunk. But he had to preserve confidence for his men, who watched him constantly. For now, the column trudged ahead using their light pila to negotiate the treacherous ground. Centurion Pilatus followed up from the rear, goading them whenever they slowed.

The centurion had acted as if the conversation with Varro had never occurred. He kept his men in line, encouraged them, and gave Varro the respect of his self-appointed leadership. This was Varro's sole relief in the unremitting aggravation of this trek through the densest forest he had ever known.

The shrouded light and unearthly silence weighed on everyone, making them whisper even when at rest. It seemed every man feared drawing attention, either from predators or malevolent spirits skulking in the endless green twilight. Yet despite their dour moods, they were all in good condition. They had taken forage where the map showed it and the more skillful hunters in the group had trapped rabbits and squirrels. They rationed their dried meats for the days ahead, where the map was all blank and foraging conditions unknown.

"Here is a good place to pause." Varro hoped he sounded as if he had come to the decision based on his experience. In fact, he had little idea of what made for a safe camp or rest area. Despite his experiences hiding in forests, he had learned little from them.

Here, at least, the stream swelled and the men could clean up and refresh themselves in it.

He and Falco removed their helmets and dropped their packs to sit on a fallen trunk now thick with green moss. Both looked off into the woods, scanning for Curio. Varro had asked him to scout ahead and coordinate with the two other men who had woodland experience from their civilian lives.

Centurion Pilatus joined them while his men went to the stream. He lifted off his helmet and set it under his arm, but remained standing.

"Sir, how long before we find that river?"

Varro patted his pack where the map now remained. "The map is blank from here to our destination. I've been filling it out with what we've found. Before we set out, send a man up into a tall tree and describe what he sees. I'll update the map and make a guess. If we continue at our current angle, I expect we will reach the river within the next day or so. That should flow west into barbarian settlements. But I can't guarantee anything."

Pilatus bent his mouth.

"I suppose no one can guarantee anything in the unknown, sir." He looked to a flat-topped stone as if seeking permission to sit. Varro nodded to it, and he settled on it with a groan.

"Sir, Centurion Curio is worrying the men."

Varro and Falco shared a knowing look.

"That's why I set him to scouting duty."

Pilatus grimaced. "It helps some, sir, when he's away. I know he's your friend. But you've got to stop him from carrying on about how we'll all go mad and the barbarian gods will eat us alive."

"I've spoken to him about it already," Varro said, wincing at the defensiveness in his voice. "Is he still talking about it?"

Now Pilatus twisted in his seat. "No, sir, but you can see it in his face. Even if he doesn't speak, he looks like he's attending his mother's funeral. That affects the men's morale."

"There's more than one man on this mission with a sour expression. But I understand. Curio has been through much. He expected to return to Rome and not be thrust back into the very place he nearly died to escape. That is more than disappointment. It's the realization of his worst fears, that he has been cursed and he'll never escape Iberia. Even his closest friends push him deeper into it."

Pilatus's expression did not yield to something more understanding. He simply nodded and looked away. Varro knew he was unconvinced, but reserved his complaints. The voices of the men cleaning up by the river had grown louder and livelier. Varro had not commanded silence. Instead, it was the forest itself that imposed silence on all of them, killing their words before they were voiced. He was gladdened to hear their banter.

After a strained pause, Curio emerged from the drab light of the forest with his two scouts. His walk was full of purpose and his worried expression was replaced with grim resolve. Varro and Falco stood, realizing he had news.

"Human tracks nearby, maybe three or four men. They seemed to have shadowed us for a time. We lost their trail ahead, where this stream curves into our path."

Varro peered ahead, seeing nothing but tree trunks that shaded off to milky gray. It looked like an endless columned gallery carpeted with dead leaves, pine needles, and twigs.

"We didn't search for where their trail picked up again," Curio said. "We'd get too far ahead of the column."

"We'll have to assume we're being shadowed," Varro said. "And hope they've not gone to fetch help."

"Or set a trap," Falco added with a falsely bright smile. "The barbarians are always good for a deadfall, rockslide, or something just as shitty."

Pilatus now stood. "I'll get the boys back in line."

"Let them rest for now," Varro said. "But let's ready our shields.

As heavy as they are on the arm, I've seen firsthand what an Iberian ambush can do. It'll come without warning and we can't be unprepared. In the meantime, Curio, take me to see the tracks."

With a crisp salute, Pilatus went to the stream undoubtedly to disobey Varro's first request to let them rest. He was born for the centurion's crest, ever ready to push his men to their limits.

Varro left Falco in command, who gave a half-hearted salute while returning to sit on the fallen trunk. "I'll stand up when there's an ambush. Don't worry. My back is killing me right now."

"That's the price of idleness," Varro said. "We can blame Flamininus when we meet him again."

He was always quick to bring up their reunion with Flamininus. It reinforced the idea of survival and a return to normal. All they had to do was bring back an addle-minded centurion who had enough charisma to persuade simple-minded barbarians to violence—something already in their blood. The actual challenge lay in getting to him alone.

He couldn't help but think of Cato's epithet of thieves and assassins and he bent his head in shame. It seemed he would not amount to anything more. His great-grandfather had warned him, but he hadn't the wisdom to hear.

As they retraced Curio's path, Varro cleared his throat.

"The men are worried about you. They say you are predicting our doom. It's not good for anyone's morale. Even mine."

Curio walked ahead of him, looking for the signs of his own passing and directing their steps.

"Are you worried? I know you hate the forest. This is the worst one yet. I should know. I can't escape it."

"Don't be foolish. You escaped it once, but Flamininus sent us back. We need success here. Otherwise, we have no life outside of the forest. Do you understand, Curio?"

"Lucian cursed me, you know. I didn't want to believe it. I begged Jupiter to protect me, but why would he listen to a tiny man like me? He let the Iberian gods have their way and now Bandua is waiting for me."

Varro grabbed him by his ragged tunic. Its hems were ripped or frayed and the belt cinched on his waist revealed it was now too big for him. His eyes were sunken and shining with a fear that bordered on madness.

"Stop this. You're shaking up everyone. The forest is frightening enough without your talking about this barbarian god."

The way Curio flinched at his rebuke caused Varro to pause. Curio had suffered through more than he had, and Lucian's manipulations had left him humiliated and doubting his own competence. So he brightened his voice and released his hold on the tunic.

"You must feel defenseless out of your armor. I'd have brought you better gear if I had been thinking. But you might be better off than the rest of us. You can vanish when danger comes. Look at me, with a shiny helmet full of feathers and a chain shirt. I couldn't hide from a blind man."

Curio searched Varro, then sighed.

"Armored or not, I won't feel right until I leave this darkness."

"I am with you." Varro now clapped his hand to Curio's shoulder. "Nothing will ever separate us again. I'm just as frightened and eager to go home as you are. But for us to have that chance, we need to keep everyone in high spirits. Nothing has happened yet. We might be tensed up for no reason at all."

With a repentant nod, Curio shrugged.

"I'll try to watch myself. I just keep remembering Lucian with that skull. It was his wife's skull. How mad is that?"

"Just smile, even if it feels false. Smile at everything. The men were expecting to meet a seasoned agent working alone in the dark of Iberia. So play that role for them, even if it's a lie. Just until we can bring down Lucian."

"That bastard will pay," Curio said, balling his fist. "His mad gods and his curses mean nothing to me."

"That's right," Varro said, again clapping Curio's shoulder. "Now let's get back."

"You don't want to see the tracks?"

"Of course not. What more could I glean than you did? I just wanted to have a private talk."

Back at the stream, Varro refined his map with help from one of his men who climbed a tall tree. He had to shout down what he saw, but by now Varro did not worry about revealing himself. Somebody was already tracking them. Once he added to the map, he admired his work with both Falco and Curio looking over his shoulder.

"Do you really know what you're doing?" Falco asked.

"I'm just adding to what is already here. I'm no map-maker. We'll need to find our way back with the silver carried on our backs. So I'm making sure we don't lose the way."

Falco snorted then spit into the bole of a tree. "It would be our luck to get all the way across this land then lose our way coming back."

"But not with a map." Varro rolled it up and had Centurion Pilatus arrange his men for the march. They now carried their shields, all freshly painted and undamaged. Even Varro and Falco carried new shields. Each one was painted differently, and those who had paid extra sported crisp designs. Varro preferred to carry a red shield, while Falco's was black. Curio was the only man without one, but since he acted as a scout it did not matter.

Once they had come to where Curio discovered footprints, whatever levity the men had drawn from their rest by the stream vanished. Varro led the march directly over the prints as if to stamp on those who left them.

The day wore on and the forest darkened. Their progress

slowed as the trees and underbrush grew so dense that they could not see more than a few yards in any direction.

Curio waited for the column to catch up to him then described the path ahead.

"It just thickens as we go," he said. "The stream is the best path to follow for now."

At first, Varro thought to follow its banks, but then realized Curio intended them to walk through the shallow water. Thanks to the design of their caligae, the water would flow through their feet rather than fill up like a boot would. So, they stepped out into the cool water and continued.

Curio did not need to lead by much while they were in the open. But he raised his hand as if to caution them. Varro then raised his to stop the column.

"In the trees," Curio said, after picking his way against the flow of the stream back to Varro and Falco. "We're being watched."

Varro stiffened but did not immediately turn to search the forest. Tall bushes, trees, masses of vines, and a chaos of greenery concealed what lay behind them. So instead he leaned out from the column and summoned Centurion Pilatus. He splashed up the stream to them, frowning.

"Sir? What's wrong?"

"Curio spotted men along the banks."

"On both sides," Curio added. "I saw them watching. They're very still, but they've camouflaged themselves. You can see them if you look closely."

All of them tried to act as if they were unaware of the stalkers as they glanced about. At first, Varro saw nothing more than the gloomy light dappling the vegetation. But as he continued to scan he saw a glittering brown eye blink. It was so unsettling he nearly jumped backward.

"I see them," Falco said. "Got branches in their hair so they blend in."

"I didn't see anything, sir." Pilatus glanced around once more. "Are we surrounded?"

"I can't say," Varro looked around once more. "But they're hesitant. So I believe we outnumber them. Otherwise, they would've attacked."

"They're just standing there," Curio said, watching. "There must be a trap ahead."

"No doubt," Varro said. "Pilatus, we're going to appear as if we're resuming the march, but as you return to your position, quietly tell the men to ready their pila. We'll rush both sides, half one way and half the other. I want to capture one alive if we can."

Pilatus saluted and Varro watched him mumble his order to ready for an attack. "Left side go left, right go right. And take them alive if you can."

He gave the last order from the rear. Varro doubted the Iberians would understand, but he still flinched at revealing the plan.

To his right, Varro searched for the blinking eye. He had seen it, but now it had vanished back into the forest. Yet he felt the intense stares radiating from the gloom. A dread hung in the air, and even the stream bubbling over his feet sounded muted. The familiar hum of animals and birds had also vanished, a sure sign of approaching danger.

Now he realized how exposed they all were. A javelin or spear might sail out of the underbrush at any moment, felling his men in a stroke. But he hefted his body-length shield and that fear diminished. He looked to Curio.

"Go on ahead, but be ready to take shelter behind us."

"I'll be all right," he said. "I'm sure Bandua is saving me for Lucian."

Falco groaned, but Varro ignored it.

Curio turned and sloshed through the water.

And Varro heard the crack of a branch and then a sudden, frantic crash like someone running through the trees.

"Fuck!" He pulled up his shield. "Attack now!"

Pilatus's voice roared out. "Charge!"

The column broke into halves, each one heading for a different bank. Varro and Falco joined the right bank, and Curio rushed toward them carrying only his pugio.

"Cast pila!"

Pilatus's bellow gave way to sixteen light pila flying ahead of the charge and into the underbrush.

Varro led his side to crash up the short bank and plow into the bushes. He heard the snap and crash of the clamoring Iberians in retreat. He glimpsed what looked like a man carrying away an injured companion vanish into the trees.

As he pushed through the foliage on the bank, the branches splashed back with blood. Something soft shifted underfoot and nearly tripped him; the warm body of a man, he guessed. With a battle cry, he leaped over it to break into the area where the Iberians hid themselves.

But there was no one there. Instead, he watched a deer leaping through bushes to escape the mad onslaught.

Eight screaming soldiers joined him, shields up and heavy pila ready for the cast. But meeting no enemy, their charge stalled.

Falco now lowered his shield and pulled on the shaft of a pilum sticking upright in the bushes.

"Looks like we'll be having deer meat for dinner."

Yanking out the pilum, the tip now bent and ruined, he threw it away then used his shield to hold the bushes aside. Varro saw a doe that had taken a pilum through her neck.

"It was a well-placed cast," Falco said with a bitter smile. "Too bad we won't have a second chance to use our pila against a real enemy. With accuracy like this, we can conquer all the tribes ourselves."

Across the stream, Centurion Pilatus's charge had ended, and the men reemerged into the stream.

"I saw them," Curio said. "They were watching us."

"They were," Varro agreed. "Only we saw enemies waiting in ambush when they were just deer."

He stood over the slain doe, her blood dripping from the leaves where she had stood frozen in place by her own terror. Then he looked to his men, their faces flushed and confused. He could not look at them long, and turned aside in humiliation.

"We're seeing things now," Falco said dryly. "We've got to get this job done before we lose our fucking minds."

15

Varro was no longer certain how long they had been in the forest. Thanks to Centurion Pilatus's skill in skinning and butchering, the venison they had inadvertently captured lasted until they all were tired of its flavor. The preserved foods stolen from Centurion Barbatus's men still remained. Also, following the river provided fresh water for cooking, eating, and bathing. It plowed through the forest, creating wide banks that were easier to follow in places, and in others more difficult.

Now the river had led them into open plains and Varro judged they must be halfway to Lusitani territory. He stood with Falco and Centurion Pilatus at the edge of a clearing. The rest of the column sat on their haunches beside the muddy banks and squinted silently into the glare of the morning sun.

Falco lifted his helmet and scratched beneath it. "I still say it's an empty village."

"We saw smoke over the trees," Varro said. "So someone is still there."

"My boys will find out, sir." Pilatus looked less impressive without his helmet feathers. Both he and everyone else had pulled them all out since the branches of the deep forest had torn them ragged.

As if they had heard Pilatus, Curio and three other men strode back across the field. He had led them through the grasses and stands of trees to get a closer and better view of the village. They now returned to make their report, and everyone leaned forward to hear what Curio and the others had learned.

"It's all empty," Curio said. "Everyone killed and left where they fell."

Falco sniffed. "Can't be long ago. I don't smell anything rotting."

"About a dozen dead, sir," one of the other scouts spoke up, looking back. "There might be more inside the huts. Blood is fresh."

"Finally, we might get to a real fight if the enemy is still near."

Whether Pilatus's statement was a jab at Varro's mistaking deer for enemies, he still narrowed his eyes at the centurion.

"Eager to get stuck in, are you? Be glad we've only wasted our pila on deer so far. Our mission isn't to battle the Iberians."

"Sorry, sir, I didn't mean anything by it." But the centurion looked to his men squatting in the shade beside the river. "It's just a lot of monotony tramping through the woods for days on end."

"Forget about it," Varro said. "Get the men ready and we're going to investigate that village."

Varro led them in two ranks, eight men wide. He had Pilatus and Falco flanking him in the front, and Curio assumed an optio's role at the rear. This was the safest spot for an unarmored and unarmed man.

Yet the caution was clearly unneeded. As the scouts had reported, bodies lay sprawled out where they fell. The small buildings, more like collapsing log huts, all lay open. Animal pen gates hung wide and the livestock was stolen or else set free.

"No one fired the place," Falco said. "Seems like something one rival tribe would do to their enemies."

Varro agreed. "Centurion, have two-man teams search the buildings. If anything useful was left behind, gather it to this center yard."

Flies had settled on bodies and blood pools. Crows lined the rooftops and tree branches, patiently watching for Varro to lead his men away. The air was foul with the stench of death, but the wind carried it away into the plains.

The searches of the homes produced nothing of value, as whoever came before them had ransacked the few huts of anything of real value, including food. Varro decided to search the area around the village with Falco and Curio for company. They easily found the trampled path the attackers had made. They had come from the southeast, approximately where Varro had come from. He looked across the plains to a line of dark trees that led into blue mountains.

"These are Roman tracks," Curio said. "Look at this print."

Falco squatted beside him. "You can't be sure of that."

Yet Curio dug a finger into the churned earth and pulled up something he held between two fingers.

"A hobnail."

The word filled Varro with dread. He snatched the dirty nail from Curio, feeling its hard coolness and the mud clinging to it. Rolling it between his fingers, he gritted his teeth.

Falco stood up. "Could have come from a barbarian boot. Maybe they use hobnails too."

"No, Romans left all these tracks," Curio said as he crab-walked along the path. "Look at the prints here on the edge. This is the hobnail pattern Consul Cato standardized for us."

Varro's and Falco's shadows passed over the clear imprint in the mud that Curio had uncovered. In the blue shadow, the outline was unmistakably the same as what Varro remembered from his own legion-issued caligae. Consuls decreed a standard pattern and number of nails to their legion cobblers. Otherwise, the footwear could vary both in cost and quality. In fact, Varro could tell who a soldier had served under just from his caligae hobnail patterns.

Varro flung the ruined hobnail into the knee-high grass that rippled with the wind. "How did Barbatus get ahead of us?"

"We wasted too much time deer hunting in the forest," Falco said, folding his arms. "Sure, it set him off our trail, but it took too long to clear. He must've taken a direct route to this river. He has the same idea we do, the cheating bastard."

With a sigh, Varro looked back at his men tossing whatever they considered useful into a pile while crows settled on corpses at the village edge.

"So Barbatus raided this settlement for food and livestock. You didn't see any cart tracks?"

Curio shook his head. "There could be some mixed in here, or farther back. Does it matter?"

"If they are burdened with a baggage train, we will have an easier time catching them."

Falco scuffed the footprints as he frowned. "Catch up with forty of Cato's soldiers? We want to avoid them."

Varro shook his head. "We won't avoid them for long. They're going after Lucian and the stolen silver. That's ultimately what Cato wants, even if he doesn't know it yet. Capturing Curio is now secondary to their mission. Barbatus is no fool. In fact, from what I've seen, he's a competent soldier. It pains me to be at odds with him."

"More likely, it will kill you. After what you did, I think the both of you have made a mortal enemy." Falco extended a hand to help Curio stand, then gave Varro a gentle push toward the ransacked village. "Come on, we've got our own competent soldier, Pilatus, to inform."

They found the centurion working alongside his men, gathering junk that had once been the property of peaceful farming families. Varro noted the children among the dead and recognized the horrific puncture wounds left by Roman swords.

"I've counted about twenty bodies, sir." Pilatus shooed flies that attempted to land on his sweaty face. "But I think many escaped or were carried off. The numbers don't square with the homes. Also, whoever attacked wasn't interested in slaves. Plenty of dead women and children here."

"It was Centurion Barbatus and his men." Varro's flat statement stopped everyone near them. Pilatus's face wrinkled in anger.

"How did he get here, sir? I didn't lead my men through all this just to have someone else steal the glory."

"I don't plan to allow him the chance." Varro glanced over the assortment of cooking pots, pelts, and half-empty sacks tossed beside ashen-faced corpses staring into the sun. "If there's anything useful, take it. Otherwise, form up to march at the double. Barbatus will leave a wide trail wherever he goes. We will follow."

Pilatus saluted and the paused soldiers returned to their work. But when Varro turned away, a strong hand grabbed him by the shoulder.

He looked into Pilatus's grim face as he stood close to whisper in a low voice.

"And when we find him, sir, what then? I'm not going to fight boys from our own side."

"And if it is fight or die?" Varro pulled his shoulder free. "Be at ease. We will evaluate our options when we catch up to them.

There's no reason to believe they have any better intelligence on where Lucian has gone. Like us, they have a wide area to search. I've no intention to meet our own side in battle, but just aim to hinder them long enough for us to claim the prize."

Falco had drawn close, bristling at Pilatus's anger. But now he leaned back, rubbing his chin with a sudden thought.

"Claim the prize but also return with it. He might be happy to let us do the work then pluck it out of our dead hands. We're a lot easier to overcome than a whole tribe of mad Lusitani warriors."

Pilatus's expression shifted from grim anger to shocked realization.

"Would he do that, sir?"

Varro raised his brow. "What do you think, Centurion? If you've served in the same legions that I have, then you know the answer. The rewards are too great, for them and us, just to let it go to the best man. So think hard about what you'll do when one of our boys runs at you with his gladius pointed for your heart."

They left the ransacked village behind for the flies and crows to feast on the corpses. Varro did not want to burn either for the same reason Barbatus did not. He feared alerting nearby settlements of trouble. They were likely in a populated area, as the plains made for good pasture and people always settled along rivers. Clouds of black smoke on the horizon would summon trouble if it was not already speeding toward them. According to Pilatus's estimations, a number of the villagers escaped. Therefore, the local tribes would be alert to danger and search for Romans to kill in revenge for the dead.

Since he had almost a full century of men, Barbatus had left an obvious path. It would lead natives to them. But Varro guessed the centurion was unconcerned about reprisals, for he did not attempt to conceal his trail. That was either hubris or a vast misunderstanding of how fast an angered tribe could mobilize. Varro reconsidered following, but he had to keep his competition in sight while they both made for the same general territory.

As the village disappeared behind the rolling folds and dips in the land, the marching column stretched out and Varro's mind wandered. He tried to imagine what Lucian would look like, and how a formerly respected member of Servus Capax could fall into such a state. Would he end up crazed like Lucian one day, unable to tell right from wrong? What if he vanished into Iberia and no one heard from him again? Who would care about his passing? His mind churned on too many questions, but none of them mattered if he did not remove the competition Barbatus introduced. Even if he lost men to the Iberians, he still outnumbered Varro's tiny force.

The fast rhythm of his marching and the monotonous high grass and cloudy sky encouraged his thoughts to wander. Everyone had fallen into a silent trance of sorts, where the body moved while the mind curled up with its own concerns.

"There they are!"

Curio had been in the lead if only to peek over the rises to ensure nothing dangerous awaited on the other side. He now lay flat in the knee-high grass, causing him to disappear from sight.

Varro, his mind rocked back to the present, raised his fist to stop the column. He crouched out of reflex, causing Falco to do the same. From behind, he heard his men setting their shields to crouch behind them as if expecting a javelin attack.

"Hold your position," Varro said to the men behind him. He and Falco then crawled forward while Pilatus took charge of the column.

"They've stopped for a rest," Curio said as Varro and Falco reached him. Now all three lay flat in the grass. Varro pulled off his helmet and rapped Falco on his.

"Don't need to flash a warning to Barbatus." He then used his elbows to hike up the top of the rise and looked across the plains.

He smiled at what he saw. Barbatus did not have his full complement of men. Some might be out scouting or foraging, but he counted thirty-two men. Curio and Falco offered similar counts.

"Great news," Falco said. "We're now only outnumbered two to one."

"They don't have a baggage train," Varro said. "So they're just as tired as we are."

Curio shielded his eyes against the late afternoon glare. "Foraging for that many men takes time. They will have less food to go on than we do."

"All right, I've seen enough. We'll stalk them until nightfall. Tonight, we'll have a look inside their camp."

"They won't fall for the gambling trick again." Falco started to crawl back down the slope.

With Curio and his two scouting partners leading them, Varro kept his men shadowing Barbatus's progress. They veered off toward the northwest, which Varro did not understand. By the end of the day, he was thoroughly confused as Barbatus had encamped outside a marsh. The ground had flattened out and the marsh bloomed from the side of the river. He set his own encampment farther away, behind a short hill and stand of trees.

After the camp had been established, they ate from their preserved rations and lit no fires. On the other hand, Barbatus had several fires lit that Varro saw as orange dots in a vast green dark below.

Falco had joined him and shook his head. "Even a civilian would know not to start a fire out here."

"Is he confident in his security or really a fool?" Varro rubbed his chin. It was careless of them to start fires. "Maybe the only food they have needs to be cooked. At least campfires aren't bright enough to be seen from afar, unlike smoke during the daytime."

"We found plenty of forage that don't need cooking." Falco

slapped Varro's back. "But we're going to take a trip down there to see for ourselves."

"Not you. I need you here to take command while I'm gone."

"Well, sir." He drew out the honorific until it became an insult. "I think you're a fool to do it. Since you've elected yourself as consul for our legion of outcasts, you need to remain in camp."

Varro had to laugh. "An apt description, but you did not change my mind. You've never been good at these infiltrations. Curio and I are better suited for it."

Falco stared at him. "You're nearly as tall as I am. Stop insulting me."

"It's not about size, but about grace in motion. You move like a stone shot from an onager."

"That might pass as a compliment in some situations. So, I'll let you have this one. But if you want to see grace in motion I'll break your jaw with an artfully placed fist. Anyway, don't get captured again."

They turned back from the edge of camp to find Curio waiting outside their tent. One of the men had provided him a brown cloak secured with a dull bronze pin. He had doubled it over to adjust the length, and pulled the extra material overhead to make a deep hood.

"I can hardly see you before my eyes," Varro said. "I'll fetch my own cloak and we're off."

They left Centurion Pilatus and Falco to manage the watches while the rest of the men slept. A bright moon painted them in milky blue light as they swept downhill toward Barbatus's encampment by the marsh. Varro shared his plan with Curio.

"I only want a look at the state of his men. If we can find a way to throw them off or slow them down, we'll take advantage of it."

"Falco was right," Curio said as they both sped low through the tall grass. "You should've left this to me and my scouts. You're our leader. If something happens to you, the whole force is in trouble."

Varro smiled. "I doubt that. I have no more idea of what I'm doing than anyone else. Flamininus gave us a hard task."

"Has he ever given us anything else?"

The question did not need an answer. As they neared the camp perimeter, both fell silent and ducked into the grass to observe the defenses. The vague scent of the fetid marsh carried on the air. Cricket song filled the night, and the breeze rustled the grass surrounding them. Blades of it brushed against Varro's cheeks as he peered through it.

Barbatus had set a standard marching camp with stakes and ditches. But he had only as many stakes as his men could carry, and there were enough gaps that he and Curio could slip through with care. He crouched low, enjoying the freedom of just wearing a cloak and tunic. Arming himself only with a pugio, he had no intention of fighting anyone.

The guards he faced, however, wore bronze chest guards and bronze helmets with their three feathers intact. Barbatus apparently hadn't led his men through the deep forests. They leaned on their body-length shields as they watched the darkness for danger.

Curio tugged at Varro's cloak, then mimed that they should circle around the camp to another side. A stand of trees and a gentle fold in the plains allowed them to get closer while maintaining their cover.

After repositioning themselves, and long moments of observing the guards, they stood bent at the waist and then rushed into the camp when the guards looked elsewhere. Though Varro's heart pounded throughout, he enjoyed the thrill. He had done this sort of work so often that unless his enemies were exceptionally observant, he was confident in passing unseen.

Now he and Curio crouched behind the first tent they encountered. It was not a large camp, and Barbatus had set his tent at the center. Both of them knew anything of worth would be there. Each watched different angles as they shifted from tent to tent toward the center. As Varro moved, he counted the tents and estimated Barbatus had lost a third of his original force.

Someone was retching at the edge of camp and stumbling back from the latrine ditch. The sound froze Varro and Curio in place behind a tent where men snored and rolled in their blankets. They saw a figure outlined in silver light doubled over and holding his stomach. But he soon reached his tent and crawled back into it.

Once again, Curio pulled on Varro's cloak. He followed his pointing finger toward the center of the camp.

Just outside Barbatus's tent, a bony man in a dirty brown tunic sat on the ground, tied to a post. He had a fuzzy gray beard and hair to match, only it was stained red where he had been struck in the head. Moonlight traced his sharp features and revealed he was also gagged.

"He must be a valuable prisoner," Curio said.

Varro considered why Barbatus had captured this man. He likely had an interpreter in his force, meaning he could interrogate the locals. Varro would struggle to get useful information from a local since he lacked any interpreters among his men. However, if he freed this captive then he might be better disposed to help Varro.

"We could use him for ourselves," Varro whispered. "Or at least deny Barbatus an asset."

They retreated from the tent they hid behind. The camp was too small to have any safe area for them to discuss their plans. But neither needed to go into details. They had worked together long enough to know what to do.

"I'll free the captive and secure him," Varro said while constantly searching the dark. "You open the way out. If we're pursued we'll head for the trees, then snake around to camp with the prisoner."

Without more discussion, Curio bent low under his voluminous cloak and vanished into the darkness between tents. Varro pinpointed the men on watch, all looking out into the vast dark. They might easily turn inside if alerted. It depended on how cooperative the Iberian was with his rescuers.

Varro crept up to the captive, who had fallen asleep despite his dire circumstance. A crust of blood matted the hair at his crown and deep bruises showed on his exposed arms. Now on his knees before Barbatus's tent, he drew his pugio and then crawled forward. He set his hand into soft sand that had been piled on the campfire, and feeling the heat, he drew it back with a start even if it was only warm dirt. He lingered a moment to gather his nerves.

Crawling the final distance, he used his razor-sharp pugio to cut the old man free. Such was the captive's exhaustion that he did not even stir when the heavy ropes fell away.

Now, Varro got to his feet, still bending low, and swept both arms around the captive and roused him.

The old man's eyes were lost in deep shadows cast by moonlight that tinged his flesh the color of cold clay. For a moment, Varro wondered if the old man had died. But then his eyes flicked open and Varro helped him up.

The old man looked bewildered as his head turned side to side in search of understanding. It seemed more like a skull wrapped in tight skin, such was his fragility.

"Have no fear, I'm setting you free. Come with me to safety."

He didn't expect the old man to understand. But his eyes widened and his mouth fell open. Varro smiled and nodded, grabbing him firmly by the arm.

But when he made to lift the man, he backed up in terror. He slapped at Varro, his bony hands fluttering like leaves in the wind.

Varro lunged at him, determined to bring him under control and explain things later.

But before he could pin the old man, he tore off his gag and screamed.

With startling speed, Barbatus's tent flap snapped open to reveal a shape emerging from the darkness within.

"Shit!" Varro cursed as he flipped his pugio around and then slammed the pommel under the old man's jaw. His head snapped back with such force that he crumpled unconscious. Varro scooped him up as the first man out of Barbatus's tent emerged to bar his path.

16

Varro hefted the unconscious Iberian on his shoulder as he faced the first soldier out of the tent. It might have been Barbatus himself, but Varro would not recognize him dressed only in a tunic. Whoever stood before him had not taken his sword, and stared in confusion that Varro exploited.

He rammed into the man, driving him back onto his tent. With a shout of surprise, the soldier folded the tent down on those still inside. Varro did not wait but sprinted away to where Curio waited.

The man on his shoulder wobbled and slipped, but weighed little more than a bundle of dried sticks. As Varro wove between tents of men still asleep, he hoped he had not killed the Iberian.

Though no alarm had come from Barbatus's tent while they sorted out the confusion, Varro's rough action caught the eye of at least one guard who was unfortunately right where he hoped to exit.

"What are you doing? What's the pas—"

The man suddenly vanished, and his call became garbled. When Varro reached his position, he found Curio struggling on the ground with him. He tried to disable the guard without resorting to his pugio.

"Forget him," Varro said as he paused over the scramble. "I've got the prisoner. Let's go."

Curio released his hold on the man but kicked him in the head before joining Varro in their escape.

The guard groaned and rolled aside, but Varro lost sight of him as he and Curio slipped into the high grass. A bucina sounded behind them, alerting the sleeping camp too late. Varro was already across the first dip and now heading for his own camp.

They reached their guard line, where the two men raised shields and demanded the password even when they should have expected Varro and Curio.

"Outcasts." Varro huffed the password as he reached the guards, who then rushed forward to take his burden. He was relieved to slough him onto another's shoulders. He felt the strain from having to duck and run with the old man flopping on his back, even though he weighed so little.

Despite the late hour, both Falco and Centurion Pilatus emerged from the tent to greet them. Both seemed surprised at Varro's prisoner, who the guards on duty deposited on the grass between them. They then returned to their posts with Varro's permission.

"He was kept prisoner," Varro explained. "I assume he is leading Barbatus toward Lucian's tribe. Anyway, we alerted his whole camp. We are safe for now. But they'll have no trouble finding us by daylight. So we'll need to pull up camp and move."

Pilatus nodded with a deep frown and turned to wake the men. In the meantime, Curio went to find a rope to secure their prisoner.

"He looks dead," Falco said as he squatted beside Varro over the frail old man.

Varro put his finger on the man's neck, finding a steady pulse.

"I gave him an artful punch to the jaw."

"Glad I could teach you something." Falco stood up and cocked his head. "I hear the bucina in the distance. It'd be a welcome sound anywhere other than this mad world the three of us live in."

"I'm not sure if I met Barbatus or not. Anyway, I'm hopeful this old man can help us. It seemed he might understand Latin. We will give him freedom in exchange for his aid."

Falco laughed. "You must be tired. Don't you think Barbatus made him the same offer? He's traded one master for another with only a broken jaw thrown into the bargain."

"I didn't break his jaw." But Varro touched it, finding hot swelling where his pommel had connected. The man did indeed seem dead, but Varro guessed he seemed that way when awake as well. "But I take your meaning. Maybe we will need to use the opposite approach."

"You mean break his fingers until he talks?" Falco again chuckled. "You're a new man, Varro. You just have to accept it yet."

He sat back at Falco's words and sighed.

"I don't know what to do with him. It's all our lives if we don't reach Lucian and the silver first."

"And defeat his tribe and stroll back across Iberia all while hoping Flamininus really did arrive and worked out a deal with Cato. You left out a few steps in your plan."

"I didn't leave out steps. I just don't want to think about it. First, we have to find Lucian. That's what I pray this barbarian can help us do. After that, I will make a new plan based on what we find. Obviously, we're not going to charge in with sixteen men and do battle. They're here for security. The three of us will carry out the mission."

Curio returned with rope then bound and gagged the old man once more. Varro at least did his best to clean his head wound and he awakened in the middle of it. After a short struggle, he vomited through the gag, forcing Varro to change it. He attempted to speak to him, but he looked away. In the end, Varro left him under guard while the rest of the camp pulled down their tents.

They resettled in a clearing within the woods they had located when foraging earlier. It would be harder to find them in the trees and made for a more defensible position if Barbatus decided to attack them. The effort left them only a few hours sleep before dawn, but everyone was glad to have it.

Varro rose in the morning twilight, his sleep too fitful to have done him any good. So he slipped from the tent, wearing only his tunic, and found the old Iberian tied to a tree. His predicament had not improved, Varro mused. But he could think of no better way to treat him.

The old man was also awake now, his gaunt face filled with twilight shadows. Even so hidden, the glare of hatred was unmistakable. A bulging bruise protruded from his jaw where Varro had struck him. He squatted before his prisoner.

"I'll remove the gag if you don't scream. Do you understand me?"

The old man continued to glare, but then slowly nodded.

"Excellent. You speak Latin. No wonder Barbatus kept you alive."

He tugged off the gag, trailing a string of spit, and the Iberian gasped at the fresh air. He looked like a skull with its jaw hanging open.

"My name is Varro. Let's not play games. I want your help and you want to kill me. You can cooperate and I'll grant you freedom as soon as I'm able. Or you can resist, and I'll force you to cooperate. I hate that sort of thing, but I'm desperate."

Varro wasn't sure how much the Iberian understood. He had tried to speak clearly so his meaning wouldn't be missed. Yet after a long silence, the old man simply glared at him.

"I'll give you time to think on it. When my men awaken, we'll need your decision. Or we will decide for you."

He made to replace the gag, but the old man turned his head aside.

"You seek the mad Lusitani. Just like the other one."

"I do." Varro lowered the gag. "Were you leading him there?"

"Yes."

Varro waited for him to say more. The old man's mouth drew tight and quivered. In the predawn light, Varro saw his eyes gleam with tears. Clearly, he had been subjected to more torment than he could have ever expected, and Varro pitied him.

"Barbatus, the centurion whose men you were leading, killed everyone in your village. He probably killed those you loved. But he spared you because you spoke to him in Latin. Why? Did you beg for your life, or more likely the life of another?"

The old man's sorrowful face now reddened in anger. His yellow teeth flashed as he hissed at Varro.

"He has my grandson. He will kill him if I don't lead him to that evil tribe. Now that you took me, what will happen to him? You killed my grandson!"

The cord-like veins on the old man's neck stood out and his eyes bulged from their deep sockets.

"So kill me! I do not care. I will not help you no matter how you hurt me. I am already dead."

Varro leaned back, shocked but unsurprised. He had guessed something like this from the old man's reaction.

"You do not want death, old man. You want to live to see your grandson grow up. You called that tribe mad? Why?"

The old man's anger seemed to shift targets and his eyes searched elsewhere.

"Anyone who enters their land never returns. They are not our tribe, and their own tribe has disowned them. They pervert the worship of the gods. And their hill is not their land, but captured from my tribe. Our leaders have often sought to reclaim it, but no one willingly goes there unless they seek death. That is what you will find there, Roman. I will speak no more of that evil place. Even if you are an enemy of my enemy, I will never aid you. You have slain my only grandson."

Varro considered the old man and realized he would get no further with him. He refitted the gag to his mouth as tears streaked down the thin skin of his skull-like face.

"I'll see what we can do about your grandson." Varro stood with a grunt, then dusted off his hands. "You underestimate your resolve. You will help me. You are one life, but I am responsible for twenty others. I don't need to consider that trade overlong."

In the moments before dawn, he returned to the tent to find both Falco and Curio sitting up. Centurion Pilatus was already kicking his men awake, unable to shout or blow his whistle for fear of giving away their position.

Falco yawned. "How's the weather outside? We've been lucky so far."

"Weather's fine," Varro said as he sat down. "The old man's grandson is Barbatus's captive. He's using him to ensure cooperation."

Falco shrugged and looked at Curio. "Do you care about torturing one barbarian if it'll help us get this done sooner?"

"Well, I don't mind slapping him around, but I couldn't actually peel off his skin or something like that."

"What?" Falco mocked shock. "You wouldn't pluck out his eyes or slice off his toes if it'd save our lives?"

"You can do it, you bloodthirsty monster."

"No, it's Varro's job." Falco sniffed and raised his heavy brows at him. "He's both consul and interrogator for our little band."

Varro was ready to shut down the inappropriate levity with a curse and rebuke, but instead, someone ripped open the tent flap behind him and he jumped in surprise.

"Sorry, sir, but you've got to see this. The barbarians are attacking."

Varro grabbed his gladius as did Curio and Falco, but the man shadowed in the door explained himself.

"Not us, sir, but the others."

He still took his gladius, finding Centurion Pilatus rushing over. His lips were pressed shut, undoubtedly suppressing a stream of curses for his man breaking the chain of command. But Varro stopped him.

"Get everyone battle ready," he said. "The Iberians have finally caught up."

He followed the soldier who explained how he had heard the battle start.

"I was at the end of my watch shift and I heard war cries in the distance. I went to the edge of the trees and saw them gathered, sir."

They reached the tree line and hid behind rough pine trunks as they searched the dawn for the enemy.

It took no effort to find the battle. The Iberians had encircled Barbatus's camp and now banged their shields and shouted war cries. Behind the ditch and stakes, Barbatus had formed a testudo formation to protect themselves from slings and javelins as well as a rush from any side. They held their shields in tight ranks all around and overhead, looking like a multicolored tortoise shell.

"There are about a hundred of the barbarians, sir," the soldier reported. "When I left to find you, they were attacking the camp."

Varro narrowed his eyes at the swarm below.

"Looks like Barbatus repelled the first attack."

"Well, they're going nowhere in that formation." Falco punched his fist into his hand. "If they try to break out like that, the Iberians will pull them down and hack them to bits."

As if they had heard Falco, the Iberians began to pull at the stakes that had repelled them. They realized Barbatus's defensive formation did not allow them to attack at range.

"We've got to get back and assemble the men," Varro said.

Falco laughed. "I can't believe our luck. Curio, you must be Fortuna's new favorite son."

"They're going to be massacred," Curio said. "Barbatus made a mistake."

"He's paying for it now," Falco said cheerfully. "Too bad we won't be around to see him suffer for it."

Varro watched the Iberians cheer the first of the stakes worked out of the ground like it heralded supreme victory. They were simple folk, and living far from the borders likely had minimal experience fighting Romans. They might be led by a handful of veteran warriors, if that much.

"We're going to open an escape route for him."

Falco, Curio, and the solider all stared with open mouths. Falco slapped both hands to the sides of his head.

"Are you mad? You led them into a trap with the Iberians. Isn't this what you wanted? They're Cato's men and our enemies."

Curio groaned and shook his head. "They want to kill me."

But Varro raised his hand. "I just wanted to throw them off our trail and delay them. They had a chance to escape that battle. Today they'll be hacked to bits."

"They fucking deserve it!" Falco looked to Curio and the soldier, but both seemed less certain.

"They're legion. We'd call those soldiers our brothers if Cato hadn't played his foolish games. Barbatus is another matter, but only one man. Anyway, we are wasting time."

Varro started back toward the camp, but Falco shouted from behind.

"Hold on! This isn't our mission. This helps our mission. Don't throw a gift from the gods back into their faces. It won't help us."

"Then you can remain behind and guard the prisoner."

All that Falco said was true, but untenable to Varro's mind. How much lower could he sink into this morass of murder and torture before he lost his way forever? He had indeed led Barbatus and his soldiers into a trap, but one from which escape was not only possible but likely. Now they faced certain destruction for the poor decisions of their centurion. Even if it was wrong for the mission, it was the right thing to do for fellow soldiers.

He resolved to accept whatever came from his decision.

"There has to be a line we refuse to cross," he shouted back to Falco. 'Otherwise we become worse than our enemies."

"Can't you wait to draw a line?"

But he reached camp to find Pilatus had everyone ranked up. His nostrils flared at the soldier who had led Varro to the edge of the woods, and he raced to take his place in the second row.

"All ready, sir. We've still got our heavy pila. Show us an enemy to stick them into."

"About a hundred have surrounded Barbatus's men. I know we have our differences with them." Varro looked to Curio, who gave a tiny nod. "But we cannot allow the barbarians to butcher them, even if they brought his vengeance on themselves. They are fellow legionaries, and they need our help."

Pilatus only gave the slightest hint of a smile.

"We will save their sorry hides, sir, and show them who are the better soldiers."

"By adding our numbers, we even up the odds in bodies. But in terms of fighting strength, one of us must equal four of them. We will hit them on the northwest side closest to the marsh. This will open an escape route for Barbatus, and form a united defense that will break the barbarians' will to fight. Otherwise, we will fall back into the marsh. This camp is our rally point for anyone who separates. Now, let's rescue our brothers."

The speech aroused the men's elan. But they had to pause while both he and Falco got into their chain armor and grabbed their own shields. Curio took only his cloak and pugio, which would serve in a close fight. When they reemerged, Pilatus had kept their spirts hot with fiery words of his own about their first battles and the greatness that awaited them on the battlefield.

Varro led the formation out of the woods with Falco and Curio at his side. Falco continued to curse him for a fool and complain. "You would've stabbed these men in the balls last night, and today we're risking our lives to save them."

"We didn't hurt anyone last night," Varro said calmly. "I've only wanted to reach Lucian before they did, not see them hacked into crow-feed."

Now back on the plains of rolling grass, Varro analyzed how the fight had developed. The Iberians had focused overlong on removing the stakes surrounding the ditch. This spoke to their inexperience. Their only threat was in numbers and knowing the land better. This error had allowed Barbatus to move his testudo formation closer to the same flank Varro planned to attack.

A thin line of dead bodies trailed out of the formation. The lucky javelin or sling cast had brought these men down. Several other bodies lay scattered around the camp, victims of the initial attack. But Varro was not certain they were all Roman.

"If they do escape," Falco said, "looks like they'll be getting closer to even numbers with us."

Varro nodded, grateful he did not say anything about their own possible losses. He could not afford a single one, and, given their heavy armor and the support of Barbatus's men, he did not anticipate any.

They hewed close to the trees as they looped around the circle of Iberians. They all taunted Barbatus while their men dismantled the camp defenses. It seemed they had decided every stake had to be extracted before they attacked. Perhaps they did not want to be hindered if they had to escape. Since they believed they had limitless time for it, the barbarians were not wrong to do so. But it gave Varro his opportunity.

If any of the enemy noticed their approach, it made no difference. They continued to taunt the Romans clustered behind their shields and threw rocks they pulled up from the ground.

"Barbatus doesn't know what he's doing," Falco said. "He could've broke out and lined up along the marsh."

"He's in charge of the treasury," Varro said. "More accountant than combatant."

It was an unfair dig, as no one reached the centurion rank without a great deal of combat experience. Yet he certainly demonstrated a lack of tactical initiative with his defensive choice. He did not know Varro was coming, and eventually, the Iberians would overwhelm the formation and kill them all.

They now left the obfuscating trees and crossed into the open. Varro ordered a fast march to reach the position he deemed best for launching their attack.

But the Iberians now noticed the threat from the rear, and some began to turn around.

"Sound the charge," Varro said, drawing his gladius as his step increased. "Let them hear their doom approaching."

17

Centurion Pilatus roared the order to charge and the sixteen hastati under his command roared in answer. Varro, Falco, and Curio added their war cries and all banged their weapons to their heavy shields as they thundered across the knee-high grass at the rear enemy lines.

Now at the same level as Barbatus's men, Varro could not see their reaction to the unexpected relief. He prayed the centurion had the sense to press the attack or else the Iberians would fold up on Varro's short line.

With only sixteen men in the small force, they charged in open formation to engage as many of the surprised Iberians as they could. Many still had not located the source of the panic in the rear. But Centurion Pilatus turned their heads when he shouted his next command.

"Cast pila!"

The heavy pila soared over Varro's head and across the short distance to the Iberian rear ranks. He smiled at Pilatus's expert timing.

The heavy shafts landed among the Iberians, impaling them

through their backs and sending them hurtling forward to splash blood on the men in front. They cried out in shock and terror at the unexpected assault, and the entire rear line bulged inward.

"There's the breakpoint!" Varro shouted. "Hit it hard, men!"

He led them with his shield up and gladius poised beside it. Curio was alone in his lack of armament, but he instead wielded his heavy cloak as a shield. It could easily entangle enemy swords and blind a foe while he struck with his pugio.

Falco outstripped him, screaming for blood as his scutum shield rammed into the first barbarian he found. That fight vanished behind the bulk of Varro's own shield. He plowed it into his own foe, driving its boss into the enemy's back and punching with his gladius. It found yielding flesh and the man crumpled.

Now underfoot lay dead Iberians leaking blood into the grass. Sunlight disappeared between the combatants, leaving them to shove and strike in shadows. The ring of bronze blades and the thump of wooden shields filled his ears along with the shrieks of the wounded and dying. A sickening tang of blood and entrails rolled into Varro's nose as he shoved deeper into the line.

A man underfoot groaned and grabbed for Varro's leg. He stomped hobnailed caligae onto his face, crushing the nose and shattering bone. Then he stabbed down behind the safety of his shield to finish the foe as he drove forward.

All the while, Centurion Pilatus bellowed off to Varro's right.

"Break 'em, boys! Don't overextend the line!"

Indeed, Varro's charge had penetrated through the thin ranks, breaking a hole into the camp.

Curio had his cloak wrapped over a smaller Iberian's head and had doubled him over. He stitched his pugio into the barbarian's side until he collapsed face down in the grass.

"Barbatus!" Varro summoned his loudest voice and aimed it at the testudo formation, which still held in place. "The way is open. Hurry, you fools!"

The Iberians had parted in fear and shock, and the grass was slick with their gore and littered with their corpses. But their masses were like a giant's finger recoiled from touching hot iron. They had flinched away to leave a wide gap, but the more clear-headed of their number were already exhorting their fellows to close it up around them.

Varro searched for his scattered men. They had not gotten far out of formation thanks to Centurion Pilatus's careful command.

"Hold the way open," Varro shouted to him. Pilatus, his face splattered with blood diluted with sweat, had a mad gleam in his eye when he nodded acknowledgment.

"Eight here," he ordered. "Line up and hold the way. "You others, there!"

This left Varro and everyone else in the center facing Barbatus's slowly moving testudo formation and standing amid dozens of barbarian casualties.

"They're rallying," Falco said calmly.

On both sides, the formerly reeling Iberians now linked up in defensive ranks. Clearly, some among them knew enough to concentrate their force. Eight men might hold against them for a short time, especially heavy infantry. But Varro would become enveloped.

Falco's voice lost its false calm. "Either Barbatus accepts our gift or we hit the marsh, Varro."

"Barbatus, it's your only chance. Hurry!"

At last, the testudo unfolded, the shields peeling off the sides to reveal the wide-eyed men sheltering underneath. The Iberians no longer had any viable shots with their slings or javelins, for a miss risked striking their own men opposite. Yet some attempted and did bring down the rear ranks.

"Pull back!" Varro ordered Pilatus, who repeated his command.

His men folded in front of the renewed Iberian attack. Varro along with Falco and Curio joined the right flank while Pilatus remained on the other.

Adding their shields to the flank stemmed the barbarians trying to lap them. Varro punched one aside, the heavy bulk of the scutum driven by a strong arm was like striking a wall at a full run. The Iberian groaned as he flopped aside. A heavy blade hammered on Varro's shoulder, turned by the chain coat. Yet he heard links snap as the force of the blow melted into the padding beneath it.

Blood slathered his sword arm as he stepped backward, each step searching before setting down on a body or dropped weapon. Still one of his men tripped, and the Iberians dragged him into their dark masses like a hungry raven snatching a scrap of meat.

"Fill that gap!" Varro ordered as he pushed left. His voice struggled with the war cries and cacophony of battle. But the rank shifted and they continued to back up as Barbatus and his men filed past.

Both of Varro's lines backed up together and met as two doors in a gate. Centurion Pilatus continued to shout adjustments, even as he bled from a deep cut over his eye.

The Iberians obligingly followed them, sticking close to bring their weight to a point but foregoing a more advantageous overlap. Once he joined with Barbatus's formation, the Roman side would overwhelm the barbarians with better weapons and tactics.

Varro fought to escape contact with the enemy and drew Curio with him, whose cloak shield had no place in a front rank. Falco raised his shield before him, then shoved him back to take his place.

"They're farmers with their fathers' swords," he shouted over the din. "Easy killing."

Varro panted and wicked blood from his gladius as he took stock of the new situation. The Iberians at the far end of the camp flooded inside, but it did not seem they immediately joined the battle. He saw tents fluttering down.

"They're looting," Curio said.

"Good for us." Varro turned to find Barbatus and his men in disordered ranks. He shook his head, wondering at how these men had come so far without more losses. He found Barbatus by the crest of his helmet, still sporting all its black feathers unlike Varro's bald helmet.

"Form two ranks with the marsh at our backs, twenty by twenty. Do you have your pila?"

All the while, Pilatus slowly worked backward and the Iberians kept in contact. Varro turned to them while he hoped Barbatus acted sensibly. Extracting his own men would hurt. This was the moment he feared.

With a glance backward to see Barbatus shouting orders at his men, Varro then made to rejoin the ranks.

"Curio, fall back and make sure Barbatus is following the plan. Warn me if he's not. And don't let him catch you, either."

Then he shoved into place between Falco and Pilatus, who had been fighting and struggling without break. All the men gleamed with sweat and blood, and their mouths hung open.

The barbarians maintained close contact but left enough space for the fighting to ebb and flow. It was the natural order of things even among the untrained. Two lines could only shove, stab, and kick at each other before breaking off for a rest before a fresh attempt. Varro had pressed in place during such a moment. A long line of dark-faced but thin and wary Iberians held up round wooden shields and brandished an assortment of weapons, from daggers to canted swords and swords that looked like gladii.

"We're making a stand at the marsh," Varro said to both Falco and Pilatus.

Even if spoken in Latin, it seemed to encourage the Iberians, who leaped forward the moment he looked aside.

The two lines crashed once more, and the tremendous weight of nearly thirty men on their fronts bowed the ends of their lines. Were it not for the mighty knot formed by the combined strength of Falco and Pilatus, the line might have broken.

Yet it held as the men groaned and both sides stabbed and cursed. Varro's shield jostled in his grip as enemy hands tried to tear it down. But he hacked and sliced off the fingers that reached around for him.

Then came the fall back in the tidal currents of battle, and it was their moment to break off.

"Fall back to the next line," Varro shouted.

Pilatus blew his wooden whistle, and the men still standing understood. As one, with Varro and Falco, they raised their body-length shields and fitted themselves into the curve. They then plowed forward with a charge that bowled over the enemies at the front.

Now they had created a gap in contact, and the line rushed backward as the Iberians struggled to redress their own scrambled ranks.

To Varro's relief, Barbatus had formed his men in a wide line before the edges of the marsh. Snatches of its fetid odors slipped through the stench of vomit and bloody entrails. Varro was satisfied they had an anchor at their back and flanks that the Iberians couldn't easily defeat.

The erstwhile enemy, Barbatus, stood out from his men at the center of his line. For an instant, Varro swore he was looking at Centurion Longinus whom he had killed. Yet Barbatus was less stocky and had a more severe face. Though he scowled at the enemy, Varro recognized the wild stare of a man who realized he had narrowly avoided his own self-inflicted doom.

Pilatus guided his line to join on their right. He met Falco there as the Iberians now hesitated as they drew up their own lines.

Falco welcomed him into the ranks. "I think the big fellow with the tattoos all over his face is the leader. If he dies, they'll break."

The Iberian Falco pointed to was larger than his kin, but not the biggest foe Varro had encountered. "Is Curio safe?"

He did not see him, and Falco simply nodded. He feared that even in this chaos Barbatus might attempt to apprehend him. But Curio had sensibly removed himself from the fight and disappeared out of sight.

With a solid line of defenders in place the Iberians now hesitated. They had suffered the worst of the battle, and while they still remained the larger force, as Falco had observed, they were not drilled soldiers but men who called themselves warriors when the need arose. The advantage now fell to Varro.

"Concentrate on the big one," he said, pointing out the warrior who now had gathered his hesitant companions into garbled lines.

"I'll handle him, sir," Pilatus said with a grin. "But he better have the balls to attack. I'm drawing flies waiting for him."

The Iberians made a show of taunting and cursing, but they approached with caution. The Roman line remained stoically silent as if every man were a rock sunk deep into the earth. Everyone knew they could not flee the lighter-armored barbarians. So they planted themselves and dared their attackers to charge.

The big Iberian at last raised his sword overhead and bellowed his war cry. His fellows joined in, though with a fraction of a delay that belied their hesitation. Pilatus growled at his men to remain steady. Varro admitted a chill from the throaty roars of the wild men arrayed before him. But, when they ran at him, his years of training took over. He raised his shield and set his knee into the curve.

The Iberian line crashed into a wall of wood and bronze, fiercely hacking and stabbing in time with their war cries. The big one led the charge, hitting the center where Barbatus stood. Pilatus cursed but was shoved back into the roaring madness.

Varro had to pull behind his shield, standing shoulder to shoulder with Falco to prevent skidding away. They both moaned against the impact, but then shoved back as one and stabbed out. The Iberians were wary of this tactic by now and leaped aside. Varro felt the relief from the front and seized the vacated space. Battles were often more about grabbing one step of ground rather than just slaying the enemy. The most decisive ones, however, included both.

This became such a battle. Varro punched with his shield, avoided the worst of the incoming blows, and stabbed into the gaps left in the enemy's defense. He found himself walking the line forward and crossing the tide mark of corpses underfoot. This caused a natural stutter in their progress, and the Iberians used the moment to break contact.

Even Varro had to restrain the urge to give chase, especially with their naked backs facing him. But instead, he shouted for the line to hold, and this repeated down the line through Pilatus and even Barbatus at the far end.

For a moment, Varro forgot about his issues with the other Romans. As one, they raised their swords and shouted triumph. The Iberians scattered back over the camp, carrying away whatever spoils they had claimed and abandoning their dead. The route was not so disastrous that they left their injured. Varro observed someone had pulled the wounded into a group, and a number of Iberians now helped them escape.

The tall leader of the Iberians actually led the retreat, and Varro smirked at the juxtaposition of a fearsome look and bravery. The two were not often found together in the same man, as was the case today.

He ordered his still intact line to advance, and when Barbatus saw this he did the same. It offered further encouragement for the

Iberians to continue to flee into the plains and behind the folds of the land.

Once the threat of a rally passed, only then did Varro relieve the formation. Another less voluble victory cry went up from both sides. Now came the accounting of loss and recovery of equipment. Without any communication between them, Barbatus's and Varro's sides separated and sought their fallen companions.

"We lost three men," Pilatus said. "The others are banged up, but will be fine."

A cut continued to seep blood over Pilatus's eye and Varro nodded to it.

"I'd send you to the hospital for that, but it's quite a walk from here. Will you be all right?

"It's nothing, sir. Just needs a bandage to keep the blood out of my eye."

Varro dismissed him to see to his men, but he paused and stared across at Barbatus.

"Whatever happens next, sir, you did the right thing. I couldn't have lived with myself running away from a fight like this."

Varro nodded his thanks. "Whether it was wise remains to be seen."

The search and recovery was a strained moment between the two sides. Varro sensed many from Barbatus's force wished to thank them, but just as many seemed reluctant. Yet they avoided each other as they recovered their casualties, of which Barbatus had suffered the most. They still outnumbered Varro, and therefore no one on his side turned their backs on them for long.

The men collected Varro's own dead away from the marsh and lined up the three bodies on the ground. One seemed to have been butchered out of frustration, likely the one who had tripped and vanished into the Iberian mob. The other two had died from clear wounds on their sides and necks.

Varro stood with Pilatus and the others to bow his head. As

their leader, he was obligated to commend their bravery and add some words for each. But a sharp call from Barbatus drew everyone aside.

He had formed his ranks, six wide and four deep. Varro's blood chilled when seeing that many shields and bronze helmets arrayed against him.

"Centurion Pilatus, form ranks to match while Falco and I go to speak with him."

Barbatus crossed the short space between them, grass churned up from battle and earth wetted with the blood of its victims. Varro glimpsed a severed hand, gray and still clutching the dagger the owner had wielded.

"We outnumber you," Barbatus said. He stood now with arms folded and head cocked. Up close, he became more of his own person rather than a look-alike for Longinus. He lacked the distinctive scar or the open demeanor. His expression was closed and cold, a man driven by his own desires and uncaring of others.

"You're welcome for coming to your rescue." Varro bluffed his confidence. He strained to look only at Barbatus and let the rows of bronze helmets backing him remain as unfocused blurs.

"We did not need rescuing."

"Strange then that you were surrounded on all sides and stuck in place. Your defensive formation was all wrong. You were about to be pulled down. That formation is only for approaching the enemy."

"Well, thank you, Scipio Africanus. I'll remember that next time." Barbatus gave a humorless smile. "Now, as gratitude for your assistance, I'll leave you all alone if you'll turn over Curio. I can forget we ever met, Centurion Falco."

Beside him, Falco cleared his throat.

"I'm Varro. And I'm afraid Curio has gone missing in the battle. He was probably captured. You better start chasing the barbarians or they'll take him away."

But Barbatus shook his head.

"You're quite the trickster. The way you fooled these men out of the garrison was impressive. The commander would like to speak to you about it, I'm sure. So, you can hand over Curio or we can capture him. Either way, we'll bring him, Lucian, and the stolen silver back to Consul Cato. That'll make for a fat reward for all we've suffered."

"Do you think to survive all of it? We've captured your guide and the Iberians have certainly liberated his grandson when they ransacked your camp. You'll be lost without him. And you don't have enough men to deal with Lucian's tribe even if you locate him."

"I have my ways," he said with a thin smile. Varro knew it for a bluff by the way Barbatus's eyes faltered with the statement.

"My ways are better. You should return to Cato with the truth of the matter—that you couldn't find Curio and sustained too many losses to continue. Let us handle Lucian, and Cato won't care what you did."

But Barbatus was already shaking his head.

"You don't understand. This is personal. Curio poisoned my men and killed some. Others would've been better off dead. We didn't come this far to let him hide behind a tree while we walk off."

"A fight will only weaken us both and let Lucian escape the justice he deserves. He's the one deserving of your hate. Curio was simply deceived."

"A fine tale to cover for your friend. But all your words are lies, Centurion Varro. I'd no more believe them than a story about talking cats. Now, I'll ask a final time. Surrender Curio to me."

He looked to Varro with mock concern.

"If only I knew where he went."

Barbatus gave the same humorless smile and looked past Varro and Falco to the men lined up behind.

"All of you were deceived into becoming deserters. Why stand with the men who ruined your future? You know where Curio is. If you give him up and join me, I guarantee Consul Cato will pardon your gullibility. Don't make a bad choice worse."

Pilatus shouted across the short distance. "A guarantee, you say?"

Barbatus gave a firm nod. "You'll share the credit with me, along with the rewards. Remember, Cato is consul now and not Senator Flamininus. He is the highest authority in the republic. I'm offering you the chance to correct your mistakes. Whatever Varro offers is as good as the lies he told you to start."

Varro had miscalculated in keeping his force so close. He originally thought to have them prepared for a surprise attack. Having never fought fellow countrymen before, he had overlooked the possibility of having his men charmed away from him.

But if he turned to look at Pilatus and the others now, it might seem he doubted their loyalty. Indeed, Pilatus had little reason for loyalty after what Varro had done to him. But he was a proud man, and Varro guessed he would be reluctant to admit his mistake before everyone. So he tightened his lips and let Pilatus answer for himself.

"It's quite an offer," he replied. "Will you throw in extra for having saved your skin from a mistake even a green recruit wouldn't make? If we go over, then I'm in charge of everything. I want to survive to see all these rewards you offer."

Whether Pilatus's demand was serious or not, it landed like a perfectly aimed javelin into Barbatus's pride.

"You've made a mistake, Pilatus!"

Then he leaped back and reached for his gladius as the men behind him pulled up their shields and started forward.

18

Reaching for his gladius, Varro backed away with Falco at his side. Barbatus's men jogged the short distance to their centurion. From behind, Pilatus bellowed.

"Raise shields! Hold your ground!"

Even though he expected it, Varro still hid behind his shield and scrambled back to his lines with Falco doing the same. Barbatus had not struck as he should have but instead sought the protection of his larger force. Falco's support had likely caused him concern.

Now that leaders on both sides were back in their formations, the true test would come.

"Hold steady," Varro said to Pilatus. "Half of them don't want this fight."

Instead, Falco growled in answer. "And half do. Where the fuck is Curio, anyway?"

"Wisely gone from here." Varro watched Barbatus walk his men to the tilting point and stop. He would have to charge or else back up in a humiliating retreat.

Pilatus called for their thirteen battle-weary men to hold the line. If Barbatus determined to make a full attack with nearly double Varro's force, they would be easily flanked and crushed. Yet to run would invite certain disaster.

"It's your last chance," Barbatus shouted. "No one has to die."

Varro closed his eyes, fearing Pilatus's choice. All of the men under his command should desert him. It was the most sensible choice. The centurion, standing beside Falco, called back in a voice roughened from the prior battle.

"Do you have a map back to the garrison? Show it to me."

"What?" Barbatus's voice was full of surprise. "We've got guides."

"Guides can die. But I can always read a map. You better back up and rethink your plan."

Once more, Pilatus hurled words as sharp as his blade and cut Barbatus's pride. His face turned red and his lips tightened to where they vanished.

"Charge!"

He held up his sword and blood-stained scutum. Twenty-four principes, the primary fighting force of the Roman legion, now charged behind him.

"Cavalry!"

Varro heard Curio's warning shouted from the rise behind them. In the fleeting instant before Barbatus struck, he saw Curio's shadow leaping madly and pointing to the southeast.

Then he staggered as a shield collided with his own, Barbatus's line arriving faster than he expected. He pushed back into the man behind him, who in turn supported him with his own shield.

A gladius licked between the gap of his and Falco's shields, and its carefully honed tip caught him under his arm, slicing a long cut that burned like fire. He shoved back with his own shield, standing now shoulder to shoulder with Falco. In the press, which was more of a shoving match than a true battle, he shouted over his shoulder at Pilatus.

"Iberian cavalry to the rear! Fall back to the marsh!"

Pilatus shouted the order to break contact. It was a strange thing for the enemy to easily comprehend his commands. So as Varro pushed, Barbatus ordered his men to stand firm.

"No escape! Capture as many as you can!"

But Varro could not protest his misinterpretation. Instead, he shouted at the rear ranks to flee. Immediately, he felt the pressure vanish from his back.

"Break!" Centurion Pilatus shouted again as he pressed forward. He shouted over his shield. "You fools, too! Iberian cavalry!"

If Barbatus countermanded Pilatus, it was lost in the groan and thud of men shoving at each other. Varro knew his side fought with only half their will and the rest simply added their weight. His own force had done much the same. Without proper unit structure and an optio at the rear to goad them, the men were free to make only a token effort to obey.

"Fuck this!" Falco roared. In concert with Pilatus and Varro, he led the push to break away.

The line buckled and Barbatus, who had cannily avoided meeting Varro or Falco in battle, collapsed back with his men.

Varro sprang away from the melee, only to turn and find death riding for him.

Nearly fifty bare-chested Iberians swooped across the grasslands on small horses. It reminded him of Numidia and the fine horse, Thunderbolt, he left there. It was a mere flash before the terror of the charge sent him scrambling toward the marsh.

On foot, the small Iberian horses seemed like mighty beasts. The cavalry swooped in with javelins poised. Their long hair flowed freely as they whooped and shouted. Their thin bodies were covered in blue designs blurred from their speed.

Varro grabbed Falco and both raised their shields together as the javelins sailed across the grass. One struck his shield at an oblique angle, shattering into thin white shards that rained over Varro's head. Others landed in the grass around him.

But far more landed among men on both sides. The cries of anguish and fear filled Varro's ears. He and Falco now ran toward the marsh, which suddenly felt miles away.

They fled wordlessly as the thudding hooves drew closer. All around, men scattered toward the marsh where horses would not follow easily.

The Iberians understood this as well, and their superior numbers allowed them to gallop around the fleeing soldiers and cut off their retreat.

"They're going for Barbatus's men," Falco said between gulps of air.

Varro could only nod as he fled. They were the largest target and made the most sense to attack while advantaged. They did not realize the Romans were divided. If only they were not, Varro knew they might survive the attack.

Centurion Pilatus was among the first to arrive at the marsh edge. How he had taken such a lead was beyond Varro. But he heard the hard beat of hooves at his left, and instinctively turned with shield up.

The Iberian had made an error in choosing Varro and Falco for his target. His long sword clanged against the bronze rim of Varro's scutum, sending a sharp shock wave through his arm. Falco, for all his size and the weight of his armor, skipped aside from the charging horse and stabbed its flank as it passed. The horse gave a horrible scream of pain, and Falco stumbled forward as it broke away from him.

But the rider couldn't bring his wounded mount under control, and so it sprang away into the wider fight.

"Ha!" Falco shouted. "I could do that all day!"

They both turned back for the marsh and Falco's wish seemed possible.

The Iberians had swooped around Barbatus to net the majority of his men. But more of the cavalry had continued past to sweep up stragglers such as Falco and Varro. Their short-lived battle had cost them the scant advantage they had in surviving the initial attack.

Now three horsemen galloped around them in a wide circle, like birds of prey over dying men.

"Have a care for your wishes," Varro said.

"Fuck. The gods never listen. Why now?"

The shuddering thunder of the circling horsemen vibrated through Varro's teeth. They toyed with them but respected their threat. Both stood back to back, hidden behind shields that limited attack angles. The barbarians' smiles were wicked and their shrill calls grated on Varro's ears. Even as they circled at such speeds, Varro still felt they seemed ill. In glimpses of their faces, their eyes appeared red-rimmed and shining as if they had fevers.

But they were young and strong, and the circle they created drew tighter with each pass.

"Ready?" Falco asked. "I hate to do this, but it's our best way out."

Varro nodded. "Now!"

Together they flung their shields into the legs of the galloping horses. The heavy scuti were rimmed and bossed with bronze and constructed in multilayered wood panels. They were new and heavy, and spun like thrown plates into the legs of the galloping horses.

The Iberians had not expected this, and the horses slammed into the shield edges, their leg bones cracking against the wood and bronze. All three animals crashed into each other in a horrific jumble of flailing hooves, tumbling men, and scattered gear. Both beast and rider let out terrified wails as their bones broke and dislocated in the crash.

Varro and Falco leaped away from the tragic pile of bodies and continued to flee for the marsh. Now unburdened, they raced faster and were soon splashing into the wetlands.

Across the small islands of grass, men in bronze helmets fled as reckless horsemen pursued. The majority of sensible Iberians remained on dry land. Their victory cries sickened Varro as he splashed alongside Falco.

"We could've fought back," he said. "We'd take their javelins on our shields, and our counterattack would've crushed them."

Falco raised his legs in exaggerated steps trying to keep dry as he fled.

"Lucky day for the barbarians, too. It's not just me getting all I asked for."

The marsh was wide and flat, reflecting the morning sunlight that spilled over Varro's shoulders. Men spread out everywhere, but he was uncertain which were his and which were his supposed enemies. All of that competition seemed pointless now. When he realized no one pursued him, he stopped with Falco on a muddy mound of knee-high grass.

It seemed that Barbatus thrived on defensive actions, for he had once more ranked up to face the cavalry that pranced around him.

"They didn't bring enough javelins for the job," Falco said through his panting. "Stupid barbarians couldn't catch a one-legged cow."

"Barbatus can't hold out against so many. Where did they come from?"

Falco now rested his hands on his knees and shrugged.

"The word is out, I suppose. There are Romans about for easy hunting. We can thank Barbatus for announcing us in grand style."

Varro grunted in agreement. "It was a mistake to sack that village. He should've avoided it or just sent men during the night to kidnap a guide."

"Barbatus doesn't have the imagination for that. Look at how he left a trail to follow. He must have tremendous faith in his men."

Once both caught their breaths, they traveled deeper into the marsh to gather up whoever they could find. Varro did not care which side they came from at this point. Behind him the echoes of battle and screaming horses faded. Barbatus and his men were meeting their end along with any chance of his escaped men surviving on their own.

The first man they found was Curio, his familiar outline waving frantically as he plodded through water and mud. They waited for him to catch up.

"You promised we'd never separate again."

As he came into speaking distance, Varro saw the genuine fear in his reddened face. Like all of them, his legs were splashed with mud from running through the marsh. But in his case, with a ragged tunic and cut up cloak, it made him appear even more pathetic.

"Am I to sleep with you too?" Falco walked forward to greet him and extended his hand as if to pull him onto dry land.

"Your warning saved us," Varro said once Curio stood with them on their mound of muddy earth. "But we had to flee into the marsh to foil the cavalry."

"You see now? The gods of this land are driving us deeper into danger. Look at this place! I'll drown here."

"If you did it's because I tipped you on your head," Falco said as he clapped Curio's back. "Not because of barbarian gods."

"There's no profit in worrying about the barbarian gods when their people are still close. Cavalry can dismount and pursue, if they are determined to see all of us dead. So let's gather whoever we can find and return to our rally point."

"Assuming we can find it again." Falco scanned the horizon,

shielding his eyes with a bloodied hand. "I've lost my bearings out here."

"I know about where we are," Varro said. "Creating the map of our route has sharpened my directional senses. But others may be as lost as you. That's why we need to act with the morning light and gather all survivors that we can."

"Those were Lucian's riders," Curio said in a hushed voice. "I can tell from their looks. They wear no armor and cover themselves in blue designs. They look sick and thin."

"Then we are close," Varro brightened his voice. "And Lucian and the sliver are within reach. With both in hand, we will follow my map back and meet Senator Flamininus for our reward—our names restored and our freedoms returned."

He emphasized the positive result, not only to encourage Curio's flagging confidence but also his own. When they found Lucian and his tribe at last, he had no clear idea of how to achieve their goals. But by now he had confidence in his own abilities to respond to uncertain situations. He would figure out the attack once he understood the landscape he faced.

They plodded through the marsh, at first gathering more black flies than fellow soldiers. But in ones or twos, he found his men. Pilatus had already gathered more to his side. Once they rejoined Varro, he counted ten men.

"Not sure about the others, sir," Pilatus said. "Maybe they didn't escape, or they tripped and drowned. Maybe they headed for the rally point. I was about to do so myself when I spotted you."

All around the wide marsh, Varro saw only a lone figure waving at them.

"One more," he said. "But after him, we should head for the rally point and recover our supplies."

"What's his problem?" Falco asked, pointing to the lone figure. "He can see us. So just join us."

"Maybe he's injured," Varro searched around, seeing only the bright sun glare bouncing off marsh water to flood the world with a golden haze. "We best not split up. Let's recover him then head back."

The small group crossed deeper into the marsh toward the shadowed man waving for help. But as they drew closer, Varro did not recognize him.

"One of Barbatus's men," Falco muttered. "Should be interesting."

"He's alone," Varro said. "We've nothing to fear from him."

"Thank Jupiter you found me!" The man continued to wave even as they arrived. "I was running and running. Thought I'd lost myself forever."

Varro drew his gladius and pointed it at him. "Keep those hands up while you're waving."

The man's wide smile vanished and his waving stopped.

"I didn't want to fight you," he stammered. "But it was orders and everyone fell in. I owe you my life. We were going to die back there."

Keeping his gladius pointed at the man, Varro stepped closer. "Seems like your centurion managed to get everyone killed anyway. He did not flee to the marsh as he should have, but stood his ground."

The man cast a fearful eye toward the direction of the sun. "They're all dead? You didn't find anyone else?"

"Only you," Varro said, keeping his sword leveled. "And everyone else scattered into the marsh or else was surrounded by cavalry. You're under my command now. I'm Centurion Varro. This is Centurion Curio. You'll treat him with respect."

The man looked anxiously across everyone assembled before him, settling on Curio.

"You're Curio? I thought you were a slave."

"Whatever grudge you hold," Varro said. "Set it aside. We must work together to escape alive. The objective is Lucian and his stolen silver. Curio has taken undeserved blame for his crimes."

The man kept his hands up, smiling ingratiatingly. "Of course I'll follow orders, sir. Centurion Curio, sir, I've nothing against you. I wasn't even part of the treasury guards. They pulled a bunch of us from different centuries for special duties, including me."

Varro lowered his sword at last, then handed him over to Pilatus to introduce him to the rest. Though he was a princeps, he had lost so much of his gear that he was indistinguishable from the younger hastati he now joined.

"Was that wise?" Falco asked.

"Will you stop questioning me? We did not rush to save these soldiers only to let them die in a marsh. He'll be fine. If he tries to cut Curio's throat in the night, he'll be sorry. Curio's sleeping with one eye open these days, waiting for the barbarian gods to yank him out of his bedroll."

Falco laughed, but Curio scowled. "I'll be better when I quit Iberia forever. Nothing but mountains and dark forests, and now lonely marshes where spirits will pull you into the water."

Varro and Falco blinked then looked to the dark water surrounding them. They marched out without another word.

Pleased to discover he had not miscalculated the path back to their campsite, Varro's step lightened. They had cut across the marsh as the quickest route back to the trees that concealed their camp. Now they climbed up the gentle slope, and Varro spotted the yellowed sides of their tents through the trees.

But they arrived at a ransacked camp.

The tents were emptied of all their gear. Their supplies were stolen or else strewn about the site. The tents themselves were either left alone or cut up with no clear pattern to the destruction. All around were hoofprints, identifying the culprits as Lucian's cavalry.

Across the camp, Varro saw the cut ropes and gag he had

placed on the old Iberian. He and the others gathered around that spot.

Falco kicked over the rope as if the old man might be hiding underneath.

"Well, I guess you don't have to worry about dirtying your hands with torture now."

A shiver flashed through Varro's body and it left behind a chill that did not leave him. He stared down with his teeth clenched.

"Gather whatever is left. This campsite has been compromised. We need to find another before dusk."

19

They recovered as much of their camp supplies as possible. Varro pitched in, searching bushes and dark places for whatever scraps Lucian's cavalry had left them. Hoofprints and human tracks were churned into the earth. The Iberians had been thorough in their work. As Varro piled their meager scraps in the camp center, he imagined the cavalry had arrived here first and might explain their delay in joining the battle. But then again, their appearance today might just be a lucky accident for the Iberian side.

By the end of the afternoon, they gave up on salvaging more than some bedrolls and packs. Their sword-sharpening tools were universally missing, which brought out Pilatus's disgust.

"Sharpen your blades with your hard heads," he yelled at his men as if they had been at fault. "A dull blade will cut your hand but never pierce an enemy's heart."

Varro pulled him aside to ask for the final tally of their recovered supplies, which was negligible.

"Whatever else you say about those barbarians, sir, they're thorough."

"I agree." Varro intended to say more, but something caught in his throat and he began to cough. It continued until Pilatus shouted for someone to bring water. Varro held up his hand.

"I think I swallowed a bug." His voice was hoarse and strained but returned to normal though the irritation remained. "I wanted to thank you for standing with me. You shouldn't have. I tricked you all into joining this adventure."

"My men don't know it, sir. They believe in the mission."

"But you know what I did."

Pilatus tilted his head. "I don't like it, sir. Not at all. But you in fact hold the map out of this pisshole. After today, I'd be fine just to return home no matter what awaits me there. I can't trust Barbatus to do that. He showed me his foolishness. You showed me something else. Not saying I'd follow either one of you on a good day, though."

"I won't question your decision," Varro said with a smile. "But I am grateful for it. The way out of Iberia will pass through darker lands before we're done. I'm glad I can count on you."

"Don't lose the map, sir. Now, I need to wring the doubt from our boys and get them marching into those dark lands."

Varro coughed again, unable to ease the pinch in his throat, and so waved him off.

After gathering what they could, Varro realized his ink bottle had been spilled. The bronze stylus was stamped into the dirt but still functional. After Falco suggested he write in his own blood, Varro devised a more practical solution.

"There's bark all around here. I'll gather some to overlay on this map. I can use my pugio to carve marks and refine them with my stylus."

He coughed again and this time accepted a skin of water recently gathered at the nearby stream. It burned going down and Varro realized he hadn't swallowed a bug but was becoming ill.

While Falco and Curio filled their packs with what meager

supplies remained, Varro turned his back as if to conceal his condition. He told himself it was just an irritating pinch in his throat that would fade after a good night's rest.

But by the time they had marched out of the camp to relocate to another, he knew a good night's rest would not help. All water he drank burned like fire and he struggled to swallow anything solid. His eyes watered and he ached all over.

"You're sick," Falco said as they watched men whittling new stakes for their camp. Their old stakes had been shattered or stolen. All the while, Pilatus hung over them and exhorted them to work faster.

"That's true," he said. "But I'll be fine after a bit of rest. Others are coughing as well. It must've been that damn marsh."

"If only we had some cabbage soup," Falco said. "It'd fix up all of you."

They stood in the long shadows of trees as dusk sapped the last light of the day. Curio sat against a trunk, whittling his own stake. He did not look up from his work and hummed his disagreement.

"It's the gods of this land. They found a way to us through that marsh."

Falco hissed through his teeth. "When did you become an old crone who lives in a cave and issues prophesies? Will Centurion Curio report for duty?"

"Don't argue about it," Varro raised his palms for peace. "No matter the cause, we have no choice but to endure it. We're close enough to Lucian for him to learn of our presence and send warriors to harass us. I won't allow sore throats and snot to hinder our progress now. Besides, we've lost most of our supplies. We need to capture what we can from Lucian to make the return trip, especially if men are too weak to forage."

Falco stared at the ground, and his expression betrayed his

thoughts. Varro always knew from his heavy, mobile eyebrows what his oldest friend was thinking.

"I told you before, I'll determine how best to get at Lucian once we study his defenses. Curio, he didn't reveal anything about where he lived?"

He shook his head. "Only that Bandua selected that place for a great city. But they're all mad. Who knows if the land would even be good enough for an outpost fort?"

"They're impoverished. That much is clear from Lucian's elaborate theft. So we won't be facing walls like Sparta's."

Falco shivered and held his sides. "Don't even joke about that. Right now, I'm not sure if I hate Iberians or Spartans more."

Curio completed his stake and set it aside. He seemed to consider something as his head tilted.

"Lucian drank a magical brew to see his gods. I got a splash of it on my lips when I knocked away his wife's skull. Just a drop of it made me dizzy. I wonder what that does to a man to drink it as often as he does. All his warriors must drink that brew, too. They were dancing like they were in a dream. They're all probably too lost in their visions to have any defenses."

Varro's fever and aches vanished under the rush of inspiration. He clapped his hands together.

"That's it! If we attack when Lucian and his warriors are in that state, it should be easy to overcome them."

Falco nodded while continuing to stare at his feet.

"Just as easy as asking if they wouldn't mind getting rotten drunk so we can pull off our surprise attack. A nice plan, Varro, but it needs something very specific to happen. Not to mention, how could we know if they were all falling on their faces?"

"You don't understand," Varro said, now sloughing off the fatigue of his illness. "Curio will show us how it's done."

He had started to stand from sitting against the tree but paused halfway.

"What do you mean by that? I don't know how to make what they're drinking."

"But you know its taste and smell. If they use it so often, then it should be to hand somewhere in their village. If we secure that brew, then we can slip it into their wine. We don't need them to be unconscious, just impaired enough to let us reach Lucian and the silver."

Falco at last sighed. "Then you better start praying for the gods to grant us invisibility. It's not like we blend in so well that we can pass unseen."

"Let's wait to see the actual conditions before we make plans or beg the gods for magic."

Curio straightened up after retrieving his sharpened stake. He pointed it at Falco like a giant wagging finger.

"That's right. I think the gods would love to see Lucian's trickery turned on him. Besides, we specialize in infiltrations like this."

"Ah, there you are!" Falco clapped his hands together. "The old crone went back to her cave."

Seeming to think on this, he gave a curt nod. "We send them to their gods in more ways than one. I do think our gods would see it done. It's a fitting end."

Varro was about to commend Curio's change of mood, but he began coughing and could not stop. A sip of water from his canteen eased the spasm but the burning throat remained.

"I know at least one of us can't go sneaking around," Falco said dryly. "I imagine Lucian would have to be stone cold before he'd miss a coughing fit like that."

Clearing his throat, Varro gave a sheepish look to both of them. "I might need to sit out this action. We'll see."

The night was not as restful as any of them hoped. Varro's fever and violent coughing kept him awake so that he heard every watch change. Curio sat up several times to check on him, but Falco snored throughout the night. He alone awakened the next morning with an expansive yawn and stretch.

"I know we're still in the shit," he said. "But I think the climate in these parts agrees with me. How are you feeling, Varro?"

"Like two millstones have been stacked on my face." He would've complained more, but his coughing ended their talk.

Curio helped Varro wear his gambeson and mail shirt. But Varro struggled into both, where even raising his arms hurt. Water streaked from his eyes and his voice had become hoarse. The weight of his mail, usually reassuring, now doubled him over. Curio stepped back to examine him.

"Can you march? You look like death."

"I will be fine." The words croaked out as barely audible. "Let's get with Pilatus and plan the day's march."

Outside the tent, he found Falco and Pilatus both in their mail shirts leaning together like two conspirators. Only half of the men were in line, including Barbatus's former soldier.

Varro's stomach churned as he and Curio joined the huddle. Pilatus stared at him with a flat expression.

"You, too, sir. No fucking good, not at all."

Falco rolled his shoulders as if still waking from his wonderful dreams of the prior night. "He's right, Varro. You're looking like day-old shit. Half the men are coughing and feverish. They have to be near death for hardnose Pilatus to let them stay in their tents."

"There's no point in bothering them, sir. Half of us are down with a fever. The other half isn't. Not sure what we should do here."

Varro covered his face as he coughed. "None of them can march?"

"Not if you want them to march again tomorrow, sir. You won't make it, either. Better to keep the healthy men away and focus on rebuilding our supplies. Not to mention, if the Iberians come for us again we're absolutely fucked. We're in no shape to go after Lucian now."

If he could stop coughing, Varro would've streamed curses until he ran out of breath. When he did recover he had to surrender to Pilatus's cold assessment.

"We are so close," he said through his constricted throat. "To be defeated like this. I can't accept it."

"Hold on." Falco put his hand on Varro's shoulder. "No one said we're defeated. We just need to wait out the fever. What did your mother do for fevers?"

Varro hadn't thought of his mother in years, but now that his body ached and eyes and nose ran with mucus he wished for her care.

"I can't remember. She gave me strong, bitter wine, I think. Someone among us ought to know what to do."

"We don't have medical orderlies in the ranks, sir." Pilatus looked at the few men standing at attention. "Only a few healthy soldiers."

Varro felt all eyes in the camp drifting to him for direction. He might look sick, but he had to pretend for the men's sake. If they thought their leader was going down, they might panic and do something foolish. With Lucian near, he had to keep his men hopeful.

"Then we will have to count on each man to make his own recovery. While they do, we'll continue to scout the area for good forage, security, and possibly any sign of Lucian's settlement, be it village or fortress."

Falco and Pilatus both inhaled to speak, but Varro guessed their protest and cut them off.

"I look far worse than I feel. I will be fine. Everyone who is able must contribute to the effort while the others recover. I'm no exception."

Pilatus gave no hint of his thoughts, but Falco rolled his eyes at

Curio, who simply shrugged. But Varro began to divide the work among them without any more protest. When he came to search for Lucian, someone in the lineup of soldiers cleared his throat to call attention.

It was Barbatus's former solider, and he looked for permission to speak, which Varro granted.

"Sir, we had an old man and his grandson captured. The old man was an escaped slave. So he spoke Latin. He told us where Lucian was located, and we were going to have him lead us directly there until you captured him. I don't know the specific location, but it is on the other side of the marsh and down the river. I remember the general directions for getting there. Centurion Barbatus made sure we all knew where we were going and how to get back."

Relief eased the burden of Varro's illness and he smiled, croaking out his thankfulness. But Falco voiced the words Varro's coughing prevented.

"Praise Jupiter, first and greatest! How close are we?"

"The marsh is not large, sir, or so our prisoner claimed. We were told a half-day crossing the marsh or a full day around it. He also said these Lusitani are not a big tribe, but followed some sort of priest into dark paths. I don't know what that means. But Lucian joined them long ago. He's famous as the Roman devil. Everyone around here knows his legend and keeps away from that tribe. Somehow, Lucian became their leader when their priest died or got sick."

Initially excited, Varro's eyes narrowed at this soldier's story.

"You know a great deal about Lucian and his tribe. How is this?"

The soldier tilted his head back. He had pale, definite eyes with a beak of a nose set between them.

"I led the interrogation, sir. I was there with Centurion Barbatus to hear everything."

"You're not withholding anything from us?" Falco asked. "You know Barbatus and your friends are all dead."

"I wouldn't keep anything back," the soldier said. "I want to get back to my century. The old man said the Lusitani live in an open village atop a hill. No one goes there. He claims the land is cursed and the tribe breeds with itself. We told the captive Lucian planned to use Roman silver to buy help for his cause. He laughed and said only the truly desperate or greedy would answer his call."

"What's your name?" Varro asked.

"Trenico, sir. First Legion, Third Principes."

"Well, Trenico, you might have saved us all. You'll come with us to scout."

They then divided up their duties, and Varro let himself be persuaded to remain in camp with the other sick soldiers. He made a show of protesting, but in the end, knew his coughing would be a liability.

While the others went out to forage or scout, Varro sat with the sick men. Some were worse than others, but they made light conversation in between coughing. Some fell asleep and others seemed animated by the stories Varro shared of his adventures in Macedonia. He enjoyed sitting with these young soldiers, who were not actually much younger than him. All his experiences had aged him. But soon, he tired and left them before they understood how exhausted he was.

The patrols returned in the afternoon, with Falco arriving first. He had taken three of the seven healthy soldiers as foragers, and they returned with berries, roots, and nuts. The roots would have to be cooked, which meant they would be saved for only the most desperate moments when they dared light a fire. With everything else combined with their own meager supplies, Falco estimated they had two days if they ate a single meal each.

"One of the boys set some snares," he said. "Maybe tomorrow we'll have some luck."

Varro coughed his thanks, and Falco leaned away and waved his hand over his nose.

"Don't give that shit to me. Go back to the tent and sleep. I'll let you know when Pilatus and Curio return."

He blew snot onto the ground, then agreed. "I haven't been so sick in years. Don't let me oversleep."

He awakened sometime later to Falco's rough shaking. Sleep stuck to him like tar, but he used his fingers to pry open his eyes. He immediately noted the golden light from the tent opening framing Falco.

"Pilatus is back, twice now. But Curio hasn't returned."

Varro sat up with a start, but it only inflicted more coughing on him. When he recovered, he grabbed Falco by his mail shirt.

"What do mean twice? Where's Curio?"

"That's my question. Pilatus went on two patrols to look for him. But he's missing along with the two men accompanying him."

"Where was he going again?" Varro staggered out of the tent with Falco's aid. Sleeping in a mail shirt was never comfortable, particularly with the pressure on his chest. But in his condition, he felt doubly miserable.

"He, Trenico, and Calvus were going to search the far side of the marsh for signs of Lucian's cavalry."

Outside the tent, five healthy soldiers sat with Centurion Pilatus at the center. The coughing of the other sick men emanated from the tents beyond them. The surrounding woods had grown dark with the onset of dusk.

"And you've not seen or heard anything from him?"

"Pilatus took four men into the marsh and fanned out to pick up whatever they could. They found prints, but nothing led them to Curio."

Varro stared at Falco's eyes glittering with low light.

"Something has happened to him. There's no time to waste. Get all healthy men assembled. We're going to find him tonight."

Falco bowed his head. "You know how he can be. I thought he was taking his time, and that you needed rest."

"There's no blame here," Varro said, his voice a thin croaking sound. "Curio found trouble, and we're the only ones who can help. So let's move out."

20

Curio hated the marsh for its lonesome expanse, the impenetrable black water, and the insects that delivered itching bites or irritating buzzing. His companions, Trenico and Calvus, were both fine soldiers but not much good for scouting work. They walked upright whenever Curio looked away.

"Don't make a profile against the sky," he would hiss at them, and then both would stoop level with the marsh grass. He felt he spent more time watching their stances than searching for signs of the enemy.

It was a desperate search, in any case. Trenico had been certain of the old man's directions, and he had no reason to lie about it. But it was thin material to work with. The marsh was narrower than its length, and crossing it at speed only cost him a few hours. He had plenty of daylight to locate horse tracks on the opposite side. But unless he was extremely fortunate, he would have to return with nothing to show for his effort other than muddy feet. For now, he ranged ahead of his two more heavily armored companions.

They carried swords and wore bronze pectorals that were

stained and lusterless. The green paint on their body-length shields had bubbled and peeled with the climate and bore bright white scars from enemy blades. They were ready for a fight if not for scouting work.

He wore only a frayed tunic and cloak and carried his pugio. Its edge needed care but it would have to wait until he escaped Iberia. He was the true scout and the others his support if they found trouble.

As they splashed between islands of mud, Curio tested the water depth with a relatively straight branch he had taken from the camp. Nothing went deeper than his knees, but he could never be certain. He feared stirring up whatever evil lurked in the waters, but he could not risk drowning or else his spirit would become trapped here forever.

They paused to get their bearings at different points in the crossing. With so few landmarks, it was easier to lose the way back. They had left a trail of sorts, with Curio marking prominent rocks or stumps with his initials. He did so now while the others sipped from their bronze canteens.

"We're almost to the other side, sir," Trenico said. "Lucian is down from the river that passes here. I can't say more than he's on a hill or something."

Curio nodded as he completed scratching his initials into a log. "We'll assume any barbarians we meet in these areas are his people."

"What are we going to do when we find him?" Trenico asked. "Centurion Barbatus planned to burn his village and drive the warriors into a prepared trap. Of course, that was before we lost half the century."

Scanning the horizon and seeing nothing but marsh and the trees on the opposite side, Curio shook his head.

"It might work for a fresh century with good supply and another century for backup. But Barbatus was going to get you killed that way. We'll use Lucian's tricks against him and not fight directly. We'll destroy him from the inside like he did with Consul Cato."

"Sir, can I ask you something?"

Trenico's hesitation drew Curio back, and he nodded.

"Did Lucian really curse you? The men all say it's true."

"Sir, I never said anything like that." Calvus stood a head taller than both of them but was reed thin. His big hands waved in frantic denial.

"It's true," Curio said. "He said this land will devour me. When Varro and Falco arrived, I thought I was escaping Iberia. Instead, I found myself going deeper into it than any Roman ever has. Lucian's curse feels true enough."

"Any Roman, except for Lucian. Right, sir?" Trenico chuckled but his smile faded when Curio did not respond.

Instead, he looked toward the trees and the gaps of light between them.

"He's not a Roman. He has forgotten who he is. Let's move out. The trees are close and we have to make this crossing again before sunset."

They traversed the rest of the marsh, and in his rush to complete his scouting mission, Curio did not mark as much of the final leg as he should. But he was confident in finding the way back. He had spent so long in the wilderness that he developed a strange sense of its logic. There were rules to nature, it seemed. Like trees did not grow up from streams even though they needed water. One side of a mountain had more vegetation than its opposite side. Deep forest trees grew branches only at their tops. Things like this became signposts for him. He was certainly no woodsman, but he was no longer a raw city man who thought forests all looked the same.

After reaching the opposite side of the marsh, they spread out to search for signs of passage. Curio wasn't certain either of his companions knew what to look for other than the most careless signs. But he did not expect the triumphant Iberian cavalry to care about hiding their path back.

As they picked a way between trees where horses would not run, Curio kept his eye on the clearing ahead. He doubted finding anything there, but it held the most promise. So he was surprised to discover Roman prints on the opposite side, freshly made.

The others gathered to him as he squatted over the tracks, fingers tracing the hobnail patterns.

"What is it, sir?" Trenico asked.

"Roman tracks. Survivors from the attack, I assume."

Now Calvus squatted opposite Curio. "It looks like they over-struck hoofprints. Was he following after the cavalry, sir?"

"It would seem so," Curio stood up and dusted his hands on his thighs. "Maybe he thought to steal food from them. I cannot imagine why a straggler would head toward the enemy."

They spread out to search the clearing, and within moments Curio's doubts cleared away.

"There are dozens of Roman tracks here," he said. "If I had to guess, at least two dozen soldiers followed after the cavalry."

Trenico looked excitedly to the northeast where the tracks pointed.

"Sir, Centurion Barbatus must be after them."

"Impossible," Curio said. "They were surrounded by superior numbers. There was no escape for him."

Now Calvus reexamined the tracks as if he might find an answer in the mud. But he stood up with a handful of grass that he let drift away on the breeze.

"I agree with Centurion Curio. There was no escape for them."

But Trenico started ahead, like a dog straining against his chain. "No, we are good soldiers. Centurion Barbatus is better than you think. He could've escaped once he had time to organize his defense."

The mystery intrigued Curio, but it seemed impossible for Barbatus to have pulled out of the envelopment. Yet what other Roman forces could be out here? Did the garrison commander send a force to recover his deserters? Given he was likely dealing with his own barbarian attacks, it seemed unlikely.

"I guess it has to be Barbatus," he said. "Or whatever remains of his century. If they're going after Lucian's cavalry, then they are bigger fools than I ever guessed. We should return to camp with the news. Varro and Falco will know what to do."

He nodded to both Trenico and Calvus, and they turned back toward the marsh.

"If it's them, sir," Calvus said. "Will it change our plans?"

"Maybe. It puts us under pressure to act fast. I think Barbatus will at least soften up Lucian's defenses for us. If they're so desperate to die, then let them."

A bright light flashed before Curio's eyes, obliterating his vision. Then cold mud and grass pushed into his face. Following this, he felt as if he were being washed away in the tide as his vision rolled and flipped. Hot coppery fluid leaked into his mouth.

He blinked through the white haze to see a smudge of two men fighting. He was staring up at them. They both had shields raised, but one staggered backward and sank lower with each retreating step.

Curio watched this figure, trying to determine who it was. Everything was black and white and overlapping in kaleidoscopic blurs. Words like distant echoes came to him.

"Why?"

It repeated over and over, growing weaker as the retreating figure dropped to his knees. His huge shield fell aside and he slumped forward as if he were asleep. The other figure hovered behind his own shield, staring at the slumped man.

Groaning escaped Curio's bloody mouth. His voice sounded

like the peal of a great bronze bell, but nothing he said made sense.

The waiting figure stood up from behind his shield, then prodded the slumped body with his sword. The body thudded into the muddy ground and was now level with Curio.

Someone flipped him over, and he now looked up into a sky too bright for his eyes. The motion made him sick and everything scrambled like reflections in a puddle.

"Sorry, Curio." The voice came through clearly as he felt arms working around him. "But Centurion Barbatus was quite clear to take you alive."

He felt his belt stripped away and his cloak removed. The shadow wavering in his sight now wrapped something about him, maybe the same cloak just removed. Then he rose from the ground and flopped onto something concave and hard. His face pointed at the sky, which rotated around a dark head hanging over him.

"And that story about being from another unit," the voice said, now close to his ear. "I lied. You nearly killed me with that poison. If I didn't have to bring you back alive, I'd have stabbed you in the back first. Now, let's go meet the others. I can't believe they've survived!"

Curio bobbed along in a state of confusion, watching the gray clouds overhead rippling in his vision.

"Calvus," he managed to say. "Trenico."

It all came back to him. A terrible, throbbing pain tore into the back of his head. He had been knocked flat from behind, disarmed, and tied up in his own cloak. Trenico had betrayed him and now dragged him along, using a scutum as a sled.

Blood pattered from his head into the curve of the scutum beneath him. He had no strength to resist or untangle himself. Even as his vision returned, he remained weakened and queasy. Still, he struggled in hopes of rolling out of the shield and fleeing.

But he was entangled and weak, unable to offer more than token resistance.

"I see them!" Trenico said. Curio was not certain how long he had dragged behind Trenico. Every rut and rock made his head shake as if he were being thrashed by a wild boar. It seemed the light had shifted to pink in the blink of an eye, hinting that he might have fallen unconscious at some point.

Now he heard challenges issued and Trenico's answer. After some confusion, it seemed these other men welcomed him.

The blurry form of a stranger hovered over him and lifted him from the shield. He then draped Curio over his shoulder. He bounced away on the shoulder of this man as Trenico stared after him. His pale eyes were bright with happiness and victory. Another Roman soldier stood with him, both framed against thin trees that revealed the marsh beyond. They seemed to celebrate with their arms around each other.

Then that scene vanished as Curio crashed to the ground, landing on his rear then flopping to his side. He lay still as muddy, bloodied feet in sandals gathered around him.

Strong hands flipped him over, and he looked into dark eyes framed with a bronze helmet and velvety dark beard. His thin lips pressed tight, and a fresh cut left a thick scab across the man's nose.

"I can't believe our luck." The man continued to stare as Curio tried to focus. But his eyes rolled uncontrollably.

"Sir, Centurion Varro captured me." Out of Curio's shifting vision, he heard Trenico give his report. "He beat me for intelligence, and I had to tell him about the old man and Lucian's location. But then he trusted me and sent me scouting with Curio of all people. When we found your tracks, I knew you had survived. I captured Curio and here he is."

The man over Curio, who had to be Barbatus, glanced away.

"You don't look beaten, Trenico. But I will not question your gift to all of us."

The cheering of a score or more soldiers stabbed Curio's ears and he rolled around, struggling to disentangle himself and block the noise. But Barbatus seized him, and despite his rocking sight, he could see the yellow teeth clenched in rage.

"Does your head hurt? It's nothing compared to what you did to my men." He gave Curio a violent shake. "You filthy, gutless poisoner and thief. If I didn't have orders, I'd cut out your liver."

Trenico's voice came from beyond Curio's narrow vision.

"Sir, there are ways for him to suffer that won't kill him and won't leave marks."

"I don't doubt you know a few tricks." Barbatus gave a wicked smile, finally releasing Curio. "But you brained him well enough. We can't have him die now, not after all we've suffered to get here."

Barbatus hauled Curio to his feet, then ripped away his cloak, spinning him so that when he finally came free he collapsed into one of the soldiers encircling him.

"Tie him properly," Barbatus said. "And get Ivonius to treat his head, as much as that sickens me. We need him alive for the consul."

Curio bounced between soldiers, his vision still a blur until he settled into a strong grip that held him in place. Once stopped, his sight settled and he found Barbatus sneering at him with Trenico staring coldly behind him.

"At last, the elusive Centurion Curio has been captured. I'll credit you for surviving this long on your own. But it's over for you now."

"Sir, does this mean we can go home? We don't need to go after Lucian anymore?"

Barbatus whirled to whoever voiced the question.

"What kind of question is that? Lucian is just as bad as Curio. We need to bring back both of them." Barbatus's fierce glare softened, and he relaxed. "Well, we only had direct orders to bring Curio back for questioning. But Lucian's head would be easier to carry, wouldn't it?"

The soldiers cheered again, and to Curio, the roar of it sounded as if a whole legion surrounded him.

He cycled through three different keepers until at last he was tied to a stake in front of Barbatus's tent, just like the old Iberian man he and Varro had rescued. Curio wished the same would happen for him but had no hope of it now. The soldier called Ivonius came to tend him after he started to hang against his bindings. By this time, his vision stabilized and he could speak clearly.

"How did you escape the Iberians?"

While Ivonius cleaned Varro's wound with fresh water, making it burn as he did, he gave a soft chuckle.

"With the blessing of Mars, that's how. We were done for, but the Iberians had spent their javelins and didn't dare us with their swords. They weren't proper cavalry swords and were too short to do the job. So after they took a few casualties, they broke off. Stupidest barbarians I've fought yet."

Curio remembered how Lucian's warriors danced in a dream-like state, and he did not doubt they could lack clear judgment. Perhaps the tribe was too poor to even outfit their cavalry with proper gear. In either case, they had failed to destroy Barbatus when they had the perfect opportunity.

When Ivonius finished he gave Curio a hard stare. "You don't look the sort to poison your fellows and steal from the treasury. But then again, what does that sort look like?"

"I stole from the treasury," Curio admitted. "But I did not believe it was stealing at the time. Lucian is a talented liar. And I didn't poison you or your companions. Lucian just assured me the treasury would be open when I got there. I was shocked to find the guards all unconscious. It was entirely his doing."

Ivonius finished wrapping Curio's head, then tugged on his

bindings to ensure they were not so tight that his limbs would be damaged.

"Well, then you were a fool, which doesn't excuse what you did. Some of my friends went blind, and others died screaming about monsters eating them alive. It was a cruel way to end a man's life, and you had a part in it. So, don't look for forgiveness here."

"Not forgiveness," Curio said. "Just understanding. Lucian led me and my men to ruin. I wish he had killed me along with the others."

"And why didn't he?"

Curio looked past Ivonius at the trees melting into darkness.

"I don't know. I think he wanted to feed me to this land like a meal for his hungry gods."

"We will at least save you from that," Ivonius said with a thin smile. "But even if Consul Cato exonerates you from everything, you're not going to live long after. Deserved or not, you're known as the man who poisoned his sword brothers to steal their pay."

He watched Ivonius walk into the gathering darkness and then up to the full moon rising over the trees. It was a good night to die or to escape.

And he knew which awaited him.

21

After dark, Barbatus's camp settled for the night. Curio hung from his post by a thin, rough rope that bit his arms and ankles. Barbatus did not order his men to trench and stake the camp as they had before. Instead, he posted double the normal number of guards. To Curio's mind, this would only leave stressed and injured men weaker the next day. He had observed an argument among the men that made the same point. But they obeyed their orders nonetheless.

Barbatus personally checked Curio's bindings before he ducked into his tent. He said nothing but patted Curio's cheek as if admiring his prize. Trenico followed. He and Curio just stared at each other. It seemed Trenico was either an optio or else part of the command group. After a long and cold stare, he followed Barbatus into the tent.

Now alone with only the full moon and cricket song for company, Curio stood straight against his bindings.

He had purposely hung forward and flexed his muscles each time someone tightened the rope. Now when he flattened against the post he had a fraction more slack than he should. With the camp silent and dark, he began to twist and wiggle. It might take all night, but he was confident he could free himself. For all of Barbatus's personal supervision, he was no sailor when it came to tying knots, and Curio felt them slip as he tested his bonds.

Each twist and pull of his ankle created more slack. No one observed him with any degree of scrutiny. The guards on watch did glance his way, but they focused on threats from the darkness beyond. The moon traveled into the sky as he patiently worked his feet out of the bindings. He stepped clear, heart racing with this minor victory.

The rope around his arms was far tighter. His right arm seemed more hopeful than his left. But now he could use his feet to lift himself against the post. It was set deep, but the earth was soft. If he chose, he could have unmounted the post by rocking around. Yet the noise from crashing over would only bring Barbatus and everyone else to him.

So he twisted and flexed, focusing on freeing his right arm. The rope burned horribly against his exposed skin, but he managed to bend the arm, creating enough of a gap with the available slack to pull it out. When it popped free, the rest of the rope around his torso went slack and he was assured of freedom.

At the same moment, Ivonius approached him. Curio stiffened against the post and held the rope to his body by tucking the slack under his free arm. He prayed his face did not betray his horror.

"How's your head?" Ivonius asked in a whisper. He seemed sleepy with small eyes ready to close. But he focused on the bandage and missed the tangle of rope at their feet.

"I'm fine," he said. "You look tired."

"I've not slept right in days. Just making sure you're still alive. A few of the men would like to cut your throat and damn Barbatus's orders."

"No one has come. You should go too before others say I've corrupted you."

Ivonius gave a small smile, reexamined Curio's bandage, then turned to leave.

He paused, looking at the rope clumped at Curio's feet.

Striking without delay or mercy, Curio slammed his knee into Ivonius's crotch, doubling him over. With his free arm, he then struck down with his elbow on the back of Ivonius's neck. He groaned and Curio kneed him once more in his face as the elbow smash drove him down. Hard bone slammed into Curio's knee.

Ivonius toppled back, and Curio desperately fought out of the remaining rope. It sloughed aside just as Ivonius staggered to his feet.

"You little bastard!"

But Curio silenced him with a punch to his throat. Half blind with fear, he dragged Ivonius to the ground as he choked, searching for the pugio at his side. He found it with Ivonius's hand atop it.

Curio pinned Ivonius on his back, clamping a hand over his mouth. He was not large enough to keep the bigger Ivonius down for long, but the shock of his brutal attack lent him dominance.

Ivonius screamed against Curio's hand, then tried to bite his fingers. But the real battle was for the pugio. With his arm bent, Ivonius lacked strength and he lost the struggle. Curio yanked the blade free so that it thumped to the ground.

He released Ivonius to snatch the weapon. The sudden freedom was just as shocking as the attack. He flipped over, arm out to protect himself.

But it exposed his armpit, and Curio plunged the blade into the soft flesh while dropping atop him again. He left the blade embedded in Ivonius's armpit, certain that his own thrashing would widen the cut on its own. Instead, he pressed both hands over Ivonius's mouth.

When their eyes met, he shifted his hands to cover Ivonius's face. He looked away as the struggling man underneath him weakened and finally went limp. A wide pool of blood spread out beneath him.

Curio waited before sitting back from the dead body. The moon reflected in the dark puddle that flowed from beneath the corpse of a man who had only come to check on his welfare. He was an enemy, and Curio knew Ivonius would not hesitate to kill him if ordered. Yet he turned aside from the corpse, and whether from disgust at this deed or from his head injury, he retched.

When he recovered, he still held the pugio in hand. He tore off his blood-crusted bandage as the white cloth would give him away in the moonlight.

The blood from under Ivonius's contorted body flowed steadily toward the command tent. Once it reached inside, it was bound to touch someone and awaken them. So he used his heel to quickly score a channel to divert it, but he was unsure how successful it was. For the moment, it flowed into the path he created.

Counting his luck so far, he did not take Ivonius's gladius. It felt wrong to take it and he would not have the sheath and harness for carrying it. But before he left, he cut a length of rope to cinch about his waist, though for now he wound it around his hands.

Like a rat, he crawled toward the darkest point of the camp perimeter. Fortuna was with him, he knew, or otherwise guards would've come to the struggle with Ivonius. He prayed she stayed with him these final yards to freedom. But the goddess was fickle.

He found two men together in whispered conversation. Their backs were to him and their attention faced the expanse of darkness. He had no time to lose, as Ivonius's blood might overflow the shallow channel and reach the command tent.

Just like a skittering rat, he shifted and crawled between tents of slumbering men to another section of the perimeter. He found yet another guard there, his side presented to Curio so that he risked the guard spotting him.

His heart thudded against his chest and the wound on his skull throbbed with the pain of his fear. He could not continue to shuffle around looking for an unguarded opening.

He pulled up a small stone from the ground, then cast it into the darkness. It did not land with any audible sound, so he dug out a larger one. Voices came from behind, and he feared other guards would arrive. Once more, he flung a stone as best as he could from prone, and this time it struck bushes.

The guard now turned aside to see what had made the noise.

Curio sprang up, rope hanging loose between his hands. In two bounds he crossed the distance then flung the rope around the guard's neck. He hauled back with all his might. It cut short the guard's anguished cry of surprise. Curio dragged the guard to the ground, then he twisted the rope until it tightened. The guard thrashed and choked, but soon went still. Curio was uncertain if he had killed him or rendered him unconscious. In any case, he heard voices drawing near, and could not linger. He left the prone guard and fled toward the safety of darkness.

Now in full flight, his fleeting shape must have caught the watchful eyes searching the darkness. He heard shouts behind him as his legs pumped for a looming shadow that soon revealed itself as a stand of trees. He dashed into these, his body fueled with terror and elation at having escaped.

He ran wherever the path was clear, and only chose a way that led him from Barbatus and his men. He was the rabbit that slipped his snare and was now mindlessly fleeing to wherever seemed safe.

But as his strength flagged and he heard the shouts becoming more distant, he slowed. Unlike a rabbit, he could not run at such speeds for long. He was thankful he had not struck a rock or rut that might have made this his final escape. After catching his breath, he continued to jog away from danger, though he chose a more careful path.

While moonlight lit the way, it would not illuminate enough to follow shadowy tracks made by a light foot. However, by morning it would be another matter. He could loop around and try to reach Varro and Falco at camp.

But he knew the two of them would not be idle. They would have gone searching for him when he failed to return. He trusted them to locate the markers he left behind, and then come upon the scene of Calvus's murder. He had dropped his Servus Capax pugio there. They would understand what happened, and might even locate Barbatus's camp.

He also knew Varro and Falco did not have the numbers to prevail in any overt action against Barbatus. So when they found the camp, they would have to stop and watch. Varro could not do the reconnaissance of the camp on his own, not with his uncontrolled coughing. Falco might be forced into the role, but he knew Varro felt he was unsuited for it. Curio disagreed, but he was not there to protest.

So as he jogged aimlessly, he considered the best way to communicate that he had escaped and finally thrown off Barbatus for good.

It did not take him long to figure out what he needed to do.

His running had taken him to the bend of a wide river. Its strong flowing water sparkled with pearly moonlight. If he followed this river, he would come to the hill where Lucian and his mad warriors waited for him.

Of course, Lucian awaited him there. Had he not cursed him and promised the land would devour him? To Curio, there was only one way that this curse could ever be lifted. There was only a single path out of Iberia. He had to destroy Lucian. Regardless that it was their mission to do so, Curio had a higher need to do it himself.

So why not lead Barbatus to where he wants to go? Why not present him with two gifts rather than one? Up on that hill, everything he had come seeking—revenge, glory, and battle—was gathered for him. He could not resist it.

And Varro and Falco must go to the same hill to find the same things.

It all ended in Lucian's twisted, mad domain.

So he stepped out of the underbrush and picked a careful path toward the river. He would be certain to leave clear tracks so that all his woes would be delivered to one place and come to a single, bloody end.

He enjoyed the fresh scent of the river as he followed its course. Thick reeds gathered along its banks, and these waved with a gentle night breeze. The full moon reflected off the water, brightening his path. From behind, he heard the distant shouts of enraged men. He was not certain if they tried to follow him or if they mourned the deaths of two more of their own. As Ivonius had promised, there would be a reckoning one day. Would Senator Flamininus be able to excuse his killing of two fellow soldiers?

But he might never have to face the consequences of his actions after tonight.

The river's flow slowed as it curled into the hilly ground. The trees now grew to the river's edge and slowed Curio's progress. Moonlight helped him find the way through trees that grew fat with moss. Hooting owls now replaced the cries of men behind him. Branches reached down for him like crooked hands eager to snatch him into the pressing darkness.

He carried only Ivonius's pugio into the depths of the forest. The blade's white edge caught what moonlight reached him here. He held it forward as if expecting danger to leap from behind each hoary tree.

In the predawn hour when the moon set and the eastern horizon glowed with faint light, Curio arrived at a ford in the river. He tested the crossing with a long branch, and upon reaching the other side, he found a place to rest. Here was the bottom of a great hill that loomed before him as utter blackness.

Weary from his efforts and his fears, he curled up into the bole of a tree and slept with his knees drawn to his chest. It was fitful and restless sleep that offered no refreshment. When dawn came, he washed in the river and considered how he might approach Lucian's village.

He admitted some interest in at last seeing the location of Bandua's dreaming city that would rival Rome. At least it was near a river, he thought. But even in the pale morning light it seemed a haunted land that invited only the mad or desperate into its ancient forests. He could never imagine anything of significance taking root in such a place. Perhaps Bandua was as mad as Lucian and his followers.

He started up a likely path between the trees that grew so close they seemed like guardsmen ranking up against him. But he slipped between their trunks, watching the way ahead as he passed.

Then Lucian's curse became reality.

The ground beneath Curio's feet rushed up to him, the land at last devouring him. Branches and leaves surrounded him, entangling him and drawing him into the canopy. He screamed in terror, trying to fight free but finding his arms pinned.

The monstrous trees thrashed him around like a wolf savaging its prey. But then it slowed and Curio realized the swinging was due to his own struggles.

He was caught in a net that was tied high in the trees.

"A snare!" he shouted uselessly at the trees above. He ground his teeth, and if he could shift his arms, he would beat his skull in rage and frustration.

He thought of his pugio, but in the shocking violence, he had dropped it. With it in hand, he could have cut himself free. But now, he dangled helplessly with it lost somewhere in the debris beneath him.

He wondered at the size of this snare and what Lucian's folk hoped to catch. While many animals might fit into a net of this size, it seemed perfectly sized for a man.

Hours passed before he heard someone calling from uphill. The gentle swaying of the net afforded him only a glimpse of their shaggy forms. But he knew the familiar calls of Lucian's warriors.

Three of them arrived beneath him. Their naked torsos were covered in blue designs that stretched up to their faces. Curio could smell their odor as they gathered beneath him. At first, they did nothing but stare in confusion.

"You've bagged a man, you fools." Curio wriggled against the net. "Cut me down. I'm tired of having my knees in my face."

While the Lusitani warriors should not understand him, they burst out in laughter at Curio's words. They started to joke among themselves in their strange tongue, and one jabbed his posterior with a spear. Curio jolted with pain and surprise, drawing raucous laughter from his captors.

After they recovered, one climbed into the tree to cut him down while the other two eased Curio to the ground. The moment his feet settled on hard ground, he lashed out in a bid to escape. Again, the Lusitani guffawed at his attempt. One held the shaft of his spear in both hands like a club, then slammed it across Curio's chest.

He collapsed with a horrified gasp, then realized if they beat him again his head wound might worsen. Tangled as he was, he could not protect himself and so went still. This drew more scornful laughter from the Lusitani, but they seemed pleased enough that Curio accepted his fate.

They hauled him off the ground then two carried him back the way they had come. The other walked beside him, speaking his incomprehensible language but sounding like a boastful hunter who had claimed a prized stag.

Through the tight weave of the net, he could not see many details. Morning light dappled the deep greens of the forest. The men he swung between were thin but strong, their faces buried in wild hair and beards. Whatever flesh was exposed was marred with face tattoos. Their strong body odor overwhelmed every other scent. But worst of all, he could see their red-rimmed, bulging eyes. These were Lucian's mad warriors.

They climbed the steep hill to reach a village that emerged from the trees. Curio couldn't see details, being unable to turn in the net and its weave obscuring his sight. Yet the entire village greeted him, or so it seemed. Children laughed and called out to him, while others hid behind the legs of adults. The scent of cooking fires hung thick in the air, and the village was brighter than he imagined it. In his thoughts, Lucian lived in a rotting land of darkness and surrounded himself with crazed men.

But from what he could see, at a superficial level everything appeared normal.

The three warriors paraded him in a wide circle while Curio stared into the blue sky. If an eye met his through the net, he looked away. He decided to show no fear. His enemies did not deserve entertainment from him. So the prodding and tentative hands that reached out to him as he passed went without reaction.

At last, they set him on packed dirt and the excited chatter of men and women around him hushed.

A shadow fell across him, and one of his bearers began to untangle him from the net. Curio braced himself so as not to roll out like a fish spilled from a fisherman's net. When the last of the net pulled away, he looked up at the man casting his shadow over him.

He squinted at the dark shape framed against the bright sky.

It was the familiar outline of Centurion Lucian.

"Now you know why I did not search for you. I knew Bandua would deliver you to me. This is where you belong. You have been called home, and together we will build something greater than anyone before us has ever dreamed."

22

Varro crouched to the ground in the clearing. The sun cast slanting shadows across the knee-high grass and sparkled on the wide spaces of the marsh beyond the trees. The path through the grass was obvious. It followed the older tracks of Roman caligae and hoofprints.

"He's buried now," Falco said from behind. "We'll say our words, then get on with the chase. There's not much light left."

Looking back at the long path of flattened grass, he lifted Curio's pugio clutched in his hand and pointed.

"It's not hard to see where they went."

Falco growled like a watchdog eager to be freed of his chain.

They gathered around Calvus's grave. Five of his companions stood with their hands folded at their laps and heads bowed. They had used their trenching tools to dig a grave for their brother, and tears mingled with sweat on their faces.

Centurion Pilatus cleared his throat.

"Calvus was a good soldier and a brave lad. He had some trouble in formation drills. But you can't expect perfection in everything. Calvus didn't deserve what he got. He'll be looking at us to claim his revenge. So let's make sure we do."

His five remaining companions nodded vigorously, sniffed, then turned away from the grave. Varro wanted to speak, but he only coughed and the moment passed.

Falco guided him from the fresh mound of earth. "Maybe you ought to return to camp with the other sick men. Someone has to tell them we're not coming back tonight."

After coughing again, Varro nodded and strained his voice to agree. "Good idea. I'll send someone back with a message, and he can assist the sick while we're gone. As for sending me back, I'm certain I was just hearing things. You didn't really say that, correct?"

Falco bowed his head. "I had to suggest it, at least. Look, you could give us all away. You make more noise than a farm cat in heat."

He looked at Curio's pugio in his hand.

"What should I tell him? Sorry, Curio, I couldn't help you because I had a runny nose?"

"How about telling all of us, sorry, everyone for giving us away and getting everyone killed." Falco pointed to the wide swath of Roman tracks. "Barbatus had some fucking luck, didn't he? No one else made those tracks. Now he has Curio. It's a three-to-one fight, and you're half dead as it is."

Varro stared at the trampled ground and the unexpected mixture of hooves and caligae tracks. Curio had found these and concluded Barbatus's men had survived. Trenico obviously did as well and stabbed Calvus in the back before knocking out Curio and dragging him off on a shield to find his old century.

"I'll have Pilatus select a man to send word back to camp. Good thing you let me sleep earlier. It will be a long night."

None of Pilatus's men wanted to return to camp, as they were all eager to avenge Calvus. But with enough cursing, he got one man to head back. The rest moved out in loose formation. Varro let Falco take the lead, and he stayed in the rear to prevent his cough from alerting enemies. Though he ached with fever, his steps did not falter as they followed the trail.

Everything he wanted was within reach: Lucian, his ill-gotten silver, and Centurion Barbatus. But he had been laid low with a sore throat and fever. He would not allow it to stop him now after Calvus and others had died to get him this close.

Lucian's madness had caused so much suffering. Varro blamed all the men he lost, the destruction of Curio's command group, and all of Barbatus's poisoned men on Lucian's madness.

He would not turn back now, nor would he leave it to another to do what must be done. He would claim his redemption and lead everyone back to safety.

Night fell too soon, for the heavy rut Curio had left behind faded into trees. Though a full moon cast strong light, the canopy prevented it from lighting the path ahead.

"I don't even know where we're headed," Falco said, pausing the small group. "I keep losing the path."

Varro sighed. "Barbatus must bring Curio back alive. But you cannot trust his men to forego their revenge. Someone has to locate his camp and not let them get out of our sight."

"Well, it won't be you," Falco said. "Let's make camp and take this up in the morning. We know they have to eventually follow the river to that hill where Lucian thinks his great city will be built. How hard can it be to find it? Curio's not sleeping on a feathered bed tonight, but he's not going to die."

Varro looked at Pilatus and his four men. Their eyes flashed with vengeance, but their postures betrayed undeniable exhaustion. His stomach rumbled and he expected others to be as hungry. As standard procedure, Varro had everyone pack three days of rations when they left camp. Every soldier went to battle with their full kit in case they became separated and had to survive on their own. However, they only had one tent among them.

"We'll use the remaining daylight to find a place to make camp."

Pilatus immediately set about locating a small clearing. They ate meager rations and then pitched their lone tent. With one man on watch at all times, the remaining six crowded together.

Despite his anxiousness, Varro soon drifted into a feverish sleep. His dreams swirled with frantic nightmares of faceless gods who reached down from the heavens as they tried to crush him. No matter where he ran, he could never escape these cloudy, vague threats.

When at last the dreams ended, he awakened but could not open his eyes. Someone was coughing beside him.

"Fuck, now we're all sick."

It was Falco's voice, familiar but deep and rough.

"How is he?" Pilatus's voice remained unchanged and was opposite Falco's.

"His fever is out of control." Falco paused to cough. "We can try soaking him in the river if the current's not strong."

Neither man spoke and Varro forced his eyes open only long enough to glimpse bright light and two blurry shapes over him.

"I'm fine." But his voice betrayed the lie. It was weak and trembling, and barely audible even to himself.

"What's that?" Falco asked.

But Varro couldn't answer. He was too tired and his whole body ached.

"At least he has stopped coughing," Pilatus said. "But what are we going to do?"

"Bring the other sick men here." Falco broke into a spasm of coughing. "No sense in splitting up now. We're halted until all the sick men recover or die."

Varro's eyes fluttered open at Falco's order. But he saw only milky light and then fell back into dreams.

From that moment, he floated in a strange twilight where time lost meaning. Things happened to him, but within moments he forgot what. Someone fed him thin, gamey broth. Other times he was aware of Falco's coughing and his voice. But the world collapsed into dreams and darkness.

He did not know how long had passed before the world took definite shape again. The sun burned a yellow disc into the tent above. One other man slept beside him and voices spoke in whispers outside the tent.

But Varro had escaped the fever's grip. He remained weak and raising his head tested the limits of his endurance. But he summoned his voice and called out for Falco.

Shadows moved outside the tent flap, and Pilatus ducked inside.

"Sir, glad to hear your voice again."

Varro smiled and set his head back. "It's rough but clearer than it has been. I am feeling much better. Is Falco here?"

Pilatus slipped into the tent to kneel between him and the other sleeping man. He glanced over his shoulder.

"Looks like he's still asleep, sir. He's gone down like you, but not as hard."

Varro's head popped up again, now staring at Falco resting beside him. His closed eyelids shimmered and his face was flushed.

"How long has he been down?"

"Let's see," Pilatus tilted his head. "About a day after you did. It's a bad illness. Had to bury two more of my boys. For a moment, I thought we'd be burying you. But Falco promised you would die in a more spectacular manner than just shitting your bedroll, sir. He cared for you like a son."

Propping up on his elbows, he stared at Falco.

"When we were children, he used to beat me up whenever we encountered each other, which felt like every day."

"The best kind of friend there is, sir. Keeps you honest."

"I'm not sure I agree with you. Is his illness serious?"

"Mild fever is about it." Pilatus shifted to touch Falco's forehead. "Nothing like you or the others. Whatever this shit is, it hasn't touched me."

"Let's be glad for that. Has anyone gone to check on Curio? Have we located Barbatus's camp?"

"Sir, it's been all we can do to tend to the sick. We've been foraging and collecting water. That's the extent of it." Pilatus shooed away a fly that whirled through the tent. "We've not had contact with any enemies."

Varro sat back and considered Curio. While he was concerned for Falco, Curio's plight was more dangerous. Also, that Pilatus had not encountered any enemy activity in the area indicated Barbatus pursued Lucian, bringing Curio along as a captive. Varro dreaded to think what might happen if the Lusitani got a hold of him.

"Help me up." He stretched an arm out to Pilatus. "Get me my cloak and harness."

Pilatus did as asked, but his eyes widened. "Sir, you are barely recovered. You cannot go chasing after Curio like this."

"Correct. Have someone prepare me a meal with meat. And if there's any wine left, I'll have that as well. I can chase Curio after that."

His limbs trembled and his eyes felt heavy. The burning in his throat had ebbed but lingered. He looked at Falco sleeping, his snoring intermittent. He should now care for him like a son, just as he had done for him. But Falco was as tough as caligae soles. If Pilatus said his illness was not serious, then he would recover.

Varro had his meal of venison, blood, and dandelions in a salty broth. The deer had been snared and butchered, providing enough meat and blood for the entire camp. Coughing came from every tent, but the men were heartened to see him again. The last of the concentrated wine had been diluted with river water the day before, and Varro finished it. It burned going down, but he took strength from it.

"You do look better after a good meal, sir." Pilatus had three men who were either not sick or recovered. "You should go scouting with at least one man."

Varro agreed and soon they were ranging beyond the camp to follow a trail now several days old. His companion brought him up to speed on the details he had missed. The biggest event had been the snaring of a doe. This was taken as a sign of the gods' favor, and Varro did not deny it.

"We offered part of the kill to Diana." His companion spoke in a rough whisper. "We'll need her blessing for the return trip. You have the map, sir. Centurion Pilatus says you've kept it updated."

"I have the map home. I'll get everyone back that I can and to good rewards. You have my promise. Make sure the others know this, too."

The trail led directly to an old campsite in a wide clearing within walking distance of the river. He found a latrine trench, old campfires, forgotten tent stakes, and other trash left by Barbatus's men. More ominously, he found two fresh graves.

Varro and his companion crouched over the packed earth. Two stones were set to mark the heads of the interred with their names scratched into the rock. A few years of rain would erase those names forever and the bones would molder in the earth, forgotten.

Patting one of the stones, Varro looked up at his companion.

"You didn't see any signs of a battle here?"

"No, sir. Maybe they died of sickness too."

Varro grunted. "Possibly. There are a hundred reasons why men might die in the field. But I wonder if this was Curio's work?"

Knowing the dead would not explain, he continued to investigate the camp. He found a deep hole in the ground about the circumference of a strong man's thigh. It seemed something had been worked out of it with a twisting motion. Scraps of rope had also been pressed into the mud where someone had stood.

"This is where they held Curio. He escaped."

"How do you know that, sir?"

Varro pulled up the rope scraps. "Cut ropes. No one wastes a resource like rope while in the field. Somehow he cut himself out of the rope, and those two buried soldiers must have blocked his escape."

"If he got away, why not return to camp, sir?"

"I don't know." Varro peered into the distance where high hills stood like blue sentinels over the land. "But he believes he suffers from a curse. Maybe he went searching for a way to break it."

The soldier stared after Varro and made a sign against evil then spit on the ground.

"Let's see if we can determine where they all went." Varro stood up and clapped the dirt from his hands. "If Curio went anywhere, then he went toward those hills to find Lucian himself. He'd be leading an enraged Barbatus behind him and away from us. He probably thought to have his enemies fight each other."

If Curio had left a trail, then Barbatus's pursuit had obliterated it. They followed that trail until they came to a wide river of fast-running, murky water. It unspooled toward the west where high, forested hills dominated the horizon.

"They have all gone there," Varro said, pointing out the hills. "Let's fill our canteens and head back."

He did not share his plans with the soldier, hoping to avoid needless panic. But days had gone by and neither Curio nor Barbatus had returned. There was a slight chance that Barbatus succeeded and missed Varro's campsite on the return trip. But from what his companion had described, someone was always out in the limited forest territory between marsh and river. A force the size of Barbatus's would be unable to conceal itself or its passing.

The same held true for the mad Lusitani. True to his old prisoner's words, none of the other tribes ventured into this land. So only Lucian's tribe would roam these parts. Yet they had not come down in any force, or else they too would've been spotted.

So Varro determined Lucian awaited him on his hill, letting his gods decide if they should ever meet.

The return trip went faster, and he found Falco awake and standing wrapped in his cloak like enduring a winter gale. When he spoke, his voice was thick with snot.

"What do you mean by going out so soon after you nearly died?" Pilatus stood beside him, arms folded and smiling.

"Glad to see you're doing well," Varro said. "I discovered where Curio went, and Barbatus as well."

He dismissed his companion to return to his fellows, and Varro led both Falco and Pilatus aside. He informed them of what he uncovered, and what he thought of the evidence. All three of them looked toward the blue-shrouded hills in the distance.

"We're finally going to meet him." Falco drew his cloak tighter as if a cold wind had just blown across him. "I can't wait to take the bastard's life and be done with all this."

Varro shook his head.

"I'm not sure it's going to be that easy. We're no longer combat effective. At this point, I will have to see the condition of Lucian's village when we get there. I might be able to make our original plan work, but with Curio missing I'm not sure it's still viable. In any case, let's assemble the men who can march and we'll head out."

In total, six of them could pursue Barbatus. They had trenched and staked the camp, more to provide a sense of security than any real protection. Only four men would remain in the camp, coughing and feverish and with enough supplies to last as many days.

Pilatus provided them his last bit of advice. "If we don't return, then we're all dead. But we're probably dead if we try to go back in this condition. So I'm taking the healthy to either glory or a glorious death in battle against a Roman traitor. Either way, you boys need to rest up and recover. Centurion Varro is leaving you the map. Guard it with your lives, since without it even victory becomes defeat."

Varro saw the desperation in the faces of the four young men to be left behind. But their coughing and overall weakness were a liability. The three healthy soldiers accompanying him did not seem more enthusiastic, but at least they were able to fight if needed.

But Varro had no plans to fight anyone. Any victory now would have to come from guile and good planning.

Gathering their supplies and saying their farewells to the sick men, Varro led his tiny force into the dark of Iberia where the dreaming gods of the land awaited his arrival and planned the toll to be paid for trespassing in the heart of their domain.

Falco took the point in the loose formation of soldiers following a days-old trail left by Barbatus's men. They had hewed close to the river of fast-flowing brown water and had done nothing to conceal their passing. But Varro, who marched along at the rear, always knew where the trail led.

The high forested hills emerged from the blue distance. Their serrated outlines cut into a flat gray sky that seemed to threaten rain. Falco had often complimented the fair weather, but now it turned gloomy as they approached the core of madness that had consumed Centurion Lucian and his tribe. The gods gathered to watch, Roman and Iberian, and their enmity showed in the bruise-colored clouds.

All along the journey, they found the detritus of Romans on the march. For all they had suffered, Barbatus's men seemed to have kept much of their supply. Judging from the trash left where they had paused to rest, they did not lack rations as Varro did.

Centurion Pilatus kept his three soldiers in line, and they suffered his scrutiny all the more for being the focus of his attention. Varro smiled whenever he complained to his soldiers, remembering his days in the ranks and how often he prayed to avoid attention from his officers. A bored centurion is more frightening than a thousand Macedonian pikemen. He couldn't recall who used to say that, but the maxim remained true.

But as both sky and terrain grew more threatening, he saw the wisdom in Pilatus's constant ridicule and demands for utter perfection. It spared the men from imagining what lay ahead of them. He distracted them with minor details that could never be satisfied so that they were more worried about marching in step than where they marched to.

Varro wished he had someone to do the same for him. Falco did not range as far ahead as Curio did when he took point. He spent more time checking behind himself than scouting the way forward. Varro knew how weak Falco was just from his posture. He bent under his chain shirt, and though he no longer carried a scutum, his shoulders slouched as if he still bore its weight. His condition worried Varro even more. Though his illness had not been as violent as the others, it could always worsen.

So they crossed the land into its dark heart beneath a gray sky. The tallest hill was undeniably Lucian's home. It was a brooding lump overlooking the river that seemed to shrink away from it as if avoiding its notice.

Falco halted them where the trees thickened and the incline to the hills began. He squatted in the grass, his head shaking.

"The trail is gone."

Varro looked down at the trampled earth underfoot where shallow prints of Roman caligae still showed. Everyone else looked down as well. Pilatus removed his bronze helmet and called a rest for his men. They immediately did the same and sat on the clumpy grass.

"You don't see where the trail picks up?"

Varro joined Falco to examine the way ahead, and Pilatus followed. Bushes and trees thickened here, as did moss-covered rocks and lichen-splattered fallen logs. Varro watched a squirrel study them before racing up a tree.

But there was no more trail underfoot.

"It's like they just flew off." Falco squinted up at the flat glare.

"The prints cluster here," Varro observed. "Then they vanish. They must have broken formation to head into the deeper trees. There are probably other prints to follow if we searched hard enough."

Pilatus let out a low growl. "I don't like it, sir. Seems unnatural that twenty men just stopped leaving tracks."

"There's a reason for it," Varro said, swishing his hands across the low grass that faded off as trees reassumed dominance over the ground. "Let's not jump to supernatural conclusions. If they broke into smaller groups, there will be something to follow, just nothing as obvious as a marching column."

They stared glumly up the hill, then all decided to rest. Varro swigged down the last of his wine, bitter and hard on the throat. Falco flattened out on the grass with his pack as a pillow. He coughed and stared up.

"What do think happened to Curio? If he did lead Barbatus here, whatever battle happened must be finished now. The good centurion didn't hike out here to have a rational talk with Lucian. So where's our man Curio?"

Varro glanced up into the dark sky and wondered about native gods and their curses.

"He's resourceful. Whatever he's up to, let's not doubt him like we did last time."

"Not doubting him," Falco said calmly. "Just wondering if he survived."

"Don't doubt that either. One man can slip away unseen better than Barbatus and all his soldiers."

Varro got them all moving ahead once more. The sudden disappearance of Barbatus's trail was strange, but not inexplicable.

Varro did not find any value in learning the explanation for it, as they had come to the same place all of them had strived so long to reach, Curio included. All questions would be answered at the summit of the hill.

Not more than a dozen yards into the deepening trees, Falco again called a halt. He simply raised his fist but said nothing as he stared ahead.

"What is it?" Varro lined up with Pilatus and his three soldiers. But it seemed a line too fearful to cross as if Falco had wandered into something that only looked like part of this world.

Falco didn't answer but looked slowly around as he backed up.

"I don't see anything, sir," Pilatus muttered.

"Neither do I, but Falco wouldn't stop us without cause. Wait here."

Only a few yards ahead, Varro joined Falco who remained with his fist up. Varro gently lowered it while he scanned around himself.

"That's all of them," Falco said. "By the gods."

Varro followed his searching gaze and found the source of his fear.

Severed heads dangled from trees with ropes tied about them. Flies hummed through the air, so thick upon some of the heads that their faces were hidden.

All the heads were secured in skillfully tied rope harnesses that held them like they would rest on their former necks. Blood had crusted at the stumps of their necks and around their mouths.

"Twenty-two heads," Falco whispered. "All of Barbatus's men."

"We can't know this is Barbatus."

"Don't fool yourself. The heads are days old. The flies aren't even done with them yet."

Varro turned back to Pilatus and signaled that he should hold. Then he pulled on Falco's chain shirt.

"Then let's see if there are any familiar faces here."

"If I find Curio, I'll faint."

Varro hadn't meant his friend, but instead Barbatus and his men. Yet it was possible Curio could've ended up hanging from a tree.

The heads swayed gently with the branches holding them aloft. None had eyes and most of the flesh was stripped away on the faces. Ravens and crows had done their gruesome work. But the heads had Roman-styled hair, at least for those heads that had not been entirely stripped of flesh. Several of the heads had been secured with ropes through the eye sockets. Varro thought whoever had done this lacked a human heart.

He came to a round head where the remaining flesh had turned the blackened green of rot. Flies swarmed in the four bloody orifices that once comprised a face. This head still had remnants of a velvety black beard that was now crusted and matted with blood. He decided this was Barbatus.

"So, the chase is over for you." Varro spoke softly to the head, which twisted on its rope as if shaking in denial. "You were a fool if you tried to fight the Lusitani. Did you try, Barbatus? I would like to know what you did, so I don't meet your fate."

"Fuck all, Varro. Don't talk to them." Falco appeared at his side, finger under his nose against the stench of rot. "I think I found Trenico's head. Can't really tell since crows ate his face and most of his nose. But it still resembles him. Who's this?"

"What remains of Barbatus."

Falco stared silently and expressionless at the head, then turned aside to cough.

"We have our answers. Let's quit this place. The smell is making me ill."

They both emerged from the copse of severed heads to rejoin Pilatus and his three men. They all waved their hands before their noses.

"You smell like rot, sir."

251

Varro stepped back apologetically. He then explained what they found, and the men started to panic.

"What are our chances, then? We should go back."

But Pilatus shouted them into order.

"Run now? After all we've done? Centurion Varro said we're not going to fight. We're just here to guard the silver he'll recover. Isn't that correct, sir?"

Varro nodded. "No fighting. You're my security team for transporting the silver and Lucian. He'll either come as our prisoner or as one of the heads hanging in those trees."

The men appeared dubious of the plan, and one still seemed ready to flee.

"We're not going to march through those heads, sir?"

"We'll go around them," Varro said. "Those heads are intended to frighten us and remind us of their strength. But their strength is limited to that of their swords and numbers. We bring less of both, but we do bring strategy and clear thought. From all I've learned, the Lusitani lack both. Lucian himself is crafty, but only when in the shadows. Rome has cast its light upon him, and his tricks are rendered useless. When we snare him, the tribe will be cast into doubt and confusion. Their numbers will mean nothing then and we shall have victory."

He searched the men and saw they still harbored fear, but the strong words had eased their immediate panic.

"Listen to Centurion Varro," Pilatus said. "The man knows what he's talking about. We're going around that mess and up the hill to claim our rewards. When this is finished, you'll never be bested for a good war story. Now, shape up!"

The three soldiers straightened their shoulders in automatic response to the command and stood to attention. Pilatus glared at them a moment before allowing a short grunt. He turned to Varro.

"Everything's in order, sir. We're ready to deliver the traitor's head and our stolen pay to Rome."

Varro never appreciated a centurion more than this moment. The men might not have complete faith in him, but they did for their beloved centurion. Pilatus was merciless in his adherence to procedure and military doctrine, but he knew how to motivate his young soldiers. His only downfall was his desire to achieve glory and medals. Otherwise, Varro guessed he would never have been able to deceive so fine an officer.

"If I may offer a suggestion, sir."

Varro raised his brows in answer. "I'm always ready to hear a good plan."

"Not so much of a plan, sir. Centurion Falco is ill and it's showing. We're heading into enemy territory. One cough from him could bring them all down on us before we can find them. So I suggest I take point on the way up."

Varro looked to Falco with his flushed face and reddened nose. He shrugged, and so Pilatus took point. But before he did, he glared at his men.

"Stay in line and stay alert. I'll warn you of trouble, so don't start imagining things. But speak up if you do see an actual enemy."

Pilatus led them in a wide circle to avoid the hanging heads. Yet all around the base of the hill skulls hung by rotting rope and bone shards collected among twisting roots. Many skulls had broken free and now sank into the earth, empty eye sockets and mouths filled with dirt.

However, these old skulls did not belong to Romans, or at least none they could prove. Pilatus could not find a way to avoid them and eventually picked a likely path up the side of the hill. The day had grown darker and the trees thicker. Progress remained slow, but Varro believed they would reach the summit within the hour. What awaited there filled him both with trepidation and hope. He fervently prayed that Curio had prepared the way for him and that he had not fallen into Lucian's hands. The end of this long journey into unknown Iberia was at hand, no matter its outcome.

They now moved through a section of thinner trees. Pilatus continue to lead the way, always checking behind to ensure his men remained in order. Vague light filtered down through the trees. Pilatus came to a level patch of ground. He held up his fist to stop them.

"What's this?" Pilatus drew his gladius, then crouched.

With everyone on edge, they all drew their swords as well. The hum of the drawn blades filled the dead silence. Varro had the men remain in place and then called forward.

"What did you find?"

"Not sure," Pilatus said. He remained crouched and eased forward. "Looks like some sort of grave."

Varro could not see past the three soldiers in front of him, but Falco was taller.

"Looks like more skulls," Falco said as he strained to see around the men. "But in a pile."

Pilatus straightened up and sheathed his gladius.

"Just a jumble of skulls on some rocks. Fuck, I'm getting as jumpy as the rest of you."

He reached out to grab one.

Then he disappeared.

In the space of a single heartbeat, Varro believed he had seen a man torn from the world by an unseen hand. The sight turned his blood to ice and his guts to water.

Then came a long, agonized scream, muffled as if it echoed from another world.

Snapping out of his irrational terror, Varro cursed and ran forward to where Pilatus had stood.

A covered pit had given way before a wide flat stone covered with weather-bleached skulls and milky green lichen. Varro peered over the edge of the pit where the screams rose from the earth.

Centurion Pilatus lay face up in a pit twice as deep as a standing man. Sharpened wood stakes impaled his left thigh, his shoulder, and his side. More gruesome but less deadly, a splinter from a spike had pierced through his ear and protruded from below his eye. The skin stood up there, making it seem like his wildly rolling eye might fall out. He hung above the dirt bottom, where white bones shined through the shadow.

"Fuck! Not like this! Not in a hole!"

"We'll get you out, Pilatus!" Varro looked back to the others. "A rope! I need a rope!"

Pilatus's screaming already started to ebb, and Varro looked down again to find the centurion still writhing on the spikes. The only visible blood flowed from his face wound, rolling into his eyes and mouth then dribbling off. But beneath him, blood shimmered with the scant light reaching into the pit.

Falco had arrived with a short length of rope and now looked into the pit.

"Gods, that's bad." He ducked back from it.

Varro snatched the rope. "We need to get him out. We can save him."

"He's dead already. Just pulling him off those spikes will kill him."

The three remaining soldiers now stood around the pit, calling down to their centurion.

But Pilatus had no more strength to scream. He let out a long groan, one hand gripping the spike through his shoulder and the other pointing up. Varro wasn't sure if he was accusing him or trying to issue an order. His clenched teeth were red with his lifeblood. He growled at the strain of keeping his arm extended. Then it dropped and the hand on the spike went slack.

Pilatus let out a final moan.

"You all hold the rope," Varro said, feeding a length through his hands. "I'll climb down and get him out."

But the rope slid through his hands onto the ground. Falco stared over the side as did the other soldiers.

"Stop wasting time!"

But one of the three soldiers shook his head. "He's dead."

"This hill is trapped. We're all going to die."

"Centurion Pilatus can't be dead!"

"Centurion Curio was right. The land has cursed all of us. We shouldn't be here!"

"Our gods are not strong enough!"

"Silence!"

Varro's shout bounced through the trees like thunder. Even Falco looked up in shock, though he had not indulged in the panic.

He glared at everyone, his head throbbing with rage and sadness. Then he picked up the rope.

"Get yourselves together. We can't let his body rot here. We've got to bury him."

Falco and the others helped him lower down to Pilatus's corpse. The earthen walls crumbled when he bumped them. He settled between the stakes that looked like the same kind used to ring a marching camp. Rather than pull Pilatus off the stakes, he planned to work them out of the earth and raise the body with the spikes in place.

He had worked two free when Falco started shouting. Varro, now slick with Pilatus's blood, looked up to glare above and found no one over the pit. He called out, hoping they had not been ambushed while preoccupied. But he heard only Falco's distant voice.

After a moment's rest against the wall, while standing in mud churned from Pilatus's blood, Varro saw Falco's head reappear.

"Just us now. Fucking gutless bastards ran off."

"But Pilatus isn't even properly buried. How could they do that?"

"With their feet, Lily. They ran. Scared for their own lives. Are you ready down there?"

Varro tied off Pilatus under his arms as best he could. He had learned how to make solid knots during his year in Numidia, where it was important to tie your horse well against it wandering off or to protect it from an opportunistic thief.

He jumped up to reach Falco's hands, but his own being slick with blood meant they had to try several times before he scrabbled out of the pit.

Hauling Pilatus up took all their effort. Not only did they fight the stakes that dragged on the earthen sides, but Pilatus was a heavy man in a mail shirt. When at last his body flopped onto the dirt outside the pit, both Varro and Falco collapsed panting in the grass.

The rope lay between them as they gasped. The light of the gray sky now faded behind the dark crisscrossed patterns of branches. Varro huffed and trembled from his effort. Falco coughed and wheezed beside him, then rolled over to blow snot from his nose.

"Fuck, I cannot bury him. Getting him out of that pit about killed me. Sorry."

"We can't let him just rot while crows eat his flesh."

"Crows or worms," Falco said through his gasps. "Something will eat him. Do you want to burn him? That'll bring Lucian's lads down in a hurry."

Varro looked toward the lump of Pilatus's mud- and blood-smeared corpse. Behind it was the flat rock of lined-up skulls, which he guessed belonged to prior victims. Just as Lucian had done, the curious had approached the grim display and then fell into the pit to vanish forever. No wonder other tribes never visited these madmen on their cursed hill, he thought.

They both remained facing the sky, their chests heaving from their efforts.

"Just me and you." Varro repeated Falco's words. "It's how every one of these missions ends."

"Varro, this mission is as dead as Pilatus. Let's find Curio and get out of here."

But Varro balled his fists.

"Not until I get what I came for, Falco. I'm going to the top of this hill and coming down with Lucian's head. I don't care what it takes."

24

Varro draped his chain shirt over a fallen log with a green cushion of moss. The links showed rust and mud, and the break in the shoulder had yet to be repaired. Restoring the shirt would take hours of skilled work. He would pay someone well to do it for him. Right now, he was so weary that even the thought of it tired him.

Beside this he set his harness that included his sword and pugio. A scuffed and dented helmet he was ashamed to call his own sat beside these.

"This is madness," Falco said then started coughing.

"You say that every time. What is not madness to you?"

Through his coughing, Falco's voice sounded squeaky and weak.

"I say it every time because you do something mad every time."

Varro looked up to the gathering darkness and the summit of the hill hidden behind brooding pine trees.

"This is the best way to get close to him." Varro straightened his tunic. The air was cooler here and goosebumps rose on his skin. "Curio said he believed in the men of Servus Capax. He wanted Curio to join him for that reason."

He held Curio's pugio and ran his thumb over the silver inlaid owl head.

"Well, maybe Curio did join him. Lucian didn't let him go, did he? So why will he do it for you?"

Varro held the pugio to his side. His hands flaked dried blood. He looked to Pilatus, whom they set in a peaceful position beneath a tree. They had tried to pull out the stakes, but they would not budge. Pilatus would carry the instruments of his death into the next life. Varro had set one of his citations for bravery on the dead centurion's chest. He had certainly earned it.

"One of us must stay back," Varro said. "You're too sick to do anything useful. So if I do not return, bring word back to Flamininus of what happened. He will work with Consul Cato to fund an expedition to this place and take our revenge."

"Normally, I'd call you mad but agree with you. But today, I just think you're mad. What's the plan, Varro? It can't just remain something you'll figure out later. You're a few hundred yards from Lucian now."

"I will get him to take me to the gods like he wanted to do for Curio. I won't swallow the poison but spit it out once he is incoherent. Then I will finish him, either with a weapon stolen while I'm there or my bare hands."

Falco's heavy brows drew together as he leaned back against the gray bark of a tree.

"The hole in that plan is big enough to fit two war elephants side by side. First, Lucian is too canny to let himself become drugged when you are not. Second, they'll probably have you restrained through the whole thing. Third, Curio talked about Lucian's warriors doing some sort of dance. You'll be surrounded. And finally, here's where those two elephants are standing. You can't carry the silver down on your own, even if you did kill Lucian and escaped his warriors. And we haven't gotten to Curio yet. Maybe he needs rescuing and you'll have to do that as well."

Varro nodded at the criticism, restraining his urge to interrupt. But Falco now rested his argument with folded arms.

"I agree with it all. But you're thinking like a rational man. Lucian is crafty but he's as mad as they come. He believes in his visions and his tribe feeds his madness. We talked about using his methods against him. I still plan to do so."

"That all hinged on Curio helping with the poison. We can't even count on him being alive now."

"He's alive." Varro looked once more to the hilltop, unwilling to let his eyes betray any doubt he held. "You see the growing darkness. The gods gather for a battle of wills. Curio has been their main weapon in all of this. If he were dead, the sky would be clear."

Falco squinted up at the glare. "The gods aren't watching us. Sure, they might for clashing armies, but not for two fools lost in the forest. If anything, they laugh at us. All I see when I look up is a gray sky and one man trying to convince himself his plan will work."

"I can't say if it will succeed. No one knows the outcome before a deed is attempted. But I will approach Lucian in defeat and humility and beg to join his cause. He will know I am the lone survivor of our group and trapped in Iberia. If I can gain even a fraction of his trust, there is an opening to exploit. Then his throat will be laid bare to me and I will not hesitate to strike. I will betray him as he betrayed Curio and his men, abuse his trust and twist his hopes to my ends."

Falco growled. "It could take months for that moment to come. By that time, the silver will be spent, Flamininus will tire of waiting for us, and I'll starve to death or become dinner for wolves."

"If I do not come down from the hill tomorrow, return to the camp and lead the sick back to the garrison with the map I left behind. Flamininus must be there by now. Report to him what happened. I'm certain he will get authorization to lead a column here and exterminate these Lusitani madmen. Cato will want his silver and his traitor returned to him."

Falco pushed off the tree, pleading with his palms out.

"That should be our plan. Go back for help then properly destroy Lucian."

But Varro shook his head before his friend could finish.

"Madness left unchecked grows in unpredictable ways. Maybe he will raise reinforcements with the stolen silver or relocate to somewhere we cannot follow. Besides, I'll remind you that Senator Flamininus is only helping us because we can deliver him an advantage over Cato. If he has to concede to Cato, then we will lose his support. We have to do this ourselves or all we have strived for will come to nothing."

"I'm not going to talk you out of this, am I?"

Varro answered by extending his pack to Falco.

"It contains the rest of my rations. Be alert for scouts or for animals drawn to the scent of Pilatus's blood."

"I'm not spending any more time with a corpse than I have to. When you go, then I'll relocate. I'll be wary for traps, don't worry. I'll return here to check for you in the morning. We will leave a sign if we miss each other. Good luck, Varro. I hope Curio is up there and able to help you."

"Don't try to learn my fate if I fail to return. Head back and bring reinforcements. If Curio and I don't make it out, at least you might have your name and life restored."

"Some good that will be with no family or friends left to spend it with."

"You have plenty of coin to buy more of both." Varro smiled and clapped Falco's shoulder. "We shall have victory, my friend. Believe in that."

He left Falco without turning back, still hearing his coughing even after moving deeper into the trees. Wearing only his torn and dirty tunic and carrying only Curio's pugio, he climbed the steep slope. After witnessing Pilatus's gruesome fate, he used a long branch to probe and sweep the way ahead. However, this side of the hill offered poor terrain for climbing and therefore made an unlikely approach for enemies. He expected the Lusitani to not bother with more traps. But he still moved with caution.

While his fever had abated, it still left him weak and the effort to extract Pilatus from the pit had exhausted him. It would at least enhance his look of utter defeat. He planned to throw himself at Lucian's mercy, and he expected it would be granted. Lucian was the kind of madman who believed in his own genius, and even if he planned to kill Varro he would still want to gloat. He would at least want to show Varro how he was misunderstood.

From his talks with Curio, Varro deduced Lucian still harbored a need for validation. He had forsaken Rome, but somehow still wanted her approval through Servus Capax. His dreams of including Curio in his plans seemed to confirm this, and his hateful cursing of him when denied spoke to his bruised ego. Any other madman would've either hunted him down or else killed him in the ambush. But Lucian wanted another of his fellows to join him in his misdeeds.

So Varro planned to dig at this wound somehow. It was why he carried Curio's pugio rather than his own. Lucian was still a legionary, proved by his ability to exist seamlessly in the legion. Therefore, he would know the details of a weapon enough to distinguish one from the other. Inexperienced civilians look at a sword and think they all look alike, but the veteran sees the war story etched in the blade.

The hill dictated his path upward, eventually circling him into the only viable approach to the summit. As expected, he found low stockade walls encircling the top, nothing like the mighty stone citadel of Lucian's mad dreams. The shaggy outlines of barbarians watched from behind it.

Varro drew a deep breath, mumbled a prayer to any god who would hear him, then stepped into the path that led to the primitive gates. He held up both hands in a universal sign for surrender. He had seen the barbarians use it themselves. The dark shapes at first did not appear to see him, but soon they were pointing and calling out.

The gate opened as Varro continued up the path, and four barbarians with spears lowered greeted him halfway up.

"Bring this to Lucian," Varro said, holding out the pugio in his open palms. "He will want to speak to me."

The barbarians were bare-chested and thin. Varro could see their ribs even in the flat light of the gray sky. Their eyes were yellow and wild, lost amid tangled beards and violent blue tattoos. He thought of Aulus and how he had the Servus Capax owl head tattooed on his face. But these men had covered themselves in sharp swirls like twisting javelins.

They laughed at his words and ringed him with the flashing leaf-shaped blades of their spears. Varro continued to hold the pugio forward.

"For Lucian," he repeated. He wondered if they knew him by that name. One foul-smelling barbarian snatched the dagger from his hand, then examined it as if he had no idea what it was. But he said something that caused his friends to laugh again.

A sharp pain jabbed his side, and he realized he was being herded inside the low walls. He kept both hands raised to the satisfaction of his captors, who walked beside him with their spears ready. The men at his sides carried them awkwardly, trying to point at him while moving forward. Varro could've easily disarmed them and broken out of the ring. But it was not his purpose.

Not yet.

The stockade walls were made of logs no bigger around than a man's arm, but the tops were sharpened to bright white points. Given any enemy would attack uphill, the walls were built to the minimum height needed to prevent anyone leaping over them. It was a frugal design and the right one for this hilltop. But as Varro passed beyond them, he could only think of how a Roman army would batter down these walls and enter as if they had not existed.

From the state of his captors and the wall defenses, Varro found the inner village as expected. Barbarian folk of every age and gender had come out of their dilapidated wooden hovels to stare in amazement. Their flesh was dark from working under the sun. The men were universally gaunt and wore their beards and hair unkempt and free. Their tunics were simple and surprised Varro with their general cleanliness. The women were the typically emboldened sort of the tribes, but wore long robes and covered their heads. Most children clutched their mothers, while others dared to come forward.

As his captors prodded him, they called out to all who gathered to the spectacle of a Roman prisoner. The boasting in their voices was unmistakable, even if the words were unintelligible to Varro's ears. Perhaps they told tales about a daring capture rather than his meek surrender. Those who heard it seemed gladdened, their wide eyes narrowing into smiles as Varro passed their homes.

The largest of the homes stood at the center of their village, where trees had been cleared away and the ground worn down to bare rock by the countless treading of feet. Several other large buildings clustered around these, and a white hearth fire smoke flowed up from them in gentle curls. Varro smelled roasting meat in the air, and his stomach growled in answer.

This drew raucous laughter from his captors, who jabbed him again as if to punish him for the insolence of being hungry. The bright pain pricked his back and sides, and he reconsidered grabbing the spear from one of them and carving a permanent smirk into their leering faces.

They stopped at the center of this barren clearing. The villagers were gathering now as news of his arrival spread. While Varro waited, he estimated maybe two to three hundred people lived atop this hill. He saw stables for horses and realized that Lucian had more warriors than workers here. So he truly needed silver to import skilled labor to build a dream city to rival Rome.

One of the gaunt men left his companions, taking Curio's pugio into the largest home. Varro straightened his back, knowing he would now come face to face with this traitor. Despite his situation, he was excited to at last face the man who had brought so much needless suffering to so many.

The wait extended until Varro felt forgotten. Even some of the villagers wandered back to their toils. He was not much of a spectacle standing amid his guards. One of them began to cough uncontrollably and Varro thought of Falco. He hoped his friend had not followed him and did as he asked. If anyone could escape this reckless plan, he could. At least one of them had to be made whole and return to Rome. But Falco was hard-headed, especially if he felt excluded from the action.

While he waited and his guards shooed flies that wove around them in a mad dance, Varro looked for Curio. He expected to find him tied to a post, locked in a cage, or even to find his severed head on display. But he found no signs of him.

The barbarian called out from the larger building where Lucian must rule his people. He waved for his companions to enter, and Varro felt the sharp spear tip brush against his back.

The inside of the house was dark and filled with cloying smoke that swirled around the rafters in search of the chimney opening. A large hearth threw smoke and heat and one sickly boy attended it. He wore no shirt and yellow light gleamed in his sweat. The whites of his eyes seemed brilliant against the dark background. Varro felt a chill despite the fire. A feeling of illness hung over this wide and dark room. It was a smell like his great-grandfather had given off in the days before his death. The thought of it summoned memories of his bright eyes and the veins sticking out of his neck.

Yet one of the barbarians shoved him forward and broke the reverie. All around were the litter of old meals, animal bones, and dirt built up into the corners of the packed-dirt floors. Hunting trophies and old weapons decorated the walls as Varro walked deeper into the hall.

Now at the back, his captors pointed to the darkness.

Lucian lay on a rough wood bed, naked though covered to his waist in a gray blanket. He wheezed through his nose and seemed to sleep. Yet he held Curio's pugio in both hands atop his chest. His face gleamed with fever and the dim hearth light reflected from his flesh.

"Centurion Lucian?"

Varro expected one of his brutish guards to strike him for his insolence. But they all stared down at their foreign leader, their brows furrowed in worry.

"You offer me the respect of a rank I no longer hold." Lucian's eyes remained closed. "Is it Centurion Varro or Falco who visits me today?"

"Varro. And I am no visitor. I'm your prisoner."

Lucian smiled, keeping his eyes closed, and chuckled.

"Never a prisoner. The men of Servus Capax are not restricted by chains or bars. We cannot be held for long, like a cat seized by the tail."

"Is Curio here? I am all that is left of the force sent to apprehend you."

"Curio?" Lucian kept his eyes closed, but now slowly rotated the pugio in his hands. "I grabbed his tail for a short time. My men brought him to me, just as they have done for you. But Curio vanished into the forest to be consumed by it. A shame to have traveled so far yet to have learned nothing."

"He escaped you, then?" Varro glanced at his captors and found them fixated on Lucian. Now he noticed more coughing from behind and realized these men might all have the same fever that had afflicted him and his own men.

Lucian nodded in answer to Varro's question.

"I offered him a chance once, but he spurned it. I thought his return to me was the will of Bandua. But it was not so. I granted him freedom and he chose to abuse it once more. He belongs to the forest now and his spirit must forever be bound to it. He cannot leave Iberia, just as I cannot."

With that statement, Lucian's eyes flicked open. They were glassy, with yellowish whites and a red rim surrounding them. They sank into his sockets, making what must have once been a roguishly handsome man look like a specter of madness.

"I have no power to bring you back, Centurion Lucian. I am but one man. This land and its gods have claimed all my men, and your warriors have claimed the other Romans sent to arrest you."

"Arrest me?" Lucian closed his mad eyes again and turned his head back to face the ceiling. "They came to make war, to destroy what cannot be destroyed, and to see what their eyes were incapable of seeing. So I joined them with the forest. You've seen them, then?"

"I saw crow-eaten heads thick with flies and blood. I assumed these were Barbatus and his soldiers."

"Now I know the name of the fool who dared bring his sword onto this sacred hill. Thank you. But you carried no weapon, nor did Curio. Instead, you bring me the gift of an old blade, one carrying the mark of our brotherhood."

Lucian ran his thumb over the silver-inlaid owl's head on the pommel. He remained with his eyes closed, but his brows drew together as if he savored the taste of fine wine.

"Do you still believe you serve, Centurion Lucian?"

Now Lucian's eyes flicked open again, but he looked at no one and indeed seemed to stare into another place.

"I serve, but not a foolish organization of small men. Instead, I serve Bandua, who showed me a vision and granted me a tribe to create that vision. But now he has withdrawn his touch and he speaks to me no more. Indeed, none of the tribe hear his voice in the storm or feel his pulse on the battlefield. We grow weak and dreaming. But Bandua's vision remains and someone must bring it to life."

"You and your tribe are ill. This illness killed most of my men, and I suspect some of Barbatus's as well. I nearly died from it myself."

Lucian continued to stare into a vaporous world.

"But you lived. And here you come to this hill, as I did long ago. No one left to support him, an outcast from his own city. A city he served with the sacrifice of his own blood and bone. He comes carrying a single dagger and a single desire to live in spite of everything arrayed against him. Then, when it seems all must be lost, Bandua finds him and proclaims him a champion of his visions."

Varro narrowed his eyes in confusion. "Do you speak of yourself? Is this why you deserted?"

Turning his head to face Varro again, he gave a feeble smile.

"Speak no more of me. You must take my place. This is Bandua's work. I was mistaken about Curio. In fact, you are Bandua's chosen. And you will remain here to carry on when I am gone. So shall the god's will be fulfilled and so shall you gain what you have journeyed so long to find."

Shaking his head, Varro replied, "I came to bring you back. And I will, even if only your plague-ridden head."

Now Lucian gave a gusty laugh, coughed, then cleared his throat. His chest sounded as if he were drowning in phlegm.

"That is what you believe you came seeking. But you seek something else, Centurion Varro. You came to find the true meaning of your life. And so you have. Now, you will go before Bandua and confirm it. Forget Curio, Servus Capax, and Rome. You have found your new home and your call to greatness."

25

Varro stood before the roaring blaze of the bonfire at the center of the village. The heat tightened the skin on his exposed flesh. The twilight sky enhanced the brilliance of the flames, obliterating the starless sky with an orange halo. As he looked upward, gentle and cold rain dotted his face. While the sky had threatened foul weather all day, Varro could not smell rain in the air. Instead, the bonfire smoke filled his nostrils with scents of burning wood.

He had spent the remainder of the day as Lucian's so-called guest, though Lucian himself slept. He had been fed a meager soup of vegetables and gristly goat meat. Guards hovered around him, as they did now. Varro discovered the freedom Lucian offered was limited to a few steps in any direction before someone lowered a spear at him.

Commoners ringed the bonfire in a wide circle. But Lucian's one hundred warriors formed the inner ring around Varro. They were naked to their waists and covered in blue tattoos. All were in various states of health and their torsos shined with sweat.

More than being sick, these warriors seemed wavering and

unstable, as if they were drunk. But Lucian admitted to having limited wine at the feast held while the bonfire was stoked. They drank and ate only minimal amounts for what was termed a feast. Though Varro had been seated beside Lucian for it, they offered him nothing.

Lucian, who seemed on the verge of death, smiled through a feeble apology. "You will see Bandua's visions clearer when you are not burdened with a full stomach."

At the conclusion of the most somber and austere feast Varro had ever witnessed, Lucian and his top guards led him to this bonfire.

"In its flames, you will see visions," he explained. "You will go to the realm of the gods and you will be shown many things. When you return, you will explain what you have seen and my shaman will confirm or deny you as my inheritor."

Lucian indicated a startlingly young man as his shaman. He stood with the other warriors surrounding their master, but his tattoos appeared even more chaotic than the rest. A necklace of polished stones and animal bones hung from his neck. He seemed to understand Lucian had spoken of him and inclined his head.

"If I'm denied, what then?"

With a weak pat on Varro's shoulder, Lucian started to laugh but it devolved into coughing. In the end, he waved off Varro's concern without an answer. It seemed to him that Lucian and his boy shaman had already made up their minds about what the gods would show him.

Lucian gestured to his shaman, who then began to call the audience to attention. The mild hum of animated conversation around the bonfire hushed while the shaman and Lucian waited.

While the shaman began to speak, Varro searched for his opportunity. Falco's words echoed through his memory and he realized he had achieved nothing this night. He would undergo whatever ceremony Lucian planned and then likely be too impaired to do more. At least he had gotten aside his enemy, who seemed to have resigned himself to his death. Varro figured if he assumed leadership of this tribe, he could at least preserve the stolen silver from being spent while Falco returned with help.

But he also expected being a newly made leader of a tribe of madmen would afford him even less freedom than if he were held in a cage.

While the shaman chanted and everyone, Lucian included, repeated the strange words, Varro looked for Curio. If he had escaped, he would not have gone far. He had proved he could survive the wilds of Iberia on his own. So Varro knew the bonfire and loud chanting would draw him close. But he saw no sign of his friend anywhere. Of course, the bonfire consumed half of his field of vision. Maybe he hid opposite of it.

At the end of the long incantation, the shaman called out and the circle of warriors parted. Two men entered carrying a black iron pot with poles. The soup within the pot steamed as the bearers set it down and then withdrew the poles. Varro smelled the reek of mold or something equally vile.

"You will drink the sacred brew," Lucian said. "Just as I did when I came to this hill years ago. We shall all share the drink and travel to the god lands together."

Varro saw scores of weapons on the hips of the warriors surrounding him. But not a single one could be captured without the direct intervention of Fortuna herself. Lucian had put away Curio's pugio rather than carry it as Varro had hoped. He understood capturing a weapon was idle fantasy, for even if armed in full gear he would not escape the ring of warriors alive. They had only to push him into the fire with their overwhelming numbers.

So he watched helplessly as the warriors drank from a wooden cup filled with the stinking brew. The shaman had an assistant, also a boy, who ladled out the drink. With a hundred men to imbibe the soup, Varro wondered if the bonfire would burn down before the ceremony began.

Now the commoners began to chant, their voices an eerie and shrill cry into the starless sky. They moved in a circle now, a slow turning like a heavy millstone. Perhaps they had all fallen under the shaman's spell, for they seemed as entranced as the warriors. Yet only a handful of men had drunk the brew. Varro wondered at how they could be so affected.

Then he realized Curio had been at work.

Just as they had planned, he must have slipped Lucian's mystical poison into the food or water supplies. Everyone moved with a strange slowness as if their feet stuck to the hard-packed earth. If the warriors drank it to excess, then they might truly be rendered helpless.

A hopeful brightness filled Varro's thoughts. Even though unseen, Curio was near and working their plan. He only had to do his part.

Now Lucian accepted something directly from his shaman. Steam flowed over his trembling hands as he carefully brought it up for Varro to see against the yellow fire.

"Here is your draught. Drink deeply, then look into the fire. You will see the path to the god lands open for you."

Cupped in both hands was a skull with the crown removed. A bowl must have filled the cranium, for within it a murky green soup shimmered with the yellow light of the bonfire.

"Curio said this is your wife's head."

Lucian gave a deep nod.

"She gave herself completely to Bandua. She was the best of our tribe, the most beautiful and wise of all the women. After her sacrifice, she gifted me her skull so that she could forever guide me to Bandua's world. I see her there sometimes, forever young and beautiful."

"Then you will leave me your skull for the same purpose?"

Lucian's jaundiced eyes narrowed at him.

"Do not make light of this solemn moment. Drink from the skull and look into the fire. My warriors will keep you from falling into it."

He proffered the skull under Varro's nose, and the rank odor made him gag. This brought a twinkle to Lucian's dull eyes, but he continued to hold it forward.

When he recovered, Varro once more looked about the circle. The villagers moved in a sluggish circle, chanting to draw the attention of their vile gods. The warriors drank from the iron pot, each in turn. Those who had already consumed the concoction now formed a new line and began a slow pantomime of combat, moving slowly through hurling javelins or raising shields to block imitations of sword strikes. It was too bizarre to watch.

"Drink, Centurion Varro." Lucian pushed the skull closer. "Once you visit the god lands, you will never want to leave. Drink. Come home."

The skull slipped into his hands, and Varro stared down into the muddy fluid. Streamers of steam still flowed off the cup rim, twirling about his hand as if enticing him to drink. Yet the smell of it made him want to dump the fluid and run.

Yet Lucian, his shaman, and his best warriors surrounded him and stared with hopeful expectation. Varro had no choice but to drink and hope the poison disabled the warriors enough that he could take some action. If he killed Lucian this tribe would fall apart. He could reclaim the stolen silver with Curio's help.

He tipped the bitter fluid into his mouth. It was gritty and tasted as bitterly vile as it smelled. A hint of mushrooms bloomed on his tongue along with a dozen other tastes he could only call disgusting. He held the drink in, despite the horrific flavor. But even without swallowing, he was hit with a mild swoon as if he had stood up too fast.

"Swallow it," Lucian said. His voice lost the gentle dreaminess and gained a centurion's edge. "I see your thin plan. You think if you do not swallow, then we shall all go to the god lands before you. Then you will escape. It's a fool's thought. The gods are calling you now, and you cannot escape. Swallow!"

With that, Lucian tapped Varro's throat hard enough that he was forced to swallow. Satisfied, Lucian took both of Varro's hands and raised the skull back to his lips.

"Drink it all."

With each gulp of the soup, it became more tasteless. It was warm and it flowed down his neck to pool in the well of his collarbone. He tried to spill as much as possible to minimize its effect. But he consumed enough to satisfy Lucian, who stood back with a gentle smile.

"Look into the fire."

Hands gripped him as Lucian stepped aside and Varro gazed into the fire. At first, it was nothing but flames twisting on dark logs. But his head began to swim and the flames twirled and spun in ways unnatural to fire.

He was aware of a sinking feeling and the fading of a distant, malign chant.

Then he awakened.

The walls of Sparta enveloped him. He stood shoulder to shoulder with Falco and Curio. They were marching through the stone paved streets, their hobnails and the hobnails of their full century clacked brightly against the din of battle around them.

Centurion Drusus, his big bear-shaped shadow, led their charge.

"We'll break them, boys! Come on! For Rome!"

Falco and Curio both shouted in response, as did the entire century of hastati surrounding them. So Varro joined in, braced his gladius against his shield, and plunged ahead down the narrow and empty streets.

Fire and smoke rose out of other alleys and roads, but their path ahead remained clear. He could not tell what they charged at, but Centurion Drusus was as enraged as Varro had ever seen him.

"We'll cut out their livers and have them for dinner! Charge!"

Varro screamed his war cry and the entire front rank occupied the breadth of the street. Now their enemy came into focus.

A full phalanx of Macedonian pikemen blocked the way ahead. Their long white pikes bristled from behind the shields of the front ranks. Yet Drusus led the charge heedless of the danger.

No one else cared for the danger, either. Both Curio and Falco screamed their war cries. The entire century was rabid to reach the fight, and so Varro flowed along with them.

The Macedonians slammed their shields to the pavement and stamped their feet in reply. It might turn another man's stomach to water, but not Varro's. Now he was primed for a fight.

The Romans crashed headlong into the pikes. One plowed through Centurion Drusus's face to burst out the back of his skull, spilling his brains over his pack. But it did not slow his attack and his voice rose above the clash even though his jaw hung by a single sinew.

"Press them, boys! We'll stomp them into bloody muck!"

Varro lifted his scutum and deflected the pike stabbing for him. He pushed into the thick ranks as easily as Drusus had promised. He seemed a madman, fighting with his helmet lost and his skull opened to the night sky.

Falco delighted in the slaughter. "We were born for this! The battle where we belong!"

Varro could not deny it. He pushed through the masses of enemies as if they were mere phantoms. Wherever his gladius struck he found exposed flesh. His hand returned to the striking position hot with fresh blood. The Macedonians were nothing more than faceless bodies that crumpled before him.

He stepped across the corpses and puddles of blood as he killed his way through the press. His vision narrowed to just the carnage before him. So that his sight filled with flailing bodies and splashes of gore as he trampled down the Macedonian line. Behind his mighty shield, he became impervious to enemy attacks. The pikes slipped around him as he drove forward.

Before his arm tired, he stepped out of the fray. He turned around and found a horrific sight.

Piled up in the crossroads of dark streets that flickered with distant orange fire were hundreds of bodies. Romans and Macedonians were jumbled together as if they had all been swept into the hand of a titan and crushed before being dropped into the street.

"Falco? Curio?"

Varro's voice echoed through the strange emptiness. The battle here was over, both sides annihilating each other in a crescendo of crazed violence. Bloodless flesh seemed to glow in the pile of armor and shields, and red rivulets flowed away between the stone pavers.

He approached the pile of bodies stacked over his head. Searching around the edges, he found bodies and parts of bodies that he did not recognize. At last, he found Falco. He had a violent gash across his throat and his tongue had fallen through it. His dead eyes seemed to stare into Varro's and he had to turn away.

Beside him lay Curio. Half of his face had been peeled back to reveal bloody teeth and a vacant eye socket. His remaining eye was wide with horror and a point of yellow light reflected from the fires raging elsewhere in Sparta.

"They're all dead."

It was Centurion Drusus's rough voice that spoke. Varro whirled to find the heavy lump of his body lying in the street, somehow outside the pile of bleeding corpses. He rushed to his old centurion and knelt by his side. His shattered head turned to face him, though the ghastly sight did not bother Varro.

"Sir, you are dead. You've been dead a long time now."

"How long?" Drusus spoke regardless of his unhinged jaw. It

moved, and a molar tumbled out of it to plop in the blood pool beneath the remnants of his head.

"Maybe six years, sir. I've lost count."

"You're too young to lose count. That's for old men. You're all we have now, lad. Take the fight forward. Don't stand and cry over the dead. You've killed them, and there's nothing that can change it now."

Varro looked back at the impossible mountain of corpses.

"I didn't kill all of them. Not Falco and Curio."

"Of course you did. You've forgotten your promise. Denying it won't change a thing. You brought us here to die, and so we have. Now, don't make it for nothing. Keep going. The enemy is just ahead and you must defeat him or I'll have you on a charge. Now, go!"

"Who are we fighting, sir? Sparta has already been defeated."

But Drusus no longer spoke. His eyes shimmered in black sockets and blood and fluid dripped from his broken face through the hole in the back of his head. The revulsion Varro had been spared now flooded into him. He turned aside and then stood.

Varro had a vague idea of an enemy. But as he stood in the blood-darkened streets of burning Sparta, he could not recall who it was. He understood a battle raged beyond his sight in other streets and alleys. He could hear the screaming and the crash of weapons. Somehow, he also knew he could never join those battles and that every street would turn on itself in an endless, empty loop. He would never escape by going back. He had to go forward as Drusus had urged him.

So he hefted his scutum and wicked the blood from his gladius, then marched forward into the shadow-shrouded street ahead of him.

His hobnails chimed as the only sound. Just enough light shined from some unspecific source to show him the way. Every door and window was barred and shuttered. He understood nothing was behind them. It was not where the enemy awaited him. That was at the end of this street.

It spilled out into a forest clearing. Ancient trees crowded him, their branches entangled overhead. Smoke rolled between them, drawing his attention to huge gouts of flame that rose in the distance. The brilliant orange haze of a forest fire danced between the black outlines of these trees. Varro felt its overwhelming heat on his face.

But his eyes were swept up to his enemy.

An Iberian warrior towered over the trees. He was a titan standing with flames lapping at his waist. He folded strong arms over a tattooed chest. His hair was long and wild, and his beard was drawn together with a golden ring at the end. He stared down at Varro, his eyes bright with the raging fire around him.

"Who are you to enter the god lands? A foreigner. A murderer. The burner of forest trees and forest friends. Answer or I shall crush you now."

The voice bludgeoned Varro backward. He looked behind to find nothing but an impenetrably black forest. With no escape, just as Centurion Drusus had ordered him, Varro straightened his back and prepared to face his enemy.

"I was sent here. It's not my choice."

The titan's laughter boomed such that the treetops bent. Yet it abruptly ended, and he drew a sword of flames that he pointed at Varro.

"You stand before Bandua, lord of war and protector of the land. Have you no humility? Do you refuse to kneel?"

"I am a Roman. I kneel before no gods other than my own."

Again, Bandua laughed and his sword of flames brightened.

"Then so I condemn you, Roman. By fire and sword, you live. By oath and honor, you die. Go back, Roman. Go back and suffer what you have earned in life. The god lands reject you and offer you no peace. Can you not see what you brought here? Fire and blood. And so to fire and blood, I return you."

Bandua swung his sword in an arc of blinding flames. Though he must have stood a mile away, the fire nonetheless splashed down to Varro. He threw his arms up to protect his face just as the intense heat engulfed him.

"Varro! Are you with me?"

It was Falco's voice.

His eyes wrenched open, and a wavering vision of Falco's concerned face hung over his. Other familiar faces hovered behind him, all peering down and all painted with a violent stripe of orange light on their right sides.

"His eyes are unfocused, sir." One of the men pointed down at him.

"He's alive," Falco said. "Get him up, and let's go."

Varro felt himself floating up and thought he might shoot into the sky, where Bandua no longer stood. In fact, he felt conflicting sensations of cool and heat as if the forest still burned in places.

Falco again appeared in his vision.

"You were not supposed to drink it, but they forced you. See why I said your idea was total shit?"

"What's happening?" Varro felt as if his mind had been plunged into a vat of tar. "Where is Bandua? How are you still alive?"

"We'll answer that later. We've got to go before our friends decide they're no longer our friends."

Falco looked down. "Take that one too. We at least need his head even if we can't take the silver back."

Coughing interrupted the rest of Falco's words, and he just shook his head. Varro noted now that his face was spattered with blood.

"Is Curio here?"

"Fuck all if I know where he is." Falco cleared his throat.

"We're in the middle of a battle. Save the chatter for when we're safe. Let's go."

Memories were all clamoring to return to Varro's consciousness. His feet dragged along the ground, but he found himself capable of walking. In fact, with every step forward the staggering confusion that bound him faded. His mind was returning from the strange dreams he had experienced.

Now he saw a real battle all around.

More properly, he witnessed mass murder. Tribesmen attacked tribesmen in a mad frenzy. He could not tell if these were Lucian's warriors or others, or both. Yet even the commoners fought. They all had weapons of some sort, from clubs to axes to swords. Some even clawed at each other's faces with bare hands.

Everywhere bodies lay in bloody clumps, locked together as if all had struck the fatal blow in the same instant. Falco jogged ahead and paused to engage a wildman who died in one stroke, such was his heedlessness.

Falco pulled his sword from the enemy's belly, then checked behind.

"You're walking? Good! Now start running. Our little alliance is ending and I don't want us to be here when it does."

26

All around Varro, Iberians slaughtered each other. The effects of Lucian's brew were swiftly diminishing and his wits returning. It seemed the magic that had caused him to witness so many odd things vanished as swiftly as it had taken effect. He tripped along with two men supporting him and realized these were his own men who had been left behind as too sick for action.

"I can manage," he said, pushing out of their arms.

Fire blazed through the village and horses cried out in terror and rage. Some warriors had mounted up and now fought from horseback. But their horses were not accustomed to the press of fighting men, and when their mounts reared in fear, eager spears knocked them off to be attacked on the ground.

As Varro staggered forward, not as steady without aid as he had hoped, he saw two more of his men running with Lucian dragging limp between them. His head hung forward and blood drizzled from his open mouth.

"What's happening?"

Falco stopped and then faced him. "You can't see? We've got barbarians to kill barbarians. I'll explain the details later. We ran into the tribe that had attacked Barbatus. They came looking for revenge on the mad Lusitani. So we managed to come to a deal to reclaim this hill for their tribe. Remember what that old fucker we captured said? Well, here is the result. Now let's go before we're chopped up like the rest."

A cloud of confusion still swirled around Varro, but he did remember the skeletal old man saying his tribe had once called this hill their own and had leaders who hoped to reclaim it. But none had been brave enough. Now, for reasons Falco would hopefully explain, they had come to do so at Lucian's weakest moment.

He looked to the centurion dangling between his two bearers. All of Falco's men were red-faced and winded, and even desperate to escape they seemed to welcome the pause.

"Is Lucian dead?"

Falco shook his head. "Seems like it. He was already covered in blood when we found you. Everyone around him was cut up like they were being prepared for soup, except for the two of you. So I suppose he's dead enough for our needs. Good thing no one thought to cut your neck, eh? Now let's go."

"We can't. We don't have the silver."

"And we can't carry it along with you and Lucian. Are you seeing this madness? We can't stay here."

Falco ranged his sword around them and Varro followed. People ran everywhere, mixed with fleeing horses and panicked goats and chickens. At every turn, someone new fell beneath the blows of a club or a sword. Flames from burning homes framed their agonies in bright light. Varro saw a young girl pierced through her stomach with a spear and realized there was no stemming this bloodlust until all enemies perished.

"Fire and blood," Varro repeated under his breath. But the

effects of Lucian's brew faded every moment, bringing him back from the questionable reality of the god lands and reality.

"Right," Falco agreed. "We're not adding our own to the lake of blood already spilled tonight. Now let's go."

"The silver is in that building," Varro said, pointing to the hall where Lucian had made his home. "It's not yet aflame. We must claim it and carry it out."

"A whole treasury pay box?" Falco whirled on him. "No. I'm in command while your eyes are still crossed. I'll drop you here and leave without you. Lucian's corpse is good enough. And when we have a moment to cut off Lucian's head, we'll be traveling light."

"It's not about command." Varro looked to the seven men who stood in a protective circle. Their crouched bodies were outlined in the light of flames blazing throughout the village. They were prepared to fight but their eyes reflected fear.

"When is it not?" Falco grabbed Varro and pulled him by the tunic. "March with us or be a fool. Not like I don't know which you'll choose."

Falco released him and then started away toward the collapsed walls of the village. The soldiers followed him, dragging Lucian along, and shooting confused and panicked looks at Varro.

"We've done what we can, sir," one said as he passed. "We're tired and ill. Let's escape while we're able."

Thus far, the Iberians were happy to murder each other and settle a generation of grudges. But as Falco noted, their fury would likely carry over to them no matter what agreement had been made. Varro watched them jogging as fast as they could with Lucian's corpse.

But Cato did not want a dead body. He would not have to explain Lucian to the Senate, but he would have to explain a missing pay box. Falco was carrying away the least valuable part of the prize, and leaving the real rewards behind. Without the silver to give to Cato, Flamininus would not have the leverage he desired and Cato would still suffer an embarrassment. No one would care what Varro and all the others had suffered to bring back Lucian.

"I'll get it myself," he shouted after Falco and the others. "Without it, you return in disgrace. You'll end up wishing you had died instead."

But the din of battle and the roar of flames seemed to have drowned out his threat, for none of them turned back.

Burning now with rage at Falco's betrayal, he turned back into the fray.

He dodged between combatants, carrying no weapons other than his freshly revived wits. He paused to pick a short sword from a fallen warrior. It was good in his hands but weighted differently from his accustomed gladius. But he held it forward and warded off attacks from lesser armed men and women.

Passing scenes of brutality and carnage, he arrived at Lucian's great hall. The fighting had concentrated in the open areas where Lusitani warriors thought to bring their cavalry to bear on their enemies. But this strategy had failed, and men fled in every direction including this hall.

Fire had also reached the west wall of this structure, and Varro realized he had no time to claim the silver. So he burst inside.

And nearly impaled himself on the spear ranged against him.

Five Iberians, either Lucian's or others, guarded the entrance against invaders. Varro deftly slipped aside, against them all, and into the hall. He had wanted to slide outside but now found himself leaping away behind long tables as the tribesmen sought to catch him.

His head was dizzy and his feet still unstable. Fortunately, these bony men seemed to be Lucian's warriors and were equally unbalanced.

He shoved a bench at two, who should've easily kicked it aside but instead toppled onto the floor. He then leaped up on a table and ran its length while the three others followed him.

At the table's end, he jumped to the ground, shoving the table back in the way of the three men. Their spears had range, and one jabbed Varro in the shoulder. Blood and burning pain flashed and he shouted out, delighting his pursuers.

There was another door, but flames already licked its frame. The Iberians seemed to understand they had cornered him.

But new enemies burst through the doorway they had previously guarded. When they turned back to the shouting of the new arrivals, Varro struck.

His sword cut a deep gash into one warrior's sword arm, causing him to drop his weapon. Without delay, he slashed aside and cut open the cheek of the other beside the first. But he continued through, and his sword slammed into a wooden pole.

It stuck long enough that Varro had to leave it and retreat from the spears jabbing for him. The newly arrived enemies now pulled attackers off of him, and he backed up.

But still heady from Lucian's brew, he suddenly toppled to his back.

The wild-haired warrior whose arm had been cut now lunged at him. He seized Varro by his throat, and despite his frail appearance, began to choke him in an iron grip.

The Iberian's yellow teeth clenched and his rheumy eyes flashed as he growled and throttled Varro.

But Varro had both hands free. He slapped them to the Iberian's face and began to clap around searching for his eyes. Even as his throat closed and head throbbed, he worked his thumbs into the madman's eyes and pressed.

He pressed long past the time a normal man would've cried out. The throttling continued, and the Iberian hung on like a hunting dog locked onto its prey. With renewed force, Varro pressed and felt one eyeball slip beneath his thumb.

At last, the Iberian fell back with a scream and Varro rolled over, gasping.

A vicious fight swirled over his head. Cries of pain and shock, curses, and bodies thudding to the floor sounded in his ears. But his vision had turned white from the throttling. He wanted to escape, but between his weakness after being ill and Lucian's brew, he had no strength to do it. He lay still, his head spinning.

"Get up."

Falco grabbed him by his arm and then hissed at his wounded shoulder.

"That's bleeding a lot. We've got to bandage it."

"It's a scratch," Varro said, smiling at the old soldier's joke. He sat up with Falco's aid, finding eleven dead Iberians draped over the disarrayed benches and tables. All of Falco's men rested on their knees, though some dripped bright blood from new wounds.

Now on his feet, he smiled at Falco, mocking his earlier statement. "Like I didn't you'd follow me."

Falco's heavy brows drew together. "One day I'll mean it, and you'll be sorry. The building is on fire, I'll remind you. Where's the silver? They're still killing babies out there, but soon it'll be our turn to face those blades."

Varro steadied himself and saw flames now brightening the far door and smoke crawled along the ceiling. He and Falco searched the other rooms at the rear of the hall. Varro discovered three heavy leather bags in one and his heart flipped.

"It's here, Falco! We have it!"

While Falco came from the other room, Varro tore open the bags to reveal the hard edges of newly minted Roman coins.

"Great," Falco said, looking over his shoulder. "I left Lucian's body at the edge of the village. Let's go take his head and be away with all of it."

Falco took up one bag and two of the strongest other soldiers carried the others. Varro and the rest encircled them as they fled the building.

Now that the battle had devolved from fighting to looting, at a glance they might appear no different than any other looter. All of them had to abandon their shields to carry their burdens. Besides their featherless helmets, nothing distinguished them as Roman. Some challenged them as they fled under the weight of their prize, but then the barbarians were distracted by other things. The chaos aided Varro's escape beyond the walls that had been torn down.

"Our barbarian allies just threw themselves on it," Falco said as Varro admired the destruction. "They were full of fight and probably so scared to come here that they went mad. The walls were like a pile of sticks to them."

Lucian's village blazed with fire, staining the clouds above with a lurid illumination. Few wails of anguish reached Varro's ears, and instead he heard the jubilation of the invaders.

Falco shook at the sound.

"They had a few who could speak some Latin, former slaves and whatnot. Between them, I was able to beg for our lives."

"They had you caught?"

"Just rode up to our camp about an hour after I returned." Falco wiped his brow and set down the heavy bag. "Shit, am I going to huff like this all the way back? Anyway, I wasn't going to follow your stupid plan. So I was going to take the men up here anyway. I convinced the Iberians that we had already weakened the Lusitani and that I could show them the way free of traps. We made a deal to fight a common enemy, as long as I could take you, Curio, and Lucian back. They could have everything else."

"Including the silver?" Varro settled onto a low stone, as did the rest of the men. They were still in danger, but all were exhausted. "It would've been a mistake to let them have it."

Falco gave a weak smile. "How stupid am I, Lily? I didn't tell them there was a fortune in Roman coins waiting for them up here. They'll only find out about it if they left anyone alive to tell them. From all the baby killing I saw tonight, my guess is they'll never find out."

One of the men sniggered at Falco's insulting term for Varro, which was supposed to never be used in front of others. But both were too tired to be angered or to apologize.

"Where's Lucian's corpse?" Varro asked. "We've got the time to cut off his head. We'll put it in one of the coin bags. I'm sure Cato won't mind blood and rotted flesh on his precious silver."

"He's right there," Falco pointed to a body resting against a tree. "You can have the honor of sawing through his neck. That's too much work for me."

But the moment Varro saw the shadow, he realized it was not Lucian. He leaped up from the rock and peered at the corpse.

"Remember how Curio told us Lucian knew how to fake his death and come back as another person?"

Falco groaned, then he and the others stood beside Varro.

All of them looked down on a young man with his neck cut. He wore a confused expression made stranger for the dancing light cast from the burning village. It was one of Lucian's boy shaman's assistants.

"Fuck, this is exactly where I left him." Falco knelt beside the body.

Varro did as well. He found the empty dagger sheath at his side and guessed what had happened.

"Lucian was just waiting for his moment to escape. As soon as you left him, he was on the move. But one of his boys had found him, and rather than leave any trace of himself behind, he grabbed the boy's dagger and cut his throat. Lucian is moving on to a new life."

Falco blew out a long sigh. "We're never going to find him now. Well, you said the silver was the more important thing. So we have that, at least. Flamininus will have to settle for it, or else properly outfit us to go on a new search for the bastard."

Varro stood up and looked out over the dark forest.

He smiled.

Lucian would never have a chance to start a new life, and he knew why.

27

———————

Curio slid beneath the jumble of fallen logs as his pursuers dashed past him. He pressed to the damp earth, its mineral scents filling his nose. The thump of their footfalls faded away as vague reverberations reaching his ear through the ground. When he was certain they were gone, he slipped out of hiding.

Days before he had again escaped Lucian. Perhaps because he was in his homeland or because he was clearly ill, he had not given enough attention to guarding Curio. Whatever the cause, Curio was glad to once more be free. When he had come into the village snared in a net, he expected a swift death. Now he was in the foothills again, this time alert for traps and deadfalls set by Lucian's men.

The night was dark and clouds hid the stars and moon. He had come to end things with Lucian and free himself of his curse. But the time had not been right for it. Somehow, he sensed that time now drew closer.

Varro and Falco would follow him and discover the slaughter of Barbatus and his men. He knew neither of them would be deterred. Between Varro's stubborn dedication to his mission and Falco's unwavering support of the man he idolized, they would climb the hill and meet Lucian on his own territory.

So Curio had done as Varro planned. He had slipped back over the low walls of Lucian's village and stolen his poison. The boys who comprised his priesthood were selected for their appeal to Lucian rather than competence. It had been a simple matter to access their poisons. Lucian may have supervised their creation, but he had not thought to guard against theft. Perhaps it was not a concern in the village.

Now that he had laced all the wine with what he hoped would be mild amounts of the poison, he had set the stage for Varro's plan. Lucian had planned a feast for Curio before he escaped. That same feast would be held when Varro surrendered himself to the same fate. Then they would drink even more of the poison than they could handle, and hopefully be rendered as ill as the treasury guards had been.

After returning unseen to the foothills, he waited for signs of Varro's arrival. It took longer than he expected, but when the bonfire was set and the voices began to chant, Curio climbed the hill once more.

Varro was there, but not Falco, who was likely bringing reinforcements. He watched from the darkness at the edge of the village. All had gathered to proclaim Varro as Lucian's inheritor. Strange how flexible Bandua was about his earthly representative, he thought. Just a few days ago that was to be Curio's role. In Lucian's mad plans, he somehow needed a Roman to lead these Lusitani. He was certain to die, either from his illness or overuse of the brew he drank to speak to his gods. By his own admission, after each time he went to the god lands he returned more tired and confused than before.

"My time is near," he had said. "And Bandua has sent you to me so that his great plans may continue."

Varro must have been told something similar.

So he watched for the battle to begin. As planned, Falco arrived but brought other Iberians with him. Curio knew better than to stay for this. So he hovered at the edges of battle and watched over the prone bodies of Falco and Lucian as long as he could. Lucian's priests and bodyguards had given their lives to defend them. Fortunately, the enemy Iberians did not realize the two of them were still alive. Curio planned to hold out until Falco could reach him.

But then he was driven off when a knot of warriors flushed him out of hiding. These were Lucian's men, and they had driven him back over the wall and into the trees. He carried only the recovered pugio he had lost when snared in the net. So he did not want to face better armed and armored men.

When the mad battle was over, he found Falco and the rest of his squad carrying away Lucian and Varro. Varro was speaking but Lucian hung like a dead man.

Curio snorted at this. Lucian had admitted to playing dead and it seemed just the sort of trick he'd use to escape his fate. Curio had never seen him take a blow during the whole time. If Varro survived, then so did Lucian.

He watched from the darkness when Falco deposited his burden to return to Varro, who had run back to the battle for some reason.

Now Curio stood and made for Lucian, who had already sat up from where Falco had dropped him.

Then three men rushed at him, spears pointed for his heart. Curio had fled, and his pursuers kept close contact. They called out for blood, but Curio led them down the hill and through the traps that had recently snared him. Yet they knew the land as well, avoiding their own snares and pressing the chase. Only Curio's desperate speed and diminutive size kept him ahead.

Then he ducked beneath the log and lost his pursuers. Now he stood alone, listening to the cries of victory and watching the flames brighten the sky above. Somewhere beneath it all, Lucian crawled like a worm in a final bid to escape his fate.

Curio considered where Lucian would flee. He could not go across his village again, but he could not return this way either. Falco had come with his barbarian allies from this direction. So he guessed Lucian would cut around the base of the hill, then flee north into the deeper forest. For a man resigned to death, he fought hard to survive.

With his decision made, Curio raced along the base of the foothill, then climbed into the night-shrouded trees in search of Lucian. The faint light from the blazes atop the hill did not penetrate here. It meant both he and Lucian had to proceed slowly.

Yet it did not take long to catch him.

Lucian hung from a net that had snared him. He twirled from a heavy branch as he struggled. Curio arrived beneath him.

"This is what you get when you have others to do your work. You don't know where your own snares are set."

"Curio, is that you? Thank the gods you have come! Cut me down."

"Of course I will," he said. He hoped to sound neutral, but Lucian suddenly went still.

"Wait, what do you intend after cutting me down? I am ill and cannot defend myself. I've come back from the god lands, you know. It leaves me weak. You have more honor than to murder a defenseless man."

"You'll find out my intentions soon enough."

The ball of Lucian in the net twisted gently while Curio sought the tie-off among the trees.

"When I went to Bandua, he promised to send me aid. And here you are! As it always has been, Curio. You are the best of all your companions. You are smarter and swifter than both. How lucky am I to count you as an ally."

"Ally? Because Bandua has said so?"

"Of course!" Lucian's net shook as he spoke. "Bandua has always guided me to you. From the start. And look at what we were so close to achieving. We can still achieve even more."

Curio found the tie-off pulled tight with Lucian's weight.

"What can you achieve? You are dying and your people are slaughtered or enslaved. Your mad dream is done."

"But a new dream blooms in its place." His voice was full of passionate excitement so that Curio wasn't certain if it was only an act. "Bandua has commanded me to return to Rome. He asks that we bring the worship of him to the great city. We will be his representatives and build a great temple to him."

"I'm so excited."

Curio cut the rope, and Lucian crashed to the ground with a holler of pain. But he began to kick at the net in the next instant. However, Curio loomed over him and brandished the pugio. This ended the struggle against the net. Lucian's voice was soft but stern.

"I have placed a curse on you. Only I can revoke it."

"Then revoke it," Curio said. "And I'll make your death easy."

"Not while I am tangled in this net. Not if I am your prisoner. Grant my freedom and I will grant you the same."

Lucian remained entangled on the forest floor, the net showing as ridges along his shadowed outline.

"If I cut you out of this net and you try to flee or attack, I'll kill you. I'll live with the curse if I must. But you belong to me now."

"Of course," Lucian said brightly, then began to cough. When it ended, he cleared his throat. "I will serve you gladly. Let us return to Rome together and fulfill Bandua's dreams. Men like you and I can become whoever we want. Whoever we need to be. I can teach you the ways, Curio. There is so much art you have yet to learn. I have recipes for poisons that can kill or make a man sleep for days. I have learned to see the gods. If we work together, all this will become your treasure when I pass on."

"Such a generous gift."

Lucian shifted in his net. "It is a gift. I will grant it to you freely. Now cut me from this net and I will show you a place nearby that no one knows. When the trouble passes, we will rejoin the legion for a short time, just enough to get back to Rome. No one will know who we are. I will show you how it's done."

"You have spent all your allies in the legion and the garrisons. There will be no one to forge your assignment this time."

"There are other ways, Curio. I have much to teach you. Now free me while we still have time to escape undetected. The other two will soon find out the body they hid in the trees is not mine."

Curio did not understand that statement, but he also did not care.

"You must release my curse. Do it, and I will free you."

Lucian's voice shifted to the familiar, confident tones of Centurion Lucian.

"Centurion Curio, I've made it clear. You will release me and then we will discuss how to proceed. Cut this net from me, now."

Curio gave a long sigh.

"If only you had shown yourself to be this mad from the start. So much death and suffering could've been avoided."

Then he savaged Lucian while he remained entangled in the net.

The pugio sliced down, strike after strike, plunging into yielding, helpless flesh, and pulling up slick with blood.

Lucian rocked and kicked, screaming, "No! No! The horror!"

But Curio did not relent. Each strike drew heat to his eyes and turned his vision red. His arm pumped without thought, relentlessly plunging the sharp blade into Lucian's entangled body. He fell atop the crumpled form even when the screaming and struggling stopped, and still he stabbed.

Whenever the frenzy ended, Curio found himself leaning against the folded-up corpse on the ground. A huge puddle of blood gathered under him, the hot wetness sucking against his legs. He was breathless, heaving as he sat against the mutilated body of his enemy.

At last, he stood, then kicked Lucian's body for good measure.

"You're really dead this time?"

He stared, waiting for an answer. Of course, he heard only the distant celebration of one Iberian tribe over another. He groaned then gathered up the ends of the net, hauling them over his shoulder.

"Fuck your curse, Lucian. You never spoke to any gods, and none of them listened to you. Roman or Iberian."

The net made a convenient bag to drag Lucian out of the woods, where the net caught on everything it could. He emerged into the clearer foothills and then circled back to the main trail, dragging Lucian's corpse with him.

In the predawn twilight, he saw almost a dozen men huddled together. Falco, being the tallest, stuck out clearly from the others.

Curio hailed them, naming himself before throwing his shoulder into hauling Lucian to them.

Varro came forward. He bore the haggard and disoriented look of someone who had imbibed Lucian's poison, and he wore a bandage dark with blood on his shoulder. Falco stood with him, unhurt but for small cuts and bruises. The other men coughed into their fists, each one bloodied, sweating, and seemingly exhausted. He noted three heavy leather bags that all of them hovered over.

Varro gave a gentle, fatherly smile that told Curio the madness was over.

"Did you bring us a gift?"

Without answer, Curio unraveled Lucian's corpse. He was dark with blood, though clear puncture wounds showed all over his body. His face had been horribly sliced with errant strikes.

Falco whistled. "By the red eyes of Mars, Curio, you just didn't kill him. He's pig feed now."

Varro patted Curio's shoulder.

"You did well. I knew you would. Now, we've got a long way home yet."

Curio smiled.

"I'm ready to go home."

28

Had Flamininus not come as planned, Varro was certain the garrison commander would have flogged all of them to death upon their return. Even as they gathered in his command room, cleared away to make space for Flamininus and his entourage, the commander stared daggers at Varro seated beside his patron. Fortunately, a square table separated them with refreshments and wine.

The senator wore a startlingly white tunic decorated only with a purple stripe at its hem. His servants and personal guards all wore the finest for their positions. Varro noted one among the guard that he had struggled with back in Flamininus's villa. But now they had greeted each other genially and even laughed about Varro and Falco's escapades.

Falco and Curio, along with the surviving hastati, also sat on the side of the senator.

The garrison commander and his adjutant sat in the middle, like a good host and mediator. Across from Flamininus was Cato himself and his staff.

Of all the shocking events Varro had experienced, the

personal attendance of the serving consul during an active campaign was the most unexpected. Varro had thought Cato might send a representative. But instead, he had come under the pretext of recovering some of the soldiers he left in this province.

Flamininus was in good spirits, smiling and laughing, toasting anyone who even looked at his wine cup. On the other side of the table, Cato's cabbage-like face folded up in anger. Varro had seen that shade of red enough to know Cato would have loved to grab a scourge and flog all of them to death.

Instead, he raised his own cup and toasted Varro and the rest.

"To your good work in recovering stolen property of the Roman legion and to bringing justice to a traitor and deserter."

They all drank. To Varro's tongue, the wine was exquisite as he had tasted nothing but stream water the entire journey back to the garrison. But both Flamininus and Cato seemed to think it was rough going down.

"So we've reached an accord," Flamininus said brightly. "Varro, Falco, and Curio, especially him, will have this entire misunderstanding stricken from any records. You will rescind the bounty on them as deserters."

Cato glared for a short time, then inclined his round head.

"I will do so gladly. This has all been an unfortunate misunderstanding."

Flamininus clapped his hands together.

"You have weighed out the silver by now. Are there any irregularities?"

Again Cato paused as if every word had to be wrenched from his mouth.

"Some spillage might have occurred in all this confusion. But nothing I care to note or anything that can't be restored from my war chest."

The garrison commander coughed, then studied the table

before him. Flamininus was about to speak, but Cato held up his palm.

"I will see to it that the garrison be reinforced for the men lost during this mission. I appreciate your willing participation in this important task."

The commander seemed astonished but smiled. "Thank you, sir. We will do everything to keep the frontier safe and intact."

After more frivolous chatter, Cato announced that he was too busy to linger. He stood and glared a final time at Varro, Falco, and Curio.

"Thanks to the three of you. Rome is fortunate to have you in her service."

All of them rose, but Flamininus did not seem satisfied yet. He gave an impish smile and then addressed Cato.

"What will you do with Lucian's head? He gave you so much trouble, after all."

Cato had received the rotting head in a box, mutilated and bloated, a draw for flies. He had sent it off the moment the lid lifted away and the stench filled the garrison parade grounds.

"I'll have the flesh boiled off and the skull set up by the treasury. He'll stand guard as a warning to other thieves until the campaign is done. After that, I will have his skull smashed to bits so that nothing remains of him. I pray you threw his body to the crows."

Varro smiled. "We left his body at the base of the hill where we found him. If crows did not eat him, then his enemies surely defiled his remains. He will never know rest, sir."

The grim proclamation ended further conversation. Cato exited with his staff following. The garrison commander looked expectantly at Flamininus.

"I'd like to use this room a while longer to meet privately with my men."

"Of course, sir." The garrison commander's voice was filled with ice.

But before he shuffled out of his own office, Varro stopped him. He held out a rolled vellum sheet.

"This is a map I made of our journey, and it is reliable. We followed it here without issue. The parts most distant from the garrison are sketchy, as I made those maps on tree bark. But it's all transferred to the vellum, and hopefully, it will be of use to you in your struggles with the Iberians."

The commander looked as if he had been offered a plate of offal, but eventually, he took the map in hand.

"We don't struggle against the Iberians. We keep them on their side of the border. Thank you for the map. I'll have my scouts review it."

When everyone had left, including Flamininus's staff, the four of them spread out at the table. The senator poured himself the last of the wine in the clay decanter. His soulful eyes gleamed with delight.

"We'll, you've made some tough enemies. Cato and everyone aligned to him are going to hate you for as long as you live."

Varro looked to Falco and Curio, who seemed as unconcerned as he felt.

"We can't be friends to everyone, sir. If we were, then we're not doing anything meaningful."

Flamininus laughed. "Well said! Still, be wary of him. Cato is just coming into his power. Things have gone very well in Iberia, particularly with capturing all the silver and iron mines. He'll be Rome's hero for a long time to come."

Varro nodded. "But we can count on another hero of Rome, can't we, sir?"

"Of course!" Flamininus raised his cup, though everyone else had to raise an empty one in answer. "You have given me a great boon once more. And it's not just me, but the Scipio family as well.

You once saved them the humiliation of their wayward relative, Paullus, back in Macedonia. You are now an enemy of Cato's and so become an even better ally to the Scipios."

"I didn't realize, sir," Varro's eyes widened and he looked at both Curio and Falco. Their mouths also hung open. "Well, I remember Paullus."

Flamininus downed his cup, then wiped his mouth with his wrist. His expression grew serious as he paused to regard the three of them.

"The three of you have been through too much. I'm seeing signs of stress and anxiety. For you to remain the excellent companions that you are, you must rest. So I've arranged for all of you for six months of nothing but pleasurable pursuits. You have deep wounds that need time to heal. I imagine that time spent in a Scipio family villa in the countryside ought to help with that."

None of them knew how to answer. Varro sat back in astonishment. But he thought back to his last so-called rest in Flamininus's villa.

"We'll be able to come and go as we please, sir?"

Flamininus laughed. "Your names are clear now. Just be aware of who is around you, as I told you. Besides, you will be honored guests of one of Rome's most influential families. I doubt you'll find much better outside of their villa, but you'll be free to verify that on your own."

So they celebrated all that they had won, recounting for Flamininus their stories one last time before the day ended. It seemed the senator could not hear enough of these, and appeared wistful for his days with his own command.

But the day churned on and soon they were all aboard a trireme headed to Rome, their names clear and Iberia vanishing behind them.

～

WITHIN DAYS OF CALM SAILING, the blue stripe of land on the horizon meant Rome was within reach. Varro, Falco, and Curio stood on the deck and listened to the drum beating time below. The salt air flowed through their hair. Varro inhaled it, loving the smell of it, for it meant freedom and a restoration of their names and rights.

They had passed the journey individually. While they slept in the same berths, during the day they separated to do their own things. Varro was beginning to wonder if he wanted to spend six more months with them exclusively. Perhaps they felt the same. It was a complex feeling, for they had endured so much together that Varro could not imagine a day without them. But at the same time, he wanted his own time and his own life. He would see how things developed.

But now they were reunited once more and standing in thoughtful silence.

Falco sniffed then spoke.

"You never told us what you saw in the god lands. Let's get that story out now. Because once we set foot on Roman soil, I never want to talk of Iberia again."

Varro saw Curio's posture stiffen beside him. Among all of them, he seemed the most fearful for the future.

"I had some crazy dreams," Varro said, staring at the ever-darkening horizon. "I saw some crazy things. I can't remember much of it."

"Don't lie to us," Falco said. "You can lie to your mother, but not to your best friends. What did you really see?"

"I saw Bandua. He stood twice as tall as the tallest tree. He had eyes that burned with fire and a sword of flames that he brandished before me."

Both Falco and Curio now turned to him, their eyes wide. Curio blinked.

"You really saw him? What did he say?"

"Do you want to know the truth?"

He looked at both of his friends, and they nodded vigorously.

"Very well, he rejected me from the god lands and said I did not belong there. But before he cast me out, he put away his flaming sword and smiled. He said, 'You are all forgiven who free my land of the Roman pretender. Deliver me his black soul, and forever shall you have my favor and blessing.'"

"Jupiter's balls!" Falco exclaimed. "You really saw him!"

"I did," Varro said serenely. He turned to Curio and put his arm around his shoulder. "I'm sorry I did not tell you earlier. There are too many hard memories of that place."

Curio's face brightened and he stood straighter.

"That's all right. I knew Lucian was a lying bastard. You met the real Bandua."

"So I did," Varro said softly and looked toward Rome and the new life it offered him.

HISTORICAL NOTES

In the First Century BC, the Lusitani and Gallaeci tribes indigenous to Iberia's west coast worshiped a pantheon of Celtic gods. Among the deities venerated during this era was Bandua, a significant god with a mysterious background. Bandua, also known as Bandi or Bandoas, was depicted as a male deity, except in one instance. Much of the information about him comes from inscriptions found on votive offerings, altars, and statues. Much of Bandua's worship and origin remain shrouded in uncertainty.

Scholars believe Bandua was associated with war, fertility, and protection, making him a multifaceted deity representing crucial aspects of life in ancient Iberia. Some theories suggest that he might have been a deity of the land, connected to the natural cycles and agricultural prosperity of the region. The Romans associated him most closely with their god, Mars. Bandua was one of the core gods of Lusitani worship alongside Reue and Nabia. Reue was the supreme god of the pantheon, and Nabia was most strongly associated with water and rivers.

The Lusitanian tribes lived in what is modern-day Portugal

and part of central Spain. They would eventually give their name to the Roman province of Lusitania in future years when all of Iberia fell under Roman control. The Gallaeci bordered them to the north, separated by the Douro River, and shared many similarities with their southern cousins. The Lusitani were a loose confederacy of tribes, each with their own rulers and territories. They would only unite in the event of an external threat. There were approximately twenty-three known tribes, and perhaps others whose names are lost to history.

The Lusitani were famous guerilla warriors, standing watch over their tribes from mountain strongholds. They were also excellent cavalrymen and served Carthage during the Second Punic War in this capacity. In fact, they replaced Hannibal's famous Numidian cavalry for battles in Northern Italy where the terrain was too rough for the Numidians. After the war, the Lusitani continued to fight Rome and would for many years to come before finally falling along with all of Iberia.

At the time of this story, the Lusitani are still strong and nominally united against Rome. Cato's efforts against them were limited, mostly because of their remote location. But they also knew enough not to stand too defiantly against the greater power of the Roman legions. One cannot help but believe they took notice of Cato's brutally efficient destruction of rebel Iberians. The tribe that I have described in this novel is utterly fictitious and falls into that previously mentioned category of tribes lost to history.

Varro, Falco, and Curio were exceedingly fortunate to survive the untamed Iberian wilderness. Not only would they have to contend with hostile natives, but the rugged terrain and wildlife would have made for thin chances of survival. Yet they have endured and live to fight new battles in new lands.

At this point in Roman history, there are a few more minor conflicts looming on the horizon, with the bigger wars still far in our heroes' future. But even with their grant of rest and relaxation in a fancy countryside villa, danger for them is always near. They have new enemies and new agendas, and as they mature, they also have a new sense of their own agency. Questions have been answered, but new ones have taken their place. The future is far from certain and their adventures continue.

NEWSLETTER

If you would like to know when my next book is released, please sign up for my new release newsletter. You can do this at my website:
http://jerryautieri.wordpress.com/

If you have enjoyed this book and would like to show your support for my writing, consider leaving a review where you purchased this book or on Goodreads, LibraryThing, and other reader sites. I need help from readers like you to get the word out about my books. If you have a moment, please share your thoughts with other readers. I appreciate it!

ALSO BY JERRY AUTIERI

Ulfrik Ormsson's Saga

Historical adventure stories set in 9th Century Europe and brimming with heroic combat. Witness the birth of a unified Norway, travel to the remote Faeroe Islands, then follow the Vikings on a siege of Paris and beyond. Walk in the footsteps of the Vikings and witness history through the eyes of Ulfrik Ormsson.

Fate's Needle

Islands in the Fog

Banners of the Northmen

Shield of Lies

The Storm God's Gift

Return of the Ravens

Sword Brothers

Descendants Saga

The grandchildren of Ulfrik Ormsson continue tales of Norse battle and glory. They may have come from greatness, but they must make their own way in the brutal world of the 10th Century.

Descendants of the Wolf

Odin's Ravens

Revenge of the Wolves

Blood Price

Viking Bones

Valor of the Norsemen

Norse Vengeance

Bear and Raven

Red Oath

Fate's End

<u>Grimwold and Lethos Trilogy</u>

A sword and sorcery fantasy trilogy with a decidedly Norse flavor.

Deadman's Tide

Children of Urdis

Age of Blood

Printed in Great Britain
by Amazon

26956982R00179